ONE BEAUTIFUL YEAR OF NORMAL

ONE BEAUTIFUL YEAR OF NORMAL

a novel

SANDRA K. GRIFFITH

SHE WRITES PRESS

Published in 2026 by
She Writes Press, an imprint of The Stable Book Group

32 Court Street, Suite 2109
Brooklyn, NY 11201
https://shewritespress.com

Library of Congress Control Number: 2025920045
ISBN: 979-8-89636-080-3
eISBN: 979-8-89636-081-0

Interior designer: Katherine Lloyd, The DESK

Printed in the United States

For my husband, Ric.
Always.

Chapter One

WHEN THE PAST FINDS YOU

One of the most important practices of a ghostwriter is to make certain you are invisible. For me, this is easy: I come from a long line of world-class deceivers. At least it seemed simple enough until a drizzly Tuesday morning in Paris when a call at four in the morning jarred me awake. A call I stumbled to the kitchen in record time to answer, only to then stare at the phone as if unsure of its purpose. *Five rings. Six rings. Seven . . .*

I didn't know then that this would be one of those moments that changes everything, but I was certain a call at that time of morning only meant one thing: Someone was dead. I closed my eyes, forced myself to take a breath, and stuttered a weak, "Hello."

At first, the only thing I heard was the sound of traffic, but a few seconds later, a soft voice said my name. My *real* name. The one I had not heard spoken in eighteen years. Something in my head suddenly shifted, and I was back to a different time. Another life. A life that had been shushed into silence, electric-shocked, medicated, and so well buried that I thought no one could ever find it. Not even me. I fought the pull of those memories, counted the pens lined up on my desk, and refocused on the phone.

The caller cleared his throat. "August Caine?"

I flinched again. "Yes."

"Okay, good," he said, audibly relieved. "This is Daniel Grant, an attorney in Savannah, Georgia. I'm sorry to wake you at such a terrible hour—"

"What can I do for you, Mr.—"

"Grant," he repeated. "Daniel Grant."

His name didn't ring any bells, but then again, nothing from my past should. Yet . . . there was something about the smooth drawl of his voice that tugged at my attention in an all-too-familiar way.

"I'm sorry to call you with bad news," he said, "but I'm afraid that happens sometimes with my job."

Slow breaths. Breathe. Just breathe. Push away—stop. One pen, two pens, three pens, four . . .

"Miss Caine? Are you still on the line?"

"I am, but are you sure you've got the right person? I have no connections to Savannah, or anywhere in Georgia for that matter."

"I'm certain I called the right number," he answered, sounding anything but. "You are August Jules Caine? Thirty years old. Born in New York, lived in Savannah for a while as a girl, and now residing in Paris, France?"

"Yes," I reluctantly answered before adding, "well, sort of. I go by Giselle Roamer now." I picked up a pen and moved a clean legal pad toward the middle of my desk. Poised and closer to ready for whatever was about to come.

"Uh-huh," he mumbled, ready to move things along. "So, unfortunately, I'm calling about your Aunt Helen."

There it was. Just like that. Impossible words. A name like a knife. *Take a breath. Say something. Anything.*

"But, she died," I said, almost choking on the words.

"Oh. You already know?" he answered gently, clearly relieved that I had served the punch line. "If that's the case, that just leaves my second reason for calling. I need to let you know a memorial service has been scheduled for your aunt this coming Saturday. If you're able to make it, we could settle her estate while you're here."

His words were simple enough, yet somehow incomprehensible. I repeated them to myself, trying to make sense of things. When that didn't help, I padded over to the window to see if the real world still existed. Two empty Bateaux Mouches puttered down a gentle, gold-lit Seine. Under a shared umbrella, a young couple meandered along the river walkway. Despite the early hour, a street vendor was hustling about, already setting up his display tables.

Everything looked normal. Everything felt upside-down.

"Mr. Grant, I'm very confused."

"Okay," he said slowly. "What part is confusing to you?"

Where to begin.

"Well, I guess for starters, I don't understand why you're just now settling my aunt's estate after all this time, but I'm even more confused by her having a funeral service. I would have thought that had been done before."

I heard paper rustle from across the Atlantic, then, "Now I'm the one who is confused. There seems to be some sort of misunderstanding here."

I mumbled, "Uh-huh," and waited, but we seemed to be at the point where neither of us knew what else to say, so we sat with all those miles between us, waiting for the other person to explain.

When the silence became unbearable, I said, "My aunt died *fifteen years* ago, and you don't understand my confusion?"

There was another long pause. A nervous laugh. And then the words that knocked the air from my lungs and made the world spin faster.

"We've somehow gotten our wires crossed," he answered as softly as the light rain on the window—more drops than I could count. "Your Aunt Helen didn't die fifteen years ago. She died fifteen *minutes* ago."

Chapter Two

MEETING HELEN

My eleventh birthday was like any other day, until it wasn't. I had gotten up, dressed, eaten a dry piece of toast, and made my mother's tray of soft-boiled eggs, juice, and pot of tea. There was no mention of this day being special; in fact, there hadn't been any mention of my birthday in the last three years before. As was customary, I left Maman's tray on the table beside her door, slipped into my backpack, and headed out for a day of self-determined studying at the local library. It was a pretty June day, like the ones before it, but I felt neither special nor particularly unique. I just felt nervous that if I didn't keep my routine perfectly in check—*Don't step on a crack, count the squares, the steps up, the steps down, don't step on a line*—on my way to and from, something bad would happen. This ritual strictness had gotten me through exactly 1,096 days without so much as a broken glass.

When I let myself back into the building through the kitchen door—*one lock, two locks, three*—I dropped my loop of keys when I saw a stranger standing at the sink, casually washing the mug I'd painted for my father a few days before his murder. "World's Greatest Dad!"

Not a burglar, I quickly surmised, snatching the little pony key fob from where it fell and taking a step backward. A suncatcher I had made for Maman during an arts-and-crafts festival at the National History Museum swayed in the window, casting gold spears of light all around the silhouette of the intruder. *How had they gotten in?* I searched the room for signs of my mother, but not a crumb was out of place, and the tray I had used that morning was back on top of the fridge, as though it had never been moved.

The light shifted just as the stranger turned, and for one impossible moment, I thought my father had come home. That there'd been a terrible mistake. Neither of us moved while I held my breath and believed in magic. But there was no magic. There were only tricks of light and wishful thinking, and when he took a step closer, the gold faded, and I saw it wasn't him. For that matter, it wasn't even a man. A tall woman who looked a lot like my father—a lot like me—stood mere feet away, her expression saying she'd rather be anyplace else.

"Hello, August," she said a few seconds later in a smooth voice that was so Southern I thought she must have been faking it. "I didn't hear you come in just now. I didn't want to meet this way, but you're here now. Anyway, I'm your Aunt Helen."

She made a move toward me and held out her right hand. I took a step back and moved my head slowly from side to side, working out the angles. I didn't have any aunts, or grandparents, or siblings, for that matter. Why would this person lie? My brain told me to run, but my legs wouldn't move.

The woman studied me for what seemed a long time before taking another small step in my direction, her hands out like a person trying to calm a wild animal.

"Everything is going to be fine," she assured me, her eyes softening. "I'm just not sure how to start this conversation. I've never had to explain something so complicated before, and I think I'm bad at this sort of thing. To be honest, I know I am. Bad at it, I mean." She blew out a loud breath and forced a smile too big to be genuine. "Let me start over with a strange question," she said. "Do you recognize me? I won't be offended if you don't."

I shook my head.

"I didn't think so. You were so small when I saw you last. Four or five, maybe."

This woman had to be my father's sister. She was tall like him, and muscular. She had his short, charcoal-colored hair. She, like me, also peered out at the world with his green eyes, which glistened with what looked like tears. I had lived alone with my mother for so long that I'd forgotten that people cry in real life. Sure, I'd seen movies when I'd get tired of studying and sneak out of the library for a matinee, but those were actors doing a job, not human beings.

"Did something happen to my mother?"

"No," she replied, closing her eyes. "Well, yes. *Something* has happened. But not like—"

"Please, just say it." I stepped toward her now, seeing some small power in her discomfort.

She eased into a chair next to the breakfast table. "Your mother is in a hospital for people who can't help themselves. She's been unwell for a very long time, probably since . . ."

The woman shifted her eyes to the window and squinted from the sun, and in that instant, I became convinced she knew everything about my life, including how much time I spent at that very window, looking out onto Central Park, watching people and seasons change outside as nothing changed inside. I had been very careful to keep every little thing the same, and was proud of it.

"A mental hospital?"

"Your mother has been sad for a long time," she said, exhaling some of her nerves now that the words she couldn't bring herself to say had been spoken. "Very, very sad and for much too long. Sometimes people can't get past that much sadness without help. They just can't. Claire needs our help, August. Your father's death broke her."

The tiles on the kitchen floor were alternating black and white, annoying for how hard both are to keep spotless. Helen had not taken off her shoes, and trace amounts of dirt drew a line between us. This was her fault. Her dirt had disturbed the equilibrium.

"It's not going to be a quick fix," she offered. "Your mother and I have never been close, but she's agreed to let me help her get through this and do what's best for you."

"Did she ask you herself?" I snapped, knowing that my mother hadn't spoken a word in three years. A test.

"This is more involved than I can explain to someone your age, August. I don't understand it myself, but the doctor I spoke to this morning thinks your mother is suffering from a combination of things that have led to a psychotic break. Apparently, she is convinced that using her voice will cause something bad to happen. This isn't true, of course, but it's what she believes, so here we are."

It made no sense to me that trying to keep something bad from happening was wrong. Our quiet life—now over—was built on this certainty.

"My age? I'm not a baby," I said, slipping off my shoes and into my house slippers before going to the counter and picking up a dish towel to redry my father's mug and put it back where it belonged. "Our life is fine. Maman is fine. She sleeps fine. She showers every morning. She eats two meals a day. I know what people with mental problems look like, and that's not her." I turned to face Helen. "It's not."

I couldn't hold her gaze, so I turned my attention to her luggage. A bag that looked brand-new was nestled next to a larger, older one. They didn't match. *A bad sign.*

She sighed and waited for me to bring my eyes back to hers. "I don't claim to understand what life has been like for you, but this isn't the way things are supposed to be," she said softly, while studying my face from a closer distance now. "This isn't what God intended for you. There are so many beautiful things in this house, but I don't see a single sign of life. There are no art projects hanging on the refrigerator. No party invitations or a calendar to keep your activities straight. No TV. There is just . . . nothing."

I pointed to the suncatcher. "That was an art project," I said. "And just because the house isn't full of clutter doesn't mean it's not full of life."

My aunt's eyes flicked all around, taking in my clothing and the bag of groceries I had left by the door as she spoke. "I also suspect that you're wandering the streets by yourself. You're a ten-year-old girl, and when I asked Claire where you were, all she could do was shrug."

"I'm not ten. I'm eleven," I corrected her. "And what do you expect from someone who doesn't talk? I don't wander around the city. I do my school assignments. I run errands. I get fresh air and sunshine in the park. I even have a bike."

That last thing was a lie, but in the moment it felt like the kind of thing a normal kid would say. "I understand my mother's needs. She understands mine. I'm a good student. Our house is clean. We are *fine*."

"So, here's the thing," my aunt said when I ran out of things to say. This was more than I had talked in a long time. "You've mentioned the word *fine* several times now, and even if that were true, is that a good standard? Are we settling for *fine*? I honestly can't imagine how you've managed to hold things together this long. It's clear to me that you've pretty much been on your own since Davis died."

Her words sounded like a question; they were anything but that. She'd already made up her mind about what was best for my mother. And for me. My life had been decided by a total stranger who just happened to share my DNA.

My aunt shook her head and motioned to the chair next to her. I slid into it and waited for her to ruin what little was left of my life.

"You were too young to realize it at the time, but your life started out so much more than just fine, August. Your life was beautiful. It was splendid. It was what was intended for you. We just need to find a way to get back as close to that as possible. Things will never be the same, but they can be so much better than this."

Before I could turn away, my aunt stroked my face. I flinched, realizing that no one had touched me in years. She withdrew and looked at me, a jigsaw puzzle without a picture.

"I know that I failed you," she said, holding my gaze. "Your mother only wrote reassuring notes, and not that often." She shook her head. "It doesn't matter now. All I can say is I'm sorry. I'm so, so sorry."

She wrote notes, I thought. Of course she did. My mother was the master of the reassuring note: to the school board, to the pediatrician, to really anyone who might question a young girl being the sole caretaker of a large brownstone and her invalid mother. Anger tore loose in my chest, but I wasn't sure where to direct it. I knew I should be furious at this woman. I knew she had been the catalyst for my mother being forced into a hospital. I watched the second hand on the clock tick down my options: *one, resist; two, give in; three, demand to see my mother; four, insist we stay here until she comes home; five—*

"Speaking of notes, Claire left one for you." She drew a small envelope from the inside of her blazer and laid it next to what looked like a legal document on the tablecloth.

Five, don't read the note.

"I've arranged for temporary guardianship of you until this is sorted out, August. You can read over the details if you want."

With that out of the way, she stood and moved back to the sink.

I held the note to my face and inhaled the scent of lavender. The only thing my mother had ever told me that she missed from her childhood was the lavender fields of Provence. "Seas of purple," she had called them, promising to show them to me one day.

I opened the envelope. A picture of my mother with a younger version of me drifted to the floor, the two of us on a small bridge, sun in our eyes and smiles on our lips. I picked it up and studied her face, desperate for clues that might help me understand how a person could appear so normal only to later break into a million pieces. Her right hand, held above her head, cast a shadow on her face, and I could see her smile was more like a grimace. I remembered this moment all too well and set the photo aside as though the sunny day had burnt my fingers.

I unfolded the note, but before reading the words, counted them twice, each time arriving at sixty-six.

My love,

Your aunt is taking you to Savannah, Georgia. She understands I have not been well, and she's forcing me to go into a hospital. I don't know how long I will be away, but I will come for you as soon as possible. You are such a good girl.

Much better than I deserve. I love you, and I am very sorry for everything.

I slipped the picture and note into my backpack before making my way to my favorite window overlooking Central Park, hoping to avoid my aunt's gaze a little longer while I thought things over.

She's forcing me.

I watched people I'd never met and wondered when or if I would ever see them again.

"What's in Savannah?" I asked, turning from the window, my stomach twisting at the thought of leaving the only place that had ever been home. Helen appeared confused again, and then something else as her eyes landed on my backpack. Her lips tightened as if annoyed, or amused, or disappointed that I knew so little about my own life.

"I live in Savannah, August," she sighed. "It's where your father and I grew up."

Chapter Three

THE BEGINNING OF THE END

I have only one photo of myself before I became someone else, taken exactly three years before Aunt Helen handed it to me in an envelope from my mother. It was taken on the Gapstow Bridge in Central Park, the day before my eighth birthday. My mother stands next to me, tall and straight, her pale eyes fixed on the photographer, while mine drift to the water below. The summer trees in the background are dappled with soft, clean light. We're smiling, or at least it looks as though we are. My mother's hand is caught mid-flight, an attempt to block the high-noon sun bearing down on our eyes.

A lifetime spent on the run from imaginary—or perhaps real—pursuers has made me highly skilled at picking up and leaving, which is what I did in the scant hours between Daniel Grant's phone call and boarding a plane to begin my journey back to America, back in time, back to Savannah. It's embarrassing to admit, but I have a go-bag like some low-budget Jason Bourne filled with toiletries, three-season clothing (you can always add a coat in winter), my passport, and two kinds of currency.

I made my way to the bookshelf, pulled down *Ulysses*, and fished that old photo from the dense pages before giving my apartment one last look and then locking up tight.

When I think about that day in the park, I can still see my father behind the camera, a hint of a grin as he leaned around it, commanding his "girls," as he liked to call us. I imagine his finger over the shutter button and then the faint click that captured that wonderfully ordinary moment, when the three of us were unaware it was his last full day on Earth.

When I think about the picture itself, my thoughts turn to an article I once read about how an image of two or more people next to each other creates the impression they share a destiny. It's called the Law of Common Fate. Once your brain creates this directional line, it doesn't matter how many people are in the picture, you're no longer able to see them as individuals. You see them instead as a single, inseparable unit, forever marching together to whatever awaits them in the distance.

I don't know if my mother suffered from a milder form of mental illness before my father was murdered, but over the days and weeks that followed, as she rapidly retreated from the world, her grief morphed into something different. Something beyond itself that eventually silenced her voice and destroyed her once-brilliant mind. And, before it was done, forever tethered that girl in the picture to the stranger with pale eyes standing next to her. Law of Common Fate.

Daniel Grant's call had changed everything in a matter of seconds. Until that jarring moment, I had existed with an unshakable certainty that my entire life had been defined by six significant events. I had even visualized these as three perfectly aligned cause-and-effect sets of two, starting with my father's murder and the mental collapse of my mother that came after. Set two began three years later when Helen came to rescue me, followed by the day my mother waltzed out of a locked facility and stole me away to France. Next came Helen's fatal car accident and my own mental collapse, a breakdown that was precipitated by a hunger strike that resulted in a lengthy hospitalization with a feeding tube and careful reprogramming.

If Helen had been alive all this time, my sets were flawed. Unreliable. If she had been alive, my life was more of a lie than I could force myself to imagine.

I settled into my airline seat while a knot of dread edged along my memory as I began to disentangle the six events, starting with my father's death.

My father was murdered the day I turned eight. According to my mother, a neighbor in the house next to ours found him by the under-stairs entrance to our kitchen when her dog slipped his leash and darted straight to his body. A detective asked me to go to my room while he and his partner spoke with my mother, and I responded by curling into a ball on my bed and wrapping a pillow around my face so tight I could hardly breathe. No matter how hard I squeezed that pillow, though, it couldn't block out the unrelenting wailing from the kitchen or the deep, low tones that assured my mother he had not suffered. His death had been instantaneous from a single gunshot to the chest. His murder was never solved.

As a child, I had no way of understanding what had happened to my mother or what the labels that had been placed on her meant: schizoaffective disorder, depression with psychotic features, delusional disorder with selective mutism. As I got older, I read anything I could get my hands on about psychotic disorders, convinced that if I could figure out how a person could go from high-functioning and fluent in two languages to dysfunctional and too terrified to utter a single word in either, there was hope of her getting better. Of fixing her. Of course, there were no answers. The delusions that silenced her didn't diminish over time. They only grew stronger.

Before my mother became totally noncommunicative, she arranged for me to be educated at home, providing me with textbooks and test requirements that I quickly mastered and became my own teacher. As long as I did my work, no one ever bothered us.

I could study at the library, the museum, or anywhere else I felt safe and at a far enough distance from my mother to convince myself she would get better. That she just needed more time. More sleep. More pills. More something.

It didn't work out that way, though. Things only got worse, and a few months after my mother stopped talking, she also stopped going out. A few months after that, she rarely left the confines of her bedroom. I quickly transformed into the role of caretaker, which included preparing most of our meals. Meals in which we silently sat across from each other, poking at the rice and vegetables that had become our staple dinner, both of us anxious for our brief time together to be over.

Time seemed to stand still, yet pages on the calendar somehow continued to turn. My mother slipped further and further into her own world, which left me no option but to do the same. Even so, without a shred of evidence, I continued convincing myself that her condition was temporary. I told myself that I had to keep her existence as stress-free as possible. So, I did just that. I became the perfect child—one who kept a spotless house, studied nonstop, grieved for her father in silence, chewed her nails until they bled, and left not a single trace of herself lying around.

A flight attendant touched my shoulder and pulled me back across time. Her lips moved without sound. I rubbed my eyes and sat up straight. She gestured toward her cart.

"Would you like something to drink?" she asked, louder. "A blanket?"

I gave her a polite smile and shook my head. She moved on to the couple in the next row, and I went back to studying my ghostlike reflection in the window. A wave of frustration rolled over me as I imagined my mother sitting in her chair at her latest accommodations, awaiting my daily visit.

It felt vengeful and right that I hadn't contacted her nurse, Etienne, to let her know I would be away. If she could punish me with a lie about Helen's death, I could return the favor by prioritizing the truth.

Had Helen been in on the fabrication? Did they talk about the ways to control my life as though I had no right to live it? And if not, then why hadn't Helen come for me? Had she never even tried to find me?

This churned around in my head for a while before I decided that Helen had come for me when I needed her most. If she hadn't come looking for the adult version of me, it didn't take away the one beautiful year of normal she had given me.

Halfway across the Atlantic, time twisted and fused into the hum of white engine noise and the murmur of soft voices as I drifted off, thinking about how sometimes, just when you have almost given up every ounce of hope in your life, someone shows up to save you.

Chapter Four

VICTORY DRIVE

Another handy tool in the ghostwriter's kit is bringing outside observation to a writer's internal process. I know my mother didn't choose the mental illness that would eventually destroy our lives, but in those earliest days, my survival depended on being able to read her intentions while respecting her silence. No such skill was needed with Helen, who seemed to fill the very air with millions of words in our first few hours together. The night passed quickly, and the morning broke early as our flight away from my studied existence began.

"We catch a connecting plane in Charlotte," Helen announced inches from my ear for the third time in the same number of minutes as we boarded. "I promise, promise, promise you'll love Savannah!"

"I'm sure I will," I offered while trying my best to smile. We hadn't argued or anything even close to that. Things just seemed forced. Strained. When I tried to get a word in, we'd start and stop at the exact same moment. "Go ahead . . . no, you go." I eventually resorted to nods and grunts.

When we found our seats, Helen shoved our bags into the overhead bin with so much force she almost caught me in the face with her elbow. My annoyance went up a click. "Why don't you take the window seat," she suggested. "Have you flown before?"

I crawled around her while I thought it over. "Just once that I remember."

"I thought this might be your first time flying, but of course you went to France with your parents," she announced, reaching for the disposable camera she'd bought as soon as we got to the airport that morning and had already used a dozen times. "Let me take your picture anyway. Be sure to buckle up."

"Yup," I mumbled, ducking the flash.

Helen had a serious aversion to silence. Pauses and lulls bothered her so unbearably that she filled them with small talk. She laughed at her own corny jokes and told me all about her career in the navy. She reeled off names and stories of famous Savannahians. Her voice was both beautiful and too much for me to handle. The more she talked, the more I twisted away from her.

"So, we had the poet Conrad Aiken," she said. "Juliette Gordon Low founded the Girl Scouts, and Eli Whitney invented the cotton gin." She held up a finger. "Good grief, I almost forgot Johnny Mercer, the singer-songwriter." She leaned closer and hummed "Moon River." I rolled my entire body toward the window and squeezed my eyes so tightly I saw flashing lights.

"I'm tired," I groaned, hoping she'd take the hint. Thankfully, the patter stopped.

For all of Helen's relentless enthusiasm and chatter, the one subject she didn't touch on just happened to be the one I cared about most. She'd not once mentioned either of my parents, and

I couldn't help but think she and my mother had made an agreement to leave the family secrets untold.

Something urged me to come right out and ask her to explain everything, especially the plan for my life and where she'd been all this time. Something else stopped me, though. Something murky and shapeless.

We boarded a small plane for the connecting flight, and the chatter started back up before the wheels left the ground. Fifty minutes later, when I looked out the window and realized the sprawling, water-laced city below us had to be Savannah, my mood lifted. The sight of it made me feel like a storybook kid on a great adventure.

Helen leaned across me and peered out the window. "Savannah will let you leave, August, but she'll never let you go," she said. "If I've been out of town for one day or ninety-five, I get the same thrill when I see it from up here."

My thoughts took a U-turn back to bleak when she said this. I wasn't home. I'd not been given a choice in the matter either. No great adventure awaited me. It was just me, a stranger who was my aunt, and the terrible knowledge my mother was locked away against her will somewhere. Likely somewhere terrible.

After the plane had rolled to a stop, Helen tugged our bags free and motioned for me to follow her, as if I were a person who needed a prompt. More clicks of annoyance. As soon as I got the chance, I slid on my backpack and made a point of huffing my way around her. If she noticed my worsening mood, she pretended otherwise.

We climbed onto a shuttle bus and rode the length of a football field before hopping off next to a sporty silver car. Helen started it with a remote, and we stood on asphalt hot enough to melt the soles of my shoes while we waited for the seats to cool. I pretended not to notice her sideways glances, but she did it so many times it made me wonder if she had a suspicion I might run.

To be honest, the thought had crossed my mind.

"Be sure to buckle up," she reminded me again.

"Yup," I replied again.

"Should we go straight to the house or do a quick tour of downtown first?"

I wasn't sure if she was talking to me or herself, but I lifted my shoulder as if it weighed a hundred pounds.

"Downtown it is then."

Helen fiddled with the radio for a few minutes until it landed on an oldies station. She only seemed to know about half the words, but she sang along as best she could while I watched fields of pines zoom by from the corner of my eye. Other than the taxi to the airport, this was my first time in a car in a very long time. The feeling was as exhilarating as it was terrifying, and I couldn't wait to get off the highway so my buzzing nerves could calm down and I could look at something other than the cars around us, waiting to crash.

Helen started out my first tour of Savannah by doing snail-paced loops around a few of the city's parklike town squares. The place hummed, and my pulse soon matched its slow motion. Moss-draped oaks and tall palms shaded the cobblestone streets and long rows of beautiful old mansions. Horse-drawn carriages clip-clopped around crowds of meandering tourists who gawked and fanned themselves with maps.

Despite the situation that had brought me there, I was awe-struck by the place.

"Can I open the window?"

"Why don't we live dangerously and put the top down," she suggested in an attempt at cheering me up. "I don't need to worry about my hair, since it's so short."

Helen drove on, block by block, explaining things the way a paid tour guide would. Savannah had the look and feel of a city frozen in time, so it would have been much the same when my father had lived there as a boy. I hadn't known he had grown up in Savannah, but my eyes blurred when I imagined him as an eleven-year-old riding his bike up and down the gaslit streets. I could almost see him sitting at a soda fountain, eating ice cream, and laughing with his friends, an old-timey tintype of a man I never really knew.

A tightness came to my throat as I thought about this. After his death, my father's name couldn't be spoken, nor could we have any reminders of him in our home. I even had to hide my mug from her at first, and then, when she stopped leaving her room, it felt like a cool betrayal in my hands. She carefully boxed up his shirts, shoes, watches—even his cameras and collection of photographs that had made him a Pulitzer Prize–winning journalist. Getting rid of his possessions effectively erased his existence, which was clearly her goal. After a while, I couldn't remember much about either of them, or how we'd lived in the before time.

A feeling that meant I was about to break out either in laughter or loud sobbing rose in my chest. *Think about something else. You can't lose it right now.*

The something else ended up not all that different. It was something Helen had brought up the day before. She had pointed out there were no signs of life in our house. No activities on a calendar. No visits from friends. It had been painful to hear, but she was right. I had no friends. My social skills weren't horrible or anything like that. When I'd been allowed to go to school, I'd gotten along fine with the other kids.

I was smart enough but not too smart, sporty but girlie, basically the kind of mix that keeps you from getting noticed. Or picked on.

No one had ever needed to tell me that I had to be careful with my words. The wrong ones would land me in foster care, so I drew as little attention to myself as possible. That meant for the most part I had stopped talking when my mother had, and other than going to the library or the corner market, I really didn't have any reason to speak.

"Hungry?" Helen asked, as though food rarely concerned her and she suddenly realized she would need to feed me. "How about we find a nice place where we can get better acquainted? There are tons of good restaurants here. It's actually hard to find a bad one. Not that you would want to find a bad one, but just saying."

I fought the urge to tell her to stop talking. Just. Stop. Talking.

My eyes drifted to a man with stringy gray hair and layers of dirty clothes, standing on the corner of Lafayette Square. He raised a plastic cup to the sky as if he were giving a toast before shuffling two steps toward our car and then two steps back.

Helen eased to a stop at the light and gave him a half-hearted wave. "That's Rag Bone," she explained. "In case you're wondering."

I twisted in my seat to get another look at him. "Why do you call him that?"

"I'm not exactly sure." She shrugged. "It's just what us locals call him."

All the blood in my body rushed to my head. "What a terrible name to call someone," I said, nearly choking on my words. "Especially someone with a life like his. I'm sure he doesn't choose to live on the street."

My aunt gave me a blank stare before looking away as if ashamed. "Until you said that just now," she said, "it never crossed my mind. But you're right. Calling him that is very insensitive."

I kept my eyes on the world's longest red light and counted the seconds.

"His actual name is Winston Krantz. You wouldn't guess this by looking at him," she added, "but he comes from old money, like your mother does. He's rich, but he sleeps on a bench and begs for money." She held up a finger. "What's weird, though, is if you try to give him cash, he won't take it. He turns and walks away. I'm not sure why he asks for it in the first place."

"Maybe he's afraid of a trap," I offered, knowing from my library research on paranoid behavior that Winston Krantz needed professional help, not my aunt's curiosity.

She nodded, considering this. "Could be. I usually drop five or ten dollars when I walk past him. He'll keep money if he finds it. He just won't take anything with a hand attached."

I wanted to ask what she'd meant by "old money," but I didn't want her to think I was dim. I also didn't want to start up another conversation, so instead I turned back toward Winston. He stood resting against the stone wall. Grimacing, he held his cup to the sky again.

A lump welled in my throat, and not just because I pitied his awful life and terrible nickname, but because a closer look made me realize the distance between him and my mother wasn't hundreds of miles—it was inches.

Chapter Five

BACK TO THE OLD HOUSE

Nine hours after leaving Charles de Gaulle, I got jolted awake by a rough landing in Atlanta. I opened the shade to blinding white light and squinted at my phone to check the time. I was about to miss my connection, and there wouldn't be another for several hours. Everything in my body ached, but I managed to barrel my way to the other side of the terminal and was in the air before I had time to catch my breath.

Two hours and one legal U-turn later, I eased my rental car to a stop at the north end of Helen's property. I'd left Paris unsure how I'd feel about being back in Savannah, and now that I was sitting in Helen's driveway, the only thing I felt was the pounding in my chest, because the hard part was still to come: The part where I had to say goodbye to one of the most important people in my life. Again.

The faint hum of traffic drifted through the trees, but the only other house within eyesight sat across Helen's graveled driveway. It had the appearance of a new place that had been built to look old. Faux old. Seeing it brought another wave of sadness because I remembered a different house there, one that looked as if it had been built during the same period as Helen's, and at least a hundred yards farther back than this new one.

I stared at the empty space and wondered what had happened to that house. More than that, I wondered what had become of the boy who used to visit there. My first real friend. My first crush.

Breathe, August. In, two, three, four—hold, two, three, four—out, two, three, four, five, six, seven. My heart was still pounding. *I am open to receiving whatever the day may bring. I am open to receiving whatever the day may bring . . .*

A sharp rap on the window brought me out of my useless mantra. Who could only be Daniel Grant stood there in a blue seersucker suit. I was definitely in Savannah. I shut off the car and opened the door to air hot enough to make me gasp.

"I'm Daniel," he said in a slow, melodic accent. "A bit swampy today." He helped me out of the car with a partial handshake, partial chivalrous assist. This close, he looked a lot younger than he had sounded on the phone. He smelled of sandalwood soap and was attractive in a boy-next-door way, with trendy square glasses and a giant watch.

"Sorry I'm late," I said, not really knowing what time it was in the greater scheme of things. My analog watch was still on Paris time, and the way the light shifted through the mossy oaks reminded me just how perplexed Southern time made me feel. "I've never driven in the States before. I got turned around as soon as I left the airport. It took a minute to get my bearings."

"It's fine." He said with a drawl that calmed me. I looked at his hand where it was still affixed to my forearm.

"I don't mean to stare at you," he went on, releasing me. "But I don't think I've seen an aunt and a niece look so much alike.

You literally look just like Helen. I suppose *uncanny* is the right word."

I had thought I'd be able to push away the fact that I had needlessly missed out on the last eighteen years of Helen's life, but hearing him say her name bordered on unbearable. I crossed one foot over the other to stop my legs from shaking.

Change the subject. "Is your office in Savannah?"

"It is," he answered. "We're not big on change around here. We've been on Montgomery Street for nearly sixty-eight years."

"Sixty-eight years is a long time to be in one place. Plenty of people would like to have that kind of security."

"For certain. Have you ever visited our office?"

"I don't think so." Even though memories had started finding me, I still couldn't find them. The more I tried to force them, the further they slipped away.

"I thought Helen might have shown you her father's old office. She had us keep it the same, right down to his phone." He mimicked dialing a rotary phone. Maybe he thought I'd never seen one.

I had forgotten my grandfather had served as a local attorney back in the day. Forgotten despite Helen's attempts to teach me everything she could about our family history. It seemed the electric shock therapy really had done the trick. Or the lithium. Or the endless hours of staring at the EMDR light bar. He was looking at me again, as if waiting for me to reboot. "She may have." I tried to brush off my lack of memory. "I was like most kids and probably didn't pay attention."

He plucked a glossy business card from his jacket and handed it over. "Caine, Becker & Grant." The sight of it brought another flush to my face, and I'd never experienced the disconnect of my life as much as I did right then. My frustration with my mother and her secrets began to simmer again.

"Is there still a Becker at the firm?" I asked.

Daniel shook his head. "No Beckers. No Caines. Has it been a good while since you were here?" he asked, gesturing for me to move toward the house.

"It has." *Pull it together, August.* One of the bad habits of living with a person who doesn't talk is you never really know when you're speaking out loud or just inside your own head. I had to be more careful.

"Helen seemed fine," he said a second later, then waited for me to respond. I bit my lip to stop the tremble until he filled the silence. "Her death was just so . . . sudden."

He gave me another awkward glance to let me know he was waiting for me to engage in normal, back-and-forth conversation. I opened my mouth to try, but I couldn't manage a single word.

I wanted to ask him questions. I could feel the weight of them in my throat. I wanted to hear every detail of my aunt's life, including the circumstances that had brought it to an end. I couldn't make myself ask him anything, though, because it took all I had to hold it together and hearing him say the words, no matter what they were, would break me.

I tried reminding myself that my mother had severe psychological issues, and her brief note—*Helen's dead. Hit a truck in the fog*—wasn't the work of a competent parent. She clearly wasn't in control of her thoughts. Still, the cold, casual way she had written it in response to my wanting to call or write to Helen, her face as expressionless as someone jotting down a grocery item, caused a smoldering in the deepest part of my soul. I'd forgotten a lot, but that note will stay with me until the day I die.

"I'm sorry about my confusion when you called," I said. "I'm embarrassed to admit this, but I got Helen mixed up with an aunt on my mother's side of the family. A long time ago, she had moved to Florida or somewhere in the South. I was told she had passed away. I don't know why, but when you called and informed me that my aunt had died, I thought you meant her."

I'm not sure why I told him this, or why I would make up a story about an aunt who never existed. Maybe I didn't want him to know how little I knew about my own family or that my mother could have done something so cruel. I emboldened the lie further by shaking my head as though I couldn't believe my own sloppiness.

Daniel looked embarrassed for me. "I understand," he said.

We came to a brick-paved path that veered onto a walkway made from small gravel and crushed oyster shells. An acoustical anomaly made the crunching noise under our feet louder than what seemed possible and shot a memory of falling on this ruthless surface directly to my knees. They'd been bloodied, and even though it had been pulled off the market due to safety concerns, Helen treated my injuries with an ancient bottle of Mercurochrome that she had likely swiped from a Civil War museum at some point. A potion created by a sadist that had stained my legs an icky orange-red long after the scrapes had healed.

I removed my sunglasses and used my hand to shield my eyes while I looked the place over. Helen's property was edged with rows of gnarled oaks, scrub grass, and a field of pines. I closed my eyes and visualized the strip of sandbars, tidal creeks, and shallow marshes that began just beyond the tree line, the topography that defines coastal Georgia. A small breeze carried the scent of sweet jasmine and a dozen other things that lured me closer to the past. A few steps later the Greek Revival house, which had been in my family for generations, came into focus.

I turned to find Daniel's eyes fixed on a large round key ring holding at least two dozen keys.

"I'm not sure which one opens the front door," he grumbled. "This is ridiculous. No one should need this many keys unless they work in maintenance. Or a jail."

I took the ring and launched a long silver key that looked familiar into the lock and turned to the right.

The door creaked open. I moved back to the stoop, and Daniel pulled a handkerchief from his pocket and blotted his forehead. I moved forward again but stopped when I suddenly remembered my mother telling me that after I left, Helen got married to an old classmate from college with two fairly young children. The house could still be occupied for all I knew.

"Wait," I said, unsure of my memory. "Is it all right for us to be here? I don't want to barge in on anyone still living here."

Daniel stared at the floor. "There must be another misunderstanding," he offered in that halting way that left me feeling he expected me to understand things I didn't. I was desperate to make it seem otherwise.

"My mother told me Helen married?" I stammered. "That she had stepchildren?"

"I see," Daniel said quietly. "But it's not correct. All she had was a cat. Perhaps your other aunt?"

"Oh." Another flash of heat rose across my face and neck. A wave of shame for being so detached from my aunt's life. For pretending we had a relationship.

Daniel glanced in the direction of his car. "I may not have mentioned this on the phone, but you're her only living relative."

Nothing made sense. And then, everything did. My jaw clenched so tightly that a jolt of pain ran through my teeth when I realized what my mother had done. What she had taken from me. She had demanded that I leave Helen alone, but I had persisted with my questions about her, even after the fake marriage, the imaginary children. I'd pushed her, so she killed

Helen off like a character in a Greek tragedy. And her terrible plan worked. I never mentioned Helen again.

Daniel turned away. He took a step back and gave his watch another long look.

Meanwhile, I wrestled down the anger that came from such betrayal and moved closer to the house that was so much more than just a house. For one beautiful, solitary year, this house had been my refuge. My salvation. Each slow step I took forward was one step back in time, and by the time I crossed the threshold, I was eleven years old again.

Chapter Six

PHOTOGRAPHS

"Make yourself at home," Helen told me, shaking the rain from her oversized jacket like a dog emerging from a pond. "I'll take your things upstairs." Our plans for a riverside lunch had been spoiled by a sudden turn in the weather, and here I stood, in an ornately carved foyer surrounded by dark, polished wood and beveled glass doors. It was a stark contrast to my mother's mid-century Scandinavian decor.

I slipped my sandals off and dusted away a few grains of sand from my feet before moving further into the house. Even though Helen had told me to make myself at home, I felt like an intruder, an unwanted time traveler deposited in her world out of a strange necessity. Out of habit, I shoved my hands in my pockets just as I always did in stores in the city, afraid of being suspected of shoplifting and bringing the authorities to my mother's bedroom door.

The storm that had ruined our lunch plans passed as quickly as it began, and my curiosity drew me into the large central room, from which the parlor and living room spread, and the curving staircase loomed overhead to where a chandelier the size of a small sofa sparkled in the midday light that poured through the tall windows. The ceiling was painted sky blue with clouds and cherubs, and the walls of the sitting rooms were a buttery yellow and a rich dusty gray that reminded me of something I couldn't quite pin down. Each room was congested with antiques, artwork, and portraits of stern-looking rich people on horses.

My first true pang of homesickness settled over me in that instant. We lived in a historic brownstone—likely built around the same time as Helen's house—but my mother had brought her *super-moderne* French sensibility to everything inside, making it sleek and modern. Stark and cold. Viewing this time capsule through my childhood veil caused a sudden shiver to overtake me, and I hurried past the stairs, though a dining room with a table that could seat twenty, and through swinging doors where I found Helen standing at the counter, squeezing lemons into a glass pitcher. It was a magic trick of some sort, as she'd changed into casual clothes, wrapped a bandanna around her head, and seemed as though she'd been in this spot all week, not just the past five minutes.

"Ah, you found me." She smiled and used her elbow to turn on an old-fashioned radio. Etta James belted out "At Last." Helen held a spoon to her mouth and sang along in a voice that spun me back to my father's ability to sing along to everything, never in tune. When he puttered around the house, fixing the plumbing or changing a light bulb, he would hum tunelessly along to whatever music was playing in his head.

Helen whacked the radio button with the spoon and things got quiet again. I looked things over. The kitchen was an airy space with white tile floors, cream-colored walls, and exposed shelves that had been loaded down with glassware and dishes in every color and size. A beam of light flooded onto a six-burner stove. I counted seventeen cookbooks that rested on the shelf above it, and shiny copper pots dangled from the ceiling. I counted nine of these while deducing my aunt liked cooking and speculating that she must be good at it.

"Did my father ever live in this house?"

"Davis and I grew up here, yes," she answered in a different voice than I'd heard for the past few hours. A voice that was relaxed. Unguarded.

"Have you always lived here?"

"Thanks to the navy, I've lived lots of places," she reminded me. "But Savannah is home. Our father grew up in this house, and so did his father. The house is even older than that, though. It was old when my great-grandfather lived here, and according to rumor," she said while reaching for two of the heavy glasses, "he won this house, two horses, a broken pocket watch, and my great-grandmother in an all-night poker game."

I gave her my best skeptical face.

She put three ice cubes into each glass and handed me one. "There are tons of fake stories about people winning places like this in poker games, but in this case, it appears to be true. Some of it, anyway." She held up one finger. "Stay right here. He lived to be ninety-eight years old, and I want you to see a picture of him so you can get the full effect. He was something to look at." She giggled. "Not in a good way."

Helen sprinted up the stairs, and I checked out the kitchen further while I waited for her to come back. Every room of the house was as beautiful as any you could find in a decorating magazine, but the kitchen was the best one of all.

An old farm table rested against the wall, and I let myself imagine my father sitting there as a young boy. It was childish, but I had a thought if I were granted three wishes I would use one to travel back in time, all the way back to the year he was the same age as me. I'd tell him about myself and ask about his life, and just when the moment was right, I'd shock the daylights out of him by revealing our connection.

I closed my eyes and tried to imagine the surprise on his face, but the memory of his face was so faint I doubted it was accurate.

I moved to the pantry and peeked behind a door full of canned vegetables with jars that had handwritten labels. Someone had also written Helen's and my father's names on the doorframe. I smiled when I noticed each penciled notch had their ages written next to their names. The door had been used as a growth chart. My father had been nearly six feet tall by the time he turned fourteen.

The next section of the kitchen had wooden panels covering the lower half of the wall. Framed photographs with brass tags identifying each location filled the upper half. Most of the prints were of old buildings and street scenes from downtown Savannah, but the center one was of a giant oak in a storm. A beam of sunlight had broken through the pitch-black sky and rested on a large branch. The mixture of shadow, light, and water created an effect both eerie and beautiful. Something about it made me sad. My chest tightened.

The subject of the photo, the actual tree, towered just outside the window to my right, a few feet from the kitchen door. I compared the portrait in black and white to the one outside. Both versions looked haunted. Tears welled up in my eyes, and I couldn't stop some from running down my face. "You're crying over a stupid tree," I whispered to myself.

"Your father took all those pictures," a voice from behind me announced. "At least he claimed he did, but he lied sometimes."

I'd been caught crying and talking to myself. I turned to face Helen to make an excuse for it, only to discover the voice belonged to someone else.

A thin woman with long blonde hair leaned against the kitchen doorframe, her arms crossed tight. Even after I smiled at her, her expression stayed blank. I took a step forward and smiled again to be polite, thinking maybe she hadn't noticed it the first time.

She tilted her head a little and blinked at me a couple of times, but that was it.

I turned back to the wall and pretended to study the pictures again. Something about her seemed familiar, but that didn't seem possible. I'd never been to Savannah before.

Still, I couldn't shake the feeling we'd crossed paths at some point.

Neither of us spoke. After a few seconds, I glanced over my shoulder, and my stomach fell when I saw she was just as she had been. The longer I stood there, the more uncomfortable things got, and something told me this was exactly what she intended.

She had called my father a liar. Who says that to someone they just met? And who says something like that without explaining what they meant?

I needed to change the dynamic. "Were you a friend of my father's?"

"That," she answered, as if the word were something jagged in her mouth, "is an interesting question."

I waited, but that was it. Five words that held the weight of a lot of stories.

I took a deep breath and counted to ten before turning to face her again. She stood still as a statue, her eyes boring holes through me. Goose bumps raised on my arms. I could tell she wanted to say or do something hurtful. Maybe she was waiting for me to say or do something to justify it.

One of us sure needed to say or do something. Our stifled

interaction was awkward to the point of torture. *Where the heck is Helen?* My mind raced, searching for something else to say. I remembered my father telling me if I found myself in a situation where I needed to make social conversation, I should just say, "Hey! How about the Mets this year?"

I suspected that it wouldn't work this time, so I asked the only other question I could think to ask: "Do you live here? In Savannah, I mean?"

"No. Not anymore."

The sharp edge to her words was unmistakable. She also spoke with a trace of an accent I couldn't place. If she intended to tell me more, her plan was ruined when Helen's foot hit the bottom step and the air stopped moving.

I distanced myself from the situation by turning back to the pictures. I didn't intentionally spy on them, but I did study their reflections in the glass.

They stared at each other, communicating without words. A style of language I'd become all too familiar with.

Helen finally broke the spell between them. "Do you . . . need something?" she asked in a voice that sounded like someone had their hands around her throat.

The woman gave Helen a long, blank look before she turned and rushed out the side door. A car door slammed seconds later, followed by the sound of spinning tires in gravel. Helen moved to the window and watched her drive away.

I stood with my mouth open and wondered what was happening. Helen kept her lips clamped tight and stared at the floor while I tried to figure out what to say. Or do.

She finally moved to put the box tucked under her arm on the counter, and the air in the room began to move again. I wondered if I should tell Helen how that woman had purposefully scared me or if I should just try to make small talk. Maybe I should ask some questions to get her mind elsewhere. The two simple questions I'd asked the other lady had upset her, and I sure didn't want to upset Helen.

But then again, some questions might distract Helen from whatever had just happened. Sometimes distraction is good. Plus, that box was just sitting there. I didn't care much about a trip down memory lane about my great-great-grandfather, but if there were images of my father in that box, I wanted to see them.

"Are there any pictures of my father in there?" I asked in a voice so low I thought she couldn't have possibly heard me.

Her gaze meandered back to meet mine. "Lots of them. We were camera-toting fools."

Phase two. "Can you tell me anything about my father when he lived here? About what he was like? I don't remember much about him."

Helen moved to the counter and slid onto a stool. Her face took on the expression people get when they are trying to draw distant memories to the surface.

"Let's see. I can tell you that Davis was a great student in everything, but he excelled in math and science," she explained. Her voice was back to normal, like nothing was wrong. "All through high school he said he wanted to go into engineering, so it was a shock when he went a different direction."

I scooted closer and waited to hear more.

"He was athletic and played all sorts of sports, but baseball was his thing. He was a bit of an introvert, but he still had a lot of friends. He liked kayaking and just about anything outdoors. Girls were wild about him, but that never seemed to faze him much." She held up a finger. "Well, girls didn't faze him much until later. Then one fazed him a *whole* lot." She laughed at this.

My heart pattered when Helen pulled a picture from the

box. The sadness that crossed her face when she looked at it turned into a smile when she held it out for me.

I reached for the monochrome photograph of the handsome young man who would someday become my father and then devoured every detail of that image from top to bottom: The grass-stained "Georgia State Champions" shirt he wore. His crooked grin and the dirt on his shoes. The way he casually held the bat the way a person does to look relaxed and unworried, whether he is or not. I examined the flock of birds sailing behind him and the scalloped edges of the photo itself, counting the bumps in my head. I even studied the sliver of sun behind the thin trees just beyond the ballfield's chain-link fence and the bend of the leaves that came from a breeze blowing at the exact moment the shutter snapped.

"I swear, you are the spitting image of your father," Helen said from somewhere far away.

I pulled my eyes from the picture and studied her face as carefully as she had mine. "So are you, Aunt Helen. When you first told me you were my aunt, I assumed you were his twin."

She smiled. "Mom always told people that Davis and I were twins born five years apart. Davis acted mad as fire whenever she said this. He'd huff and puff around and shout something like, 'I don't look like her or any other girl!' He only pretended to be annoyed. He played a role, you see."

She slow-nodded as if she had just figured this out about her big brother at that very moment. "Keep that," she murmured, her gaze straying back to the window, her expression once again edged with worry.

Later that afternoon, I held up my father's face next to mine in the hallway mirror and did something childish. When I saw the similarities, I practiced making his expression, trying to look more like him. Just when I had an almost perfect image of his face, it got overshadowed by a flashback to my life at home. After my father died, my mother kept the shades down during the day and dimmed the lights at night, often leaving us surrounded by nothing but a faint yellow glow. The only explanation I had been able to come up with was that light bothered her eyes. She suffered from terrible headaches, and when she sensed one coming on, she insisted on total darkness.

When I stared at my father's image next to my face, I realized it wasn't light she had tried to keep out. It was instead the one constant, unbearable reminder of him she had not been able to tuck away in a box, hide in a desk drawer, or set out on the curb to be taken away.

Me.

Chapter Seven

SONGS IN THE KEY OF MEMORY

After Daniel Grant left, I spent the rest of the afternoon getting reacquainted with Helen's house. I did the same slow walk around the main floor as I had that first day, nineteen years earlier. She'd replaced some of the furniture, but other than that everything appeared pretty much the same. The same as it had a hundred years earlier, for that matter.

I drifted from one room to the next in a fog, my footsteps echoing behind me and waves of memories rising and retreating like unpredictable rip currents. At one point, I found myself standing in the middle of the kitchen, my face wet, trying to revive a memory of Helen in her best element. Helen was a fantastic cook, and she loved having people over to eat. Her friends were the most diverse, eclectic group imaginable. At any given time, people of all ages and stages were in her kitchen, on the porch, or scattered in the yard. She was comfortable in all worlds and wanted everyone to feel that way in hers.

Helen had always let me help in the kitchen, and those memories made me smile. I'd loved playing chef, hostess, and waitress. But what I loved most was how Helen had acted as if I belonged, no matter who else was around. She had presented me to her friends like I was an adult rather than some pesky kid she had the misfortune of getting saddled with just because she had drawn the familial short straw.

I remembered how, while pretending she didn't realize I was standing within hearing distance, she had bragged about me to her visitors. She would go through this whole elaborate act, looking around for me and lowering her voice. Even then I understood she had wanted me to hear. She was always trying to make me feel better about things. About my situation. My future.

Her friends often stayed after dinner to play cards or hang out on the porch. There had been a lot of raunchy jokes and loud laughter. And music. One night Helen had arranged for a string band to perform under the canopy of trees behind the old carriage house. There had been something unreal, almost dreamlike, about Helen grilling steaks in old cutoff shorts and a T-shirt while men in crisp tuxedos played classical music under a skyful of stars.

I was still shell-shocked around other people, and when I think back on that night, I think of animals who live in the dark for so long their eyes need extra time to adjust. By the end of that evening, my eyes were wide open and ready for all the light the world could offer. That night had been incredible in so many ways. Everything about Helen and her life and this house had seemed magical.

I moved next to the farm table and tried to remember the sound of Helen's voice. There had always been a subtle difference in the tone and cadence of her voice whenever she talked to me and we were alone. I never could put my finger on what it was specifically, but I'd thought a lot about it over the years.

Helen had been like that in so many ways. Mysterious and layered. Clear and indecipherable. Just when you thought you'd figured something out about her, she pitched you a curveball.

I moved on from the kitchen and picked up a framed print on the hall table: A picture of me with Helen on Tybee Island. Seeing my face next to hers reminded me of how often she had stuck a camera in my face. She found every excuse in the world to snap the shutter.

Without saying her reason, I knew she wanted to make up for the years when no pictures had been taken. "The years when I didn't exist," as I later called them. If Helen thought I had missed out on something important in life, she tried to make sure it happened while I was living with her.

I held the picture under the light. The frame had recently been oiled. Helen and I stood shoulder to shoulder with our arms hooked together, wearing matching oversized straw hats and identical smiles. In the haze of years, I'd forgotten how much I looked like her. She had an athletic build, whereas I'd always been too thin. "Scraggy," as Helen described it. She had kept her hair short, while mine was typically shoulder-length or a little longer. Those things aside, seeing that picture was like looking at myself at two different ages.

I put the frame down and moved to the parlor before the anger swelling in my chest consumed me. I'd learned to tuck my feelings about my mother away a long time ago, because nothing good ever came from them.

"She did not choose mental illness. It chose her," I whispered to myself as I had thousands of times over the years. These nine words had become my life vest, my compression chamber, my imaginary Xanax. Anything they needed to be in order to keep my lid on straight and to accommodate my mother's madness.

Helen's piano brought another tangle of memories. She had been a talented musician when it came to playing instruments, but her singing was the worst I'd ever heard. She couldn't, as they say, carry a tune in a bucket, but that never seemed to discourage her from trying. Sometimes I would hear her playing a beautiful piece of music only to ruin it by adding crazy lyrics or singing off-key in an exaggerated manner. She would play Christmas carols in July. Church hymns during card games. Any song at any time was fair game. She once banged out the "Happy Birthday" song, and when I asked whose birthday we were celebrating, she shrugged and told me it was lots of people's birthdays. Just because they might be strangers didn't mean we shouldn't celebrate their special day.

It didn't occur to me until years later that Helen's impromptu performances likely weren't so common before I came to live with her. Or after. Perhaps they had been for my benefit. Another way for her to be funny and silly and interesting. To make me laugh and find joy despite everything bad in my life.

In hindsight, Helen had done everything she could to be the opposite of my mother. Even before the loss of my father, my mother didn't do fun or silly. She had allowed only classical music in our house. Everything had to be high-end and formal. Manners, etiquette, and proper protocol were always required. Even a complete breakdown couldn't alter this.

I hit a few random notes before closing the lid.

The day had faded, so I made my way to the porch as I had with Helen so many times before. The porch had been our spot. Each of us in our corner, reading a book or talking about the one we had just finished. It was the place where she had told me stories about our family and the history of Savannah. I had loved every word and minute we shared there.

But eighteen years had come and gone, and she was gone. I was alone.

I listened to a marsh wren call for its mate for a while and then reached for the phone to call Cort, my significant other until a few weeks ago. The man who was about to marry the woman he loved before me and whose apartment was still just thirty-nine steps from my front door. His apartment might as well have been a million miles away, though, considering his fiancée had already moved in with him. Or, in this case, *back in* with him, since she had lived there before.

I laid the phone down. Cort had moved on, and I had no one to blame but myself. Calling to tell him where I was "just in case something came up" was nothing but a thinly veiled excuse to keep a connection with him. A connection I still wasn't sure why I'd severed in the first place.

A jogger appeared on the side road, and without breaking stride, gave me a friendly wave. I threw my hand up to her and then turned my attention to the old dog stretched out in the grass at the neighbor's house. The dog raised his head and studied me for a few seconds before yawning and looking away.

Something about the convergence of that jogger's youth with the dog's gray, worn-out face made me think about all the loneliness stretched out in front of me and what the next fifty years might hold. And then, whether I truly cared.

Think about something else. Anything else.

I closed my eyes and conjured up the childhood ghosts of Helen and my father. In my mind they wore faded jeans and soft cotton shirts as they ran across the lawn on a night lit by fireflies and a yellow-white moon slicing through the pines. I wanted to imagine their laughter, but that wren warbling in the distance distracted me.

Sitting in the exact spot where my father once had, separated by mere decades while seeing the very things he once saw, brought a long-familiar ache to my soul. But there are thoughts and memories and imaginings that are too much to bear all at once, so I opened my eyes and moved away from the longing that settled in me the day he died.

I stayed while the tangerine-streaked sky dimmed to something bleak but just as beautiful, and my mind raced and trotted to places that could make things only worse. It was too early for bed, but I was jet-lagged, emotionally drained, and on the verge of getting one of the migraines I'm prone to when my sleep is disrupted.

I pulled myself from the chair the way a person three times my age would, checked all the windows and doors, set the alarm, and headed upstairs.

I stood in the doorway of my old bedroom for a good while, looking things over before making my way to something on the bookshelf that had caught my attention. On my first night in Savannah, Helen told me a story about the mythical Cygnus, and she'd made an origami swan to remind me of the story. That paper swan was still sitting on the top shelf, right where I'd left it eighteen years earlier.

Little had changed since I'd left. I was glad for this.

I opened the window and wrestled fresh sheets onto the bed that had been my father's before it had been mine. The mattress was new, but it had the same feather softness as the old one. Trying again to remember the sound of Helen's voice, I fell on the bed, watched the slow, hypnotic wave of the curtains, and listened to the cadence of crickets and night birds.

Helen once told me crickets can tell us the temperature. You need only count the number of chirps for fifteen seconds and then add that number to thirty-seven. I tried it twice, and both times came up with seventy-one. The weather app on my phone confirmed it was seventy-one degrees. I smiled and whispered to Helen that, as usual, she was right.

Chapter Eight

MONTGOMERY STREET

The sound of a backfiring lawn mower shocked me from an uneasy sleep, and it took me a full minute to remember where I was—my father's childhood bedroom, in my dead aunt's house. *My house.* I stumbled to the window to see a man on a giant Green Machine zipping across the back lawn. He threw his hand up and waved, and I dropped the curtain.

I turned on the shower, and while the hot water took its time making it up to the second floor, I went down the hall to Helen's room to find something of hers to wear. I'd left my bag in the car. Plus, I'd always loved the way she dressed in contrast to the Southern belle programming: in sharply pressed tailored shirts, flat-front slacks or shorts, and usually a small scarf tied around her neck that she would occasionally untie and use to dab sweat from her brow. The smell of her perfume hit me with a wave of nostalgia when I opened her door: Joy—a scent I had smelled often in the years since, but never specifically identified as *Helen* until that moment.

As the shower pounded the exhaustion from my body, the dream that caused me to toss and turn all night flooded back in fragments: Helen and I on a beach, somehow both of us teenagers at the same time. The night sky above us was dotted with long-ago burnt-out specks of the past—all an illusion. Was she only ever a dream?

I'd never believed dreams are filled with hidden meanings, at least not in a mystical sort of way. The human brain is wired to pull fragments of information together into something that makes sense. Things you heard get paired with things you suspected. Things you saw get mixed with neural firings and random stimuli.

Still, Helen's phantasmal visit had left me unsettled. Was my brain trying to pull something to the surface? Something that needed to be set right?

Whatever it did mean, or didn't, this was a rabbit hole I couldn't go down. I had too much to deal with in the real world, so I pulled on the smart navy capris and a short-sleeved pinstriped button-down that fit me as though tailored to my body, and armed me with Helen's formidable strength. I slicked a little color on my lips and studied myself in the mirror. No longer a girl, I had the first strokes of the family gray in my hairline, the first signs that I was more Helen than I would ever be Claire.

"Claire," I said out loud, and grabbed my phone from the bedside where it lay charging. Three texts from Maman. I swiped the pull-down and hit "Clear all," before shoving the phone deep into my pocket. I made the bed and folded my discarded clothes, opened the top drawer of the small dresser and smiled: My T-shirts and shorts from all those years ago were still there, just as they had been. It was as if I'd never grown up and never left. When my mother grabbed me that hot June day, she hadn't brought any of my possessions. I left with the clothes

I was wearing and the few meager things that were already in my backpack.

I moved the clothes aside and saw my father's mug was also right where I'd left it. I slammed the drawer shut before the swelling in my chest could consume me.

The feel of my bare soles on each carpet-wrapped step brought a flood of memories ancient and impossible. I bounced on the bottom stair to see if it still creaked, and I smiled for the second time when it did.

In the brisk light of midmorning, I could now see that Helen had changed some of the walls to a sedate cream and white, but other than that, everything gave me the feeling of being the same.

While I made my way to the kitchen, another flood of memories came over me: A houseful of guests, laughing at the piano at Helen's terrible voice. Playing cards snapping apart and back together in clean arcs and then passed into tidy bridge piles as I served trays of cookies and coffee. Book clubs by the fire in deep winter with a particularly pointed observation that *Midnight in the Garden of Good and Evil* was marvelous and the best thing for Savannah tourism ever.

Much to my surprise, there was a fancy coffee maker on the kitchen counter. Helen had always been fussy about doing things the old way—recipes from scratch, heirloom vegetables, real cream and butter. I remembered an old-fashioned stovetop percolator that I was so fascinated by that I took up drinking coffee at the age of eleven so I could watch the glass dome darken as it boiled. It made me feel sophisticated. Without any effort, I located the aluminum pot and prepped it, the muscle memory taking over.

While the coffee perked, I called Daniel's office.

"Caine, Becker, and Grant," a young-sounding happy voice pierced my ear. "This is Sharla, how may I help you today?"

"Hello, this is Gise—August Caine," I began.

"I know who you are, sweetie," Sharla broke in. "Mr. Grant told me to expect your call. He's available for you in about an hour. How does that work for you?"

"That's fine," I said, pouring coffee into a travel mug. "See you then."

With twenty minutes to spare, I found the office on Montgomery Street. I looped around to a small parking lot in the back and inspected the building, hoping it would spark a memory, but nothing about the square, three-story, nondescript structure looked the least bit familiar. If Helen had ever brought me here or pointed it out as the family law office, I had no recollection of it.

The law offices of Caine, Becker & Grant occupied the entire third floor. When I got off the ancient elevator, petite, very blonde Sharla was waiting with a bottle of water and a giant smile.

"I am so *pleased* to meet you," she cooed, her ornately manicured hand outstretched. Each perfect almond shape was a slightly different shade of beige, which matched her likewise gradated pantsuit, blouse, and heeled pumps. "I just *loved* your aunt. She was a hoot!" She led me down a hallway to a dimly lit room where Daniel waited at a conference table big enough to seat sixteen.

"I'm glad you could come in so soon. I'd make small talk about the weather, but if you don't mind, something has come up and I need to leave in about fifteen minutes." He stood and pulled out a chair for me before handing over a paper. "Starting with this. Helen wrote her obituary while she was in the hospital," he explained.

A lump rose in my throat.

"She was on a ton of sedating medications, so if you could look it over to see if everything is correct, that would be helpful."

I couldn't read Helen's obituary without sobbing, and I wasn't about to do that in front of her lawyer. Besides, reading it would be pointless. I was eighteen years removed from her life.

"I'm sure this is fine." I handed it back to him without a glance. Sharla had set herself up at the far end of the table with a pad of paper, silently taking notes while pulling occasionally on a smoothie. I found her note-taking curious.

Daniel placed the paper to his left and picked up the next one. "This is the order of the service, if you want to look it over. Helen's only instruction was that it shouldn't be too fussy, crappy, sassy, or sappy."

I shook my head and refused to take the paper. He tucked it back into a folder and jotted something on his legal pad. "We'll go with it as is." *Check. Check.*

"Next. A few of Helen's friends have offered to serve lunch at the house after the service. The church reception hall is available if that works better for you."

"Her house is fine," I said. "Helen loved having people over. 'The more chaos the merrier' was her motto."

Daniel gave a polite smile and looked at his list. "The service is graveside, with military honors, at Bonaventure Cemetery. And one more thing," he said. "As her only living relative, Helen asked for you to do the eulogy."

My mouth turned to sand, and I reached for the water bottle after glancing a thank-you to Sharla, who gave me a soft look in return. I couldn't imagine why Helen had chosen me to speak about her life.

"I'm not sure I can do that," I said, trying to come up with a reasonable excuse, besides acute agoraphobia combined with a terror of public speaking. "I'm sure there must be someone who knew her better . . ."

"How about this?" Daniel leaned forward. "Try to do it. If you can't finish, I'll take over for you," he offered. "It's what she wanted."

A sudden, inexplicable urge to hug him came over me. I ignored it and decided instead to ask some of the questions I'd been avoiding. Before I lost my nerve, I blurted, "How exactly did you find me, Mr. Grant?"

"Call me Daniel," he said, smiling. "We're practically cousins since our grandfathers started this firm together."

Another piece of the puzzle slid into place. The Caine name was still on the firm sign because Helen owned her father's shares, not because of some nostalgic codicil.

He sat up a bit straighter in his tall chair. "And, I didn't find you. Helen gave me your information a few days before her procedure."

My stomach seized. Helen had *known* where I was. She could have reached out, but didn't.

"Then why—"

He held up a finger. "Let me start by explaining what happened to her. Medically, I mean. I'm not sure how much you want to hear about her condition, but . . ."

"Tell me everything," I said with more bravado than I intended.

He laid his glasses on the table. "Helen had a significant valve blockage and underwent a routine stent procedure earlier in the week. Unfortunately, she developed a clot about twenty minutes into the procedure and had to be moved to the ICU. Sometime during the night, she had two more embolisms, both of which went to her kidneys, and by the next morning, she was in renal failure. She spiraled from there and passed two days later."

I couldn't let myself linger on his words. The images. I had to switch gears and fast.

"We hadn't been in touch, so I'm curious how Helen found me."

He half smiled and shook his head like he couldn't believe what he was about to tell me. He slid his glasses on and leaned closer. "I'll tell you what she told me by posing this question. What significant event happened in your life three years ago in May?"

I scrolled through my memory. "I bought an apartment in Paris."

"How did you pay for it?"

I suddenly knew where this was going. It was headed back to when I made the first real break from my mother. Not a complete break, but a significant one. I had found an insurance policy in my mother's possessions, payable to me, for a large sum of money. I called the bank holding the account, moved every cent to my bank, and bought an apartment with the desire of never moving again. My mother passive-aggressively responded by checking herself into a long-term care facility for the well-to-do mentally unwell five blocks away.

"I paid for it with an insurance trust my father had set up."

Daniel nodded like I was a student who'd come up with a difficult answer. "Helen was the designated trustee of that policy while you were a minor. After that, you were able to do whatever you wanted with it, but she was still notified when the account was closed out. Once she had that information, she tracked down your attorney."

"In Colmar?" I asked, barely interested in what Daniel was saying now. *My father chose Helen as my trustee over my mother . . . What did he know even then?*

"I'm not sure what Helen did from there," he explained, "but she somehow managed to get her hands on something that showed an account in Paris. An account in the name of Giselle

Roamer." He spread his hands wide, like a magician proving no coins or scarves were hidden there.

"From there, she simply googled that name." His voice was the shiny coin that had been hidden in plain sight. "When she came across a fiction ghostwriter named Giselle Roamer, she knew it was you."

"Then why didn't she try to contact me?"

"That I do not know." He shrugged. "Helen gave me your number in the event things went south during her procedure. She didn't give me a lot of details, but she told me enough to convince me she cared a great deal about you."

Daniel nodded to Sharla, who lifted a file box from a side table and placed it in front of me.

"Here are copies of everything she left you. Deeds for the two houses, her insurance policies, the title to her car, bank accounts, stock portfolio, and various other holdings, including her shares of this law firm." Sharla handed him a small ring of keys. "Oh, and safety deposit boxes. More keys."

I tried to smile at his reference to the day before, but my brain was overloaded by this new set of information. *Two houses, car, accounts, stocks, keys? Two* houses*?*

"I wasn't aware she had a second house. Where is it located?"

"Tybee Island," he said, after consulting his legal pad. Meanwhile, Sharla pulled something from a folder, walked the length of the table, and handed me a copy of the deed. The purchase date was listed just a few days before Helen had come for me on my eleventh birthday. I wasn't sure what to make of this.

"Look, I know this is a lot," he said, examining my face after a quick glance at his watch. "These documents will likely help you more than I can. I remember Helen from when I was a kid, but I moved away for law school and only moved back two years ago. I didn't realize she had a niece until she specifically asked for help with this."

We stood and reached for the box at the same time.

"I can get it."

"I insist," he said, already halfway to the door with it.

Chapter Nine

SUMMER OF CHANGE

My new life at Helen's started slowly, as though I needed to be eased into the tremendous changes that were about to come. That first night, after a quiet meal on the screened-in porch, I stretched my arms over my head and announced my bedtime.

"It's late," I said, the drone of cicadas and crickets increasing as the pink-tinted sky slowly darkened above the trees. I set the *National Geographic* magazine I'd been studying back on the coffee table between us and stood up, slow as molasses.

Helen looked up at me over her slim reading glasses, pencil poised above a crossword. "Late? The sun's just set," she chuckled, as though sleeping in daylight was unheard of. Her demeanor had been slightly sullen ever since the stranger in the kitchen, and it made me feel weirdly at home.

Helen was my aunt, but we were strangers, and I wasn't comfortable prying into her personal life, so I tried to think of a clever way to ask her what the deal was without being too direct. I was too exhausted to come up with much of anything. The day had taken a toll on me, including my ability to form clear thoughts. I covered a yawn with the back of my hand.

"Would it be okay if I go on to bed? Early or not, I'm really tired."

"Sure. Head upstairs and pick a room. Doesn't matter which one. Well, not the last bedroom down the hallway. I want to keep that one if you don't mind. After all these years I've gotten sort of attached to it."

I didn't need to see the bedrooms; I knew exactly where I wanted to be. "Which one belonged to my father?"

Her smile turned to a cheesy grin. "To tell you the truth, I already put your things in his room. Follow me," she said in an overly dramatic voice. She led me to a sage-colored bedroom at the top of the stairs. Twin beds with old quilts filled the corners, one with a neatly folded nightgown and a pair of small slippers set up at the end. St. Louis Cardinals pennants lined the walls, and a desk with built-in shelves was loaded down with trophies and bobblehead baseball players.

"Until you told me earlier, I didn't know he played baseball," I said, picking up a worn leather glove from a shelf. It was warm, as though he'd stopped using it five minutes ago.

"Your mother, being French, found it *stoopeed*," Helen said, in a voice that was perhaps an impression of my mother. "He loved her very much."

"I believe he did," I whispered, picking up a nightgown draped across a chair.

"I didn't see any summer pajamas when I packed you up yesterday. That should fit. Let me check my bedroom for something else just in case."

She returned a minute later with another gown draped over her arm, but I'd already scurried into the soft, sleeveless one she'd left. She motioned for me to follow her to the window.

"Come take a look at Twisted Oak Row. Not the most original name in the world, but it is highly accurate."

I moved next to her and inhaled an intoxicating mixture of her perfume and basil from the pasta she had made us for dinner. It had been a very long time since I had been close enough to smell another person, or to feel the warmth of a body so near my arm.

My eyes stung, and I reflexively took a step to the side and focused on the two massive rows of trees bordering a straight, wide path. Gnarled branches reached out to other gnarled branches—a sharp depiction of how alone I felt.

"Move this way and take a look at the ceiling." She pointed to a cluster of dots painted on a square of indigo blue that covered half the room. "Your dad painted those constellations in perfect order. He was space-crazed. Read everything he could about the technology that would give our country an edge." She sighed. "After all this time, your father's stars still glow. They're faint now but wait until it gets dark."

"He'd take me up to the roof of our house and promise one day we'd live someplace where we could see the Milky Way," I said, remembering the warm, soft tar long ago beneath my bare feet. "He also explained that looking at the night sky was like looking back in time. That the light from most stars has traveled hundreds, sometimes thousands of years across space before reaching Earth, so the gleam and shine we see is already long in the past."

Helen smiled at this. "His favorite was Cygnus, the Swan," she said.

I squinted at the ceiling. "That's the same thing as the Northern Cross, right?"

From the corner of my eye, I saw my aunt smile again. "How old are you again?"

"I am eleven years and two days. And I have a membership to the Hayden Planetarium at the Natural History Museum."

"You're smart," she said, appraising me. "And clever, like him. He was so brilliant I sometimes thought I lived in his shadow. Everything came easy to him. Me, not so much."

My face and neck heated up again, but in a good way this time. The kind that came from hearing something like that about my father. And as much as it embarrassed me to admit, having her say something like that about me. I covered my mouth to hide a smile.

"Are you familiar with the story of Cygnus?"

"Not entirely," I answered, though I'd read *Metamorphoses* multiple times. A bedtime story seemed like the perfect way to end the day, and I didn't want to be alone just yet.

"Good," she said, pulling back the covers to the bed. "If you'd heard it already, I would need to hush. Then where would we be?"

I laughed and squirmed into the tightly tucked sheets. "Then I for sure never heard the story."

"Okay, two Greek men, Cygnus and Phaeton, were best friends, but they liked competing. One day they challenged each other to a race around the sun, but they got too close, and their chariots caught on fire. Cygnus survived the fall, but Phaeton's body got trapped at the bottom of a river.

"Cygnus kept diving, but no matter how hard he tried, he couldn't reach his friend, and finally begged Zeus for help. Zeus offered Cygnus a solution. He would turn him into a swan so he could dive down far enough to get him. But there was a catch. There's always a catch. Cygnus would have to give up his immortality to make this happen."

"Cygnus took the offer, became a swan, pulled Phaeton's body from the river, and helped move him on to the afterlife.

Zeus was so touched by the sacrifice Cygnus made, he burned his image into the night sky."

"That is so sad," I offered, gazing at the constellation. "But if Zeus was so moved, why not give Cygnus his immortality back? Better yet, why not help him without making him ask?"

Helen looked impressed and concerned. "Life doesn't work that way. Maybe it should, but it doesn't."

She lifted the quilt and tucked me into bed as if I were a small child. I was hypnotized by her slow, syrupy voice. A few faint memories of my parents tucking me in rumbled around in my head, but I'd mostly forgotten about that part of our lives.

Helen patted the bed like a finished task. "Turn the lamp off whenever you want. Or leave it on. I'm just a few steps down the hall if you need anything. The last room with the wide door."

The exact number of steps to her room was twenty-seven. I didn't dare say this out loud. She'd just given me a compliment, and I didn't want to spoil her opinion of me. She might change her mind if I told her about my habit of counting. Instead, I thanked her for everything she'd done for me.

She gave me another long look and stood to leave. She turned at the door. "Good night, sweetness. Sleep tight. Don't let the bedbugs bite."

With that she disappeared, and I spent the next few minutes wondering what in the world bedbugs were, but more than that, contemplating the thought of my father painting those tiny stars on the ceiling.

One thing was for sure: The more I learned about him, the more I wanted to learn. And I needed to find out everything I could as fast as possible. My mother might get released at any time. She would come for me, and everything associated with my father would be banished once again.

I turned the lamp off and began to drift, my mind shifting

moment to moment, unable to stick with any one thing, but somehow always circling back to the thought that I should be home with my mother. She needed me.

My eyelids grew heavy as anchors, but I willed myself to stay awake so I could see the ceiling in full darkness. I must have dozed off, though, because when I opened my eyes again a million stars burned across my father's painted sky

From down the hall, Helen's grandfather clock chimed twelve times, and I smiled at the thought that no matter how brief our time on this earth might be, we always leave something of ourselves behind.

Chapter Ten

WHEN MEMORY FINDS YOU

My trip to Daniel Grant's office, coupled with jet lag and an extremely hot Georgia morning, left me incapable of deciding what step to take next. So instead I sat in the car with the AC blasting and tried to narrow my focus to one thing at a time, starting with Helen's recent attempt to find me.

It was possible she'd known exactly where I was and how to reach me for many months, if not years. By the look of the box on the seat next to me, she had decided long ago to be prepared if something happened to her, but had she ever actually tried to call?

No longer able to postpone the inevitable, I fished my cell phone out of my pocket and unlocked it, which instantly caused a cascade of texts and message alerts. For someone who preferred muted solitude, my mother certainly found ways to express herself when pointedly ignored. Swiping and deleting everything without reading, I then scrolled through the "Missed Calls" log from a week earlier. *One, work; two, work; three, work; four, work; five . . . a US area code.*

I pressed it and hit the speaker button.

"Hello, thank you for calling the Regional Heart Center of Savannah," a weary-sounding woman announced. "How may I direct your call?"

"Sorry, wrong number," I said, and hung up.

Six, same number, one hour earlier.

I laid my head back and wondered if Helen had called from there or if she had asked Daniel to do it for her. Either way, why hadn't someone left a message? The phone, in response to my disappointment, buzzed in my hand with a text notification.

appelez-moi maintenant

I swiped it away, tapping my nail ten times on the screen.

est-ce que tu mort?

Swipe. Tap, tap, tap, tap, tap, tap, tap, tap, tap, tap.

ou vas-tu????

Swipe. Delete. Power off. I knew I could only expect more of the same demanding texts. There had to be over two dozen since I last turned on my phone. I put it aside and ran my hand over the smooth cardboard top of the file box. *Maybe just a peek*, I decided. Enough to let some furies fly while keeping hope inside. My memory was repairing too rapidly, at a pace that I had no interest in speeding with Helen's meticulous record-keeping. And yet I couldn't ignore the answers that box held forever. I popped the lid and it fell to the floor of the car.

Right on the top was a dog-eared copy of Ovid's *Metamorphoses*. I held it to my nose for a moment, then opened it to a page with a bookmark. "Cygnus, his sacrifice, his triumph." Was it possible Helen knew before going into the hospital that she wouldn't make it out? Perhaps, but how could she be so certain that I would come to pick up the pieces she so carefully left behind?

A file tab marked New York caught my eye, and within it, a letter addressed to Helen from Detective Hector Sanchez, Manhattan Borough, dated nearly three years after my father's murder. The name sounded familiar, but I had no specific recollection of him. I said his name out loud. It didn't nudge my memory, so I started reading.

Ms. Caine,

My name is Detective Hector Sanchez. I have been trying to contact you for some time. As you may recall, I am the lead detective in your brother's unsolved homicide. It is not my intention to make problems for your sister-in-law or cause her undue grief. I am compelled, however, to speak to you about some issues with her as they relate to her daughter, August. I am not writing to you in an official capacity, but rather as someone who is concerned for your niece's well-being.

Protocol dictates I report my concerns to child protective services, but I would like to speak with you first regarding possible options. I'm enclosing my card with contact information. Please get in touch with me as soon as possible, even if only to inform me you don't wish to be involved. Or if there are any other family members I should reach out to, that information would be appreciated as well.

I had contemplated many times over the years what would have made Helen hop on a plane to New York. Why, after three years, had she suddenly decided to disrupt her entire life? All our lives.

The letter from Detective Sanchez explained a lot. Helen had read it and understood she was my only chance to avoid foster care.

A vague impression of the detective kept pushing forward, but it wouldn't form into anything solid, so I googled him. His face, though many years older and grayer, ignited a rush of terrible memories.

"Hello, August," he'd said to me in the softest of tones. "We need to speak with your mother for a bit, so would you mind staying in your room?" Another, lankier detective was already in the living room with Maman, so I nodded and did as I was told. Eventually a female detective came to my room and sat on the end of my bed, waiting for me to fall asleep. I closed my eyes and pretended, but she didn't move all night, and I didn't sleep.

When the sun finally came up the next day, I went to the living room, where my mother was curled up tightly on her favorite chair, not talking or crying or blinking. It was the first time I knew you could run dry of tears, and it scared me. Detective Sanchez returned, and the lady cop left. The first few days there were cops and detectives crawling all over us, but Sanchez was the only constant, and the only person who could get my mother to speak. His eyes always followed my mother, and when she moved into another room, they shifted to me, an unspoken question always seeming to hang between us.

As my father's case got colder and my mother got angrier and less talkative, the detective came to visit less and less. New York's a big city with a lot of murders. We quickly slid down his list of priorities as no breaks happened, no clues emerged.

Why hadn't he reached out to Helen sooner? My mother talked when he first came, but within the next three weeks she had stopped entirely. He must have realized she was getting worse. After reading his letter, I wondered, not for the first time but for the first time in a long time, if he had ever considered her as a suspect in my father's murder.

I certainly had.

My father was killed as he came through the below-stairs entrance of our building right before dinner. My mother had run out to the corner store to get candles for my birthday cake—something she seemed to forget every year. His key to the gate was missing, and Detective Sanchez arranged to get the locks changed. Not that my mother ever used a key again.

Over the years I had often wondered if our lives would have turned out differently if my mother hadn't appeared almost completely sane the moment any outsider stepped into the house. On those days her hair and makeup and clothing were perfect. She'd turned into something mechanical: A robot-parent programmed to do one thing over and over. She knew exactly what to write down on a pad, how to make direct eye contact and pour a welcoming cup of tea from a large tray. I played my part by explaining her inability to talk in as brief and unquestionable a manner as possible. My mother had suffered everything from a rare thyroid disease to an industrial accident that crushed her voice box.

Our interactions outside of the house were minimal, but we certainly intersected with people. Dentists, pediatricians. Bankers and lawyers. Would one of them have stepped in long before Detective Sanchez had she not been so elegant and lovely in her silence? Had I not been a spotless, admiring, and scholarly child?

The reality of our situation was stark: She rarely left our house, and by the time Helen came to fetch me, my mother wouldn't even come out of her bedroom. If anyone had seen her curled into a fetal position on her bed, it might have made a difference. Or it might not have mattered at all. The delicate mask my mother wore was so beautiful even I hadn't always been able to see how much damage was hidden behind it.

Detective Sanchez must have seen it, though. He had to have shown up at the house when I wasn't there, or noticed something off about her that first day, because he had wanted to help in a way that wouldn't further damage my mother's psychological state. Or land me in foster care.

I placed the letter back in its file, unable to absorb any more information from this box of dynamite, and secured the lid. Clearly it was going to take some time and strength to wade through the murky past.

I drove back to Helen's house in a daze. *Two houses. Car. Deeds. Policies. Stocks.* The box next to me practically hummed these words in a loop until I pulled up the drive and parked in front of the garage—an old, converted double-door stable a short walk from the house.

The old convertible and a new Jeep waited behind the doors. The ancient hearse was gone. I bent down to grasp the Jeep's left door handle, but it wouldn't give.

"Keys," I said aloud, startling myself. "Of course she locked everything up." I stood there, turning in a slow circle. *Car. Two houses. Deeds. Policies. Stocks . . .* The enormity of what Helen had left me became overwhelming, so I decided a long walk might help clear my head.

I wandered between the garage and the house, and out into the salt marshes. As I walked, memories poured over me. I detoured through Twisted Oak Row (ten trees, five each side, aching to reach each other) and past Helen's prize heirloom tomato garden ("They don't do well here, August. I have bags of soil hauled in each spring, and even then, Mother Nature sends the squirrels to spoil my joy."). I was saddened to see that her garden had since gone fallow.

I came upon a clearing in the high grass where I expected to see a wooden table, but where now rested an ornate metal one. I eased onto the top and took in the incredible view of the marshlands for a while, without thinking of anything else. My mind eventually twisted back to Detective Sanchez, though, because his letter had answered the question of why Helen had come for me in New York when she did, but it had created a whole new set of mysteries. My father had been murdered twenty-three years earlier, yet my mother never appeared interested in the search for his killer—she only wanted to run away, again and again. At times I convinced myself there was a good reason for this; at other times, I thought her mind was broken by her grief.

Helen was more of a mystery to me. She hadn't reached out to us before the day she showed up at our apartment. Based on the correspondence from Detective Sanchez, Helen hadn't reached out to him either. If she had, he wouldn't have introduced himself. The lack of interest on my mother's part could be explained away by her psychological issues, but what of Helen's?

Her fierce personality didn't fit with the passive, hands-off approach she took regarding her brother's murder. Then again, they had little to no contact for years prior. Her ability to do much of anything would have been limited.

A covey of birds flew off as soft, even footsteps approached from behind me. I turned to see a man with sandy brown hair and a friendly face. I could tell we were about the same age, even with a ball cap and sunglasses hiding his eyes.

"You mowed Helen's lawn," I said, visoring out the sun over his head to try and see him better. "I appreciate that."

"I've been doing that for a while," he countered, his voice low and kind. I'm cautious around strangers, but something about this man put me at ease. *He belongs here*, I thought.

"Well, I'll likely need to keep you on for a while," I said. He sat down on the table about a foot away, which seemed both forward and welcome.

"How are you holding up, August Caine?" he asked. He took off the cap with one hand, smoothed his disrupted waves with the other, and just as effortlessly replaced the cap.

"Okay," I answered. Helen must have mentioned me to him over the years. "And you?"

He nodded as if he had all the time in the world, while I racked my brain for something else to say. "How long have you worked for Helen?"

"Well, I wouldn't call it work." He laughed. "Just being neighborly. I've been mowing for her on and off since I was a boy." He gestured in the direction of the house across from Helen's with the big dog who never strayed from the porch.

I tried to fake my way into more information. "How is everyone doing over there?"

He shrugged. "Grams has dementia, fades in and out. No one has told her about Miss Helen. I need to tell her, but I'm waiting for the right time."

Grams . . . Still nothing. I nodded like I understood.

"If she found out, she would be devastated," he explained. "Then she would forget about it, and then she'd be upset all over again."

"I'm sorry," I offered, knowing a lot about keeping secrets. "Then why even tell her? Just say Helen's on a trip?"

"Can't do that." He shook his head as if he couldn't think of anything else to do. "That's the cost of doing business in this life," he said. "None of us get out untouched."

"That is a sad but practical way of viewing things."

"Hey," he added, "that would be me all the way around. Sad but practical."

I smiled and looked away.

"I'm awful sorry about your Aunt Helen."

I should have asked his name right away. Now it was awkward, but something told me he would be insulted if I admitted he was a stranger to me.

A few seconds later, he covered his face with his hands. "I'm so embarrassed," he moaned, laughing. "I just realized you don't know who I am."

"I know you," I said defensively. I still had no idea who he was. "You're the guy who cuts a stranger's grass because he's a good person *and* who visits his grandmother because he's a good grandson."

"I gave you the first one when I mowed." He chuckled again. "I gave you that second one when I called her Grams."

I tried to keep a straight face. "You do make an excellent point."

"Well," he said, "you and I aren't strangers. Not by a long shot." He twisted toward me again and took his sunglasses off so I could study his face. I took mine off so I could do a better job of it. I shaded my eyes with my hands and looked him over. Handsome. Straight white teeth. Big, curious eyes that hinted at things both hard and kind. Laugh lines that managed to be different on each side of his face.

Still nothing.

I wasn't sure what to expect, but him stretching out flat on the ground wasn't on the list of possibilities. I wasn't sure what came next, but I was curious to find out.

He motioned to me. "Come stand over me."

I took a few slow steps until I was next to him. I thought this might be the part where I found out he was a serial killer who lulled his victims by way of friendliness and distraction. A bit of wariness kicked in, so I took a big step back.

He grinned at me. A grin that tiptoed along the perimeter of my memory. A memory full of giant holes contrasted with razor-sharp edges.

He motioned me closer. "Scoot around behind my head."

"This can't be good," I moaned.

"Oh, it's good," he said. "I'm going to say something, but I want you to imagine it coming from a twelve-year-old boy who just got plastered in the face by a fastball."

Another sliver of memory whispered something in my ear, but I couldn't make out the words yet. *Tommy?*

He looked nothing like that boy, and besides, Tommy was much younger, couldn't be more than . . .

I slid another step back. The silence that followed lasted so long I thought I must have missed what he said.

But then, "I love you, August Caine."

I stared at the grown man at my feet and saw that tenacious cowlick and the charming smile. In that instant, my mind transformed him into the kid who came to visit his grandmother next door, in a house that no longer stood. The boy who rode his bike into Helen's yard and turned my summer into a whirlwind of playing Ping-Pong and board games and climbing the tallest trees. The boy who insisted I come to his game on my twelfth birthday because he had a surprise waiting for me. And the boy with a head injury I saw at that moment on the ballfield, and this man reliving that moment right then, but whom I had not seen in between that moment to this.

As my mind pieced things together, one minute we were twelve and I was running out onto the field to check on him after getting clocked by a fastball, and the next minute, eighteen years had vanished like a vapor. I inspected this new version of my old friend a little longer. No wonder I hadn't recognized him—he was forever frozen in my memory as a boy.

I can't remember a time when I believed in fate, or destiny, or karma, or any of the words that imply life is anything other than a random collision of events, genetics, luck, timing, and circumstances. If I did believe in such things, I would unquestionably believe that the fourth day of June held some special meaning for me. That fate had placed us on a strange, winding course together.

I could easily let myself believe there was something more than statistical improbability at play, since the four most significant events of my life all happened on the fourth of June.

It was the day I was born.

It was the day—eight years later—my father was murdered.

It was the day Helen showed up on my eleventh birthday to take me home with her.

And it was the day, one year later, my mother came for me, fleeing with me so quickly to France I didn't get a chance to tell anyone goodbye. Not Aunt Helen or any of her friends. Not my teachers. Not even the sweet boy-turned-man lying in the grass who was the only real friend I ever had.

Chapter Eleven

THE TOUR

My first day as a ghostwriter—or more specifically, a writer of ghost stories—began with a bugle playing "Reveille." I shot out of bed and staggered to the top of the stairs to see what in the world was happening. My aunt stood stiff as a pole at the bottom landing, wearing fatigues and a deadpan expression. She clutched the bugle to her chest and gave me a crisp salute. I could tell she was trying not to laugh.

I rubbed my eyes. "What time is it?"

"Time to rise and shine, buttercup!"

"Okay, but what time is that exactly?"

She smiled and honked the bugle again. "A little after seven, and breakfast is ready, sir!"

I covered my ears. "I'm a girl," I groaned, pointing out the obvious.

"Yes ma'am, sir!"

I groaned again and rolled my eyes. "Be down in a few."

An unfamiliar, mouthwatering aroma floated up the stairs. I threw on some clothes and hurried to the kitchen to investigate. Enough food to feed ten people stretched across the farm table. With a pencil in her mouth and an intense look on her face, Helen sat at the farthest end, staring at a notebook.

"Is someone joining us for breakfast?"

"Just us chickens," she said, glancing up at me from over the rim of her glasses.

I let my eyes travel over everything again. "What is all this?"

She lifted a massive biscuit from the basket and held it in the air like a trophy.

"Have you heard the saying 'When in Rome'?"

"Sure."

"Well, when you're in the South, you eat like you're in the South. We got biscuits and sausage gravy. Hash browns and scrambled eggs. Oh, and some heart-healthy fruit salad."

I eased into the chair next to hers and tried to remember the last time anyone had made breakfast for me. I couldn't recall, but I was sure it'd not been anything like this. Dad had been our chief cook and bottle washer, so it had been at least three years.

"Well, that's the menu," I said. "What's on the agenda?"

She reached for the coffee pot. "Well, it just so happens I'm working on something I thought you might be able to help me with. How do you take your coffee?"

At home we only drank water, skim milk, and hot tea. No soda or sugary drinks. I'd never tasted coffee, even though I lived in a city where you couldn't go five steps without smelling a Starbucks.

"With cream and a little sugar," I answered, as if this were my usual. "What do you think I can help you with?"

My aunt poured another cup and handed it to me. "Remember how I told you I retired from the navy last year?"

I nodded.

"I'm lucky to have had a career where you can retire before you're old," she said with a long pause. "But then I woke up and realized that I had a lot of empty time in front of me, so I started a business. I'd always wanted to do it, but never really had the time."

I took a sip of coffee. It was hotter and smoother than I expected. "What sort of business?"

My aunt gave me a lopsided grin like she was half proud and half embarrassed of what she was about to say. "Well, people down here just love to hear ghost stories, and they also love to see where all the horrible things that have happened in Savannah took place. So, with that as the backstory, I am proud to inform you that I am the owner and sole proprietor of Caine's Famous Ghost Tours."

I thought she must be joking. She sure acted serious enough.

"The problem is," she added, without waiting for me to comment, "there is a lot of competition, plus I'm starting to get repeat customers. I need new material, and you seem like the kind of girl who could help me with that."

I set my cup down and studied her face. Not a joke. "Wait. People pay you to lie to them?"

My aunt threw her head back and laughed. "I don't lie, August. I just take bona fide ghost stories and shine them up a little. People choose to believe what they want to believe."

"I'm not sure what I can do to help," I said warily, "but I'll be glad to do what I can, unless it involves dressing in a costume. If it includes that, count me out."

Helen clapped like a toddler. "Grand," she said. "I'll take you around to my usual haunts and give you the outlines of a story. You take notes and then add details to make the narrative more interesting. The scarier, the better. I want us to be unique and the best in town."

"Let me check my availability." I pretended to flip through a date book. "You're in luck. Looks like I'm wide open."

"Super. We'll get started right after breakfast. I'll show you around the property before we go into town. Deal?"

I gave a quick nod.

"I almost forgot," she added. "This might be a good starting point."

She handed me an old book with a scent that took me right back to the New York Public Library system, an aroma I liked to think of as "dusty mold."

The Unrested Spirits of Savannah.

"I almost forgot this too," she said while I examined it. "I made you an origami swan this morning in honor of Cygnus."

"Thank you," I said, and meant it. It was beautiful, and I was flattered she'd gone to all that trouble of making me something.

"You're very welcome. Now finish up so we can get cracking," she instructed, as if pleased with the way things had gone.

I'd been in Savannah less than twenty-four hours and it already felt like a second home.

After we washed the dishes and restored complete order to the kitchen—clearly a shared hereditary trait—Helen sprayed my arms with sunscreen and my ankles with an oily bug repellent that smelled like it might kill me right along with the chiggers—a terrifyingly tiny bug I'd never heard of and certainly had no desire to encounter. Give me a giant cockroach any day, right out in the open where I can kill it and move on.

We made our way down a worn path that cut through long rows of oaks and pine trees. In her back pocket she just happened to have an aerial photo of the property, so she showed me how the Wilmington River had become a braided maze of marshes, canals, and tidal streams running along the edges of the mudflats. She pointed out the birds, plants, and insects that had survived there for millions of years before us, and likely long after.

We eventually came to a small clearing that seemed a strange place for an old wooden picnic table, but there one sat. She settled herself on the top and motioned for me to sit next to her. Her face glistened with sweat, and she removed her sunglasses to clean off the lenses. "I haven't brought any customers here," she explained, "but I'd like to work it into the tour. There are a lot of troubled souls that linger in these marshes."

Helen untied a bandanna from around her neck, and I mirrored her movements with the one she had given me. We used them to wipe our faces and necks while she rambled on about glowing green balls that could sometimes be seen at night, carried, according to her, by the souls of people who had died from the yellow fever outbreak of 1820. Many of the bodies had been thrown into the marshes when they couldn't keep up with the burials. Grim.

Green balls. Yellow fever. Bodies in marsh. Got it.

Helen leapt off the table with surprising agility. "We need to go to the grocery store this morning. We're having company tonight."

I slid from my perch, the heat of the day already plastering my shorts to my thighs. I was half afraid she would say it was the angry woman from the other day who would be coming, and half hopeful it would be. I was dying to find out more about her.

"Since you like reading so much, I thought we could start a book club. I don't have any friends with kids your age, though, so you might be dancing with the oldies."

I thought this over. "Dancing with the oldies" must have been an expression that had been around before my time. "People in book clubs talk about books they're reading, right?"

"That would be the general premise," she said, walking back toward the house.

"I'm sure we're not all reading the same book," I pointed out, "especially because the only thing I'm reading is the book you gave me, and it was written more than thirty years ago."

My aunt gave a dismissive hand wave. "Details, details. Quit your grumbling and think of this as the planning stage. Everything in life starts somewhere."

Starts . . .

One gnarled tree, somewhere. Two gnarled trees, planning. Three gnarled trees.

I'm not going home anytime soon.

Four, five, six, seven, eight, nine, ten gnarled trees.

Just ask her about going home.

"We'll get you set up nicely here," she said, as if able to read my mind. "More books and writing supplies. A library card. You're also going to need more summer clothes than what I was able to pack on short notice. Seems you weren't very outdoorsy."

Weren't. I translated her words into, *Get comfortable. You're staying for a while, and you will not live as you did.*

"Will we go back-to-school shopping?" I asked, prying up the lid on my fear of never seeing my mother, or New York City, again.

"Let's wait and see." She stopped and looked at me, and then off into the distance, as though the truth was too heavy to lift. "Let's get some doughnuts!" And off she went, her strides so swift that I had to jog to keep up with her.

"Sure!" I shouted, even though we'd just had breakfast, and I wasn't used to eating so much sugar. Still, I was a kid.

"Can I ask you a personal question?" she asked without turning around.

A familiar dread wrapped around me. Because she had mentioned I needed more summer things, her next question would likely be related. If it was related, this likely meant I would be staying for a long time. Part of me hoped this was true, and part of me wanted to get on the first plane back to New York. It would solve a lot of problems if my mother could come to stay with us in Savannah. I wouldn't have to keep a foot in both worlds.

"What did you do about doctor appointments?" she asked. "Going to the dentist? Getting the things you need, like clothes or medicine?"

"I'd gone for an annual checkup right before my father died. My mother took me the next year. She would still leave our apartment back then. Once we got to where we were going, I lied and said she had damaged vocal cords from an old accident. I haven't been since."

"You're lucky your teeth are beautiful and that you're healthy," she mumbled. There was something disapproving in her tone. She kept her back to me. "So you're due for a visit now? With a pediatrician and dentist?"

"I guess."

"I'll make an appointment for you. We'll get your records sent here."

We'll get your records sent here.

"One more thing," she said. "You squint a lot. Did your mom take you to the eye doctor? If not, let's put that on the list too."

Before I could give her an answer, the sound of tires crunching across the gravel driveway and the low rumble of an engine interrupted the conversation. Helen ran around the corner of the house and yelled, "Thank you, Big Ed!"

"Keys are in it!" a man with the highest pitched voice I'd ever heard from a male shouted back to her as he got into a waiting car and drove off.

Helen motioned to me. I caught up to her, out of breath.

"Not something you see every day," I wheezed, unable to say more about the long black station wagon with oversized side and back windows. "Wait a sec, is that a *hearse*?"

"Isn't she a beauty?!" Helen squealed, clapping her hands together as if all her dreams had suddenly come true—the pumpkin *was* a carriage. "It's a 1980 Ford Granada, retrofitted with bench seats where the casket should go." She opened the back hatch to reveal the handiwork. "Ta-da!"

"What's it for? I mean, I know what it's *usually* for, but why do you have it?"

"Caine's Famous Ghost Tours!" she chirped. "I'm gonna grab my pocketbook and then we can go for a spin." Helen sprinted off to the house, and I circled the shiny black car, amazed by how much a life can change in twenty-four hours. I was also fascinated by how much a grown woman can talk and move, and felt my usually low-key spirits lifting even in the sweltering morning heat. The hearse sat low to the ground, yet the top of it was higher than my head, with enormous windows that would show off a coffin just fine. Helen was right; she was a beauty, polished to a shine that made my eyes narrow, which is why I must have missed the young man creeping up on me.

"Are you August?" he asked, and I spun around, clutching at my chest like I was ninety.

"Yes," I said, and waited for my pulse to slow down. "You scared me half to death!"

"Oh gosh, I'm sorry." He pointed to the big house across the lawn. "I'm Tommy Reese from next door. I'm staying with my grandmother some this summer."

I said, "Okay," and gave him a good look over while I waited for him to say more. He was a full head taller than me, with sandy-brown bangs peeking out from under a red cap with the letters *AB* in script across the front. He wore white Reebok tennis shoes that looked brand-new except for a black smudge on his right toe.

"Okay, okay," he mumbled like he had a script worked out and I had just ruined it. "Okay. Good."

"Do you need something?" I glanced toward the house, hoping Helen would spring back out like Houdini to save me. My face felt even hotter than it had, but my hands had gone cold and clammy.

"No. I don't guess I do." He shrugged. "Well, sort of. I came over to see if you want to maybe hang out or something. Miss Helen said I could."

"Hang out?" This was a foreign idea to me, and I couldn't help the feeling that Helen, despite her claims, had already grown tired of my company and was trying to pawn me off on the closest living child she could find.

Tommy Reese blew out a loud breath and glanced around like this had been the worst idea ever. "Hang out as in ride bikes. Go rollerblading. Play Ping-Pong or maybe some video games?"

My face got hotter. I was an only child. Before my father's death, I had attended a small private academy. There had never been a point in my life when I'd been around a lot of other kids. In the last three years, I'd not been around a single person my age. *Sheltered*—that was the word for what I was. Even when my father was still alive, I wasn't exactly encouraged to play well with others. Someone showing an interest in me, especially a boy, was not something the world had prepared me for in the least.

"I can't do a single thing you listed," I said.

He stared at me like he was thinking of what to say next, then walked past me. I could see his tanned face was likewise flushed. "Nice ride," he whistled. "What's her name?"

"Her name?"

"You do know cars have names, right? Like pets, except it's almost exclusively a girl's name." He shook his head as though a lesson had begun and he expected me to fail the quiz at the end. "I know a good one. Morticia!"

"I've never had a car, so how could I possibly know they have names?"

He locked eyes on mine in the window's reflection of us. "I do believe I've insulted you in some way. Where are my manners?" He doffed his cap and turned to face me. "Forget the stuff I mentioned. We can do whatever you want instead," he said, his voice crackly. "What do you do for fun?"

"I read." This was the second time in as many days that I was standing close enough to another person to feel their body heat, and I took a small step back.

"Read? As in books?"

"No, like fortunes," I answered like a terrible brat, embarrassed by the clumsiness of my answer.

Tommy Reese scratched his head and kicked an invisible rock before glancing back toward his grandmother's house across the way. "Well then, what else do you do?" he asked, evidently trying to decide whether to go home or salvage the original plan of hanging out with me.

"I write." This wasn't exactly true, but it was the first thing I thought of since Helen suggested it for her ghost tours. Plus, I thought it might end the idea of spending another minute outside. No one sits out in the heat writing.

"Well, it's certainly been a pleasure," he clipped while turning to leave and replacing his cap, decision made.

"Is that you, Tommy Reese?" Aunt Helen yelled from behind us.

He turned back. "Yes, Miss Helen." He just as swiftly removed the hat again, and the sun caught in his hazel eyes. I experienced an odd relief that he hadn't gone.

"What are you two doing standing around in this heat?" Helen had changed into a flowing floral sundress and had put on an apron.

"I was waiting for you to go on that ride," I said, confused by her change of costume and plans.

"I changed my mind," Helen said, glancing between me and Tommy. "I have too much to do to get ready for tonight."

I sensed a setup. Helen motioned for us to follow her into the house. "Come in and get something to drink. I just put some cookies in the oven. There's snickerdoodle, sugar, and chocolate chip. Tommy, our new book club is coming over tonight and that pack of women can sure put the sweets away. The booze, too, if I leave it out where they can get their grimy paws on it."

"Thank you, Miss Helen. I don't want to be a bother," he said while keeping pace with her. "I was just admiring your new car. Have you named her yet? I have a cool name if you need one."

We entered the house by way of the kitchen, which did indeed smell of cookies. There weren't any mixing bowls or bags of flour on the counter, though, which made me even more suspicious of Helen's sudden change of plans.

"I'd love to hear some names!" She put on an oven mitt and rescued a sheet pan of small, sad-looking discs. I searched the room for clues until my eyes landed on an empty Toll House cookie wrapper poking out from under a dish towel and an unwashed knife resting in the sink. *One cookie, she's up to no good. Two cookies, I don't need a friend. Three cookies, he's kind of cute. Four cookies, five cookies, six cookies, seven, eight, nine, ten.*

"Morticia is perfect!" Helen clapped her hands together. "You're very clever, Tommy Reese."

"I thought August might want to hang out or something," Tommy explained, reaching for the cooling rack.

Eleven cookies.

"I see," Helen said, as though she wasn't in on this plot. "How nice. It would do her good to be around kids her age,

Tommy. She's eleven years old going on ninety-seven." Loud, fake laugh. "What did you have in mind?"

"I thought we could ride bikes." He shrugged. "Maybe roll-erblade over on the side road."

"I can't do either of those things," I interrupted a bit too loudly. "And I'm not ninety-seven."

Helen and Tommy Reese looked at me and then each other as though I were an algebra problem to be solved.

Helen twisted back around to him. "Tommy, maybe you could just start out with the bikes?"

"Sure."

"I don't know how to ride a bike," I said, assuming this logic would end all the foolishness. "And I'm not putting any wheels on my feet." I'd spent a ton of time in Central Park watching other children riding, falling, and bleeding. I'd decided long ago that none of that was for me. I couldn't risk the injury, the questions, the foster home.

"Now, August, don't be coy," Helen admonished me. "You told me yourself in New York that you have a bike."

"Yes," I muttered through my teeth, betrayed by my own lie. "But I don't *ride* it." I'd played out every scenario that could land me in a hospital and disrupt my carefully ordered world. I'd even found a word for this in the dictionary: *hypervigilant.*

If the word fits . . .

"I'll teach you. You can borrow my sister's bike," Tommy offered. "She's at a nature camp on Tybee Island. One of those overnight things. Not one of those juvenile delinquent camps, but with Liz, it could be." Another shared, loud, fake laugh.

Helen nodded. "That might work," she said as though considering all the possibilities and the incredible luck of him having a sister at a nature camp for the day. "That is very nice of you," she added before turning her attention my way. "Isn't that nice of him, August?"

My reluctant, nearly inaudible grunt earned me a stern look from Helen.

"Yes. That is very nice of you. Thank you."

Helen clapped her hands. "I read both of our horoscopes this morning, August. Yours indicated this was a good day to try new things. How great is that?"

"Super great," I said like my soul had been sucked out and replaced with something mechanical.

My aunt turned to the sink as though the matter had already been settled. "Don't wander off too far," she said with a flick of her hand.

"Yes, ma'am," Tommy answered before grabbing another cookie—*ten cookies*—and motioning for me to follow him. "Come on," he said. "I'll show you how to make a whistle from blades of grass after you tell me what the deal with Morticia is."

"Get her back here in one piece by dinner, Tommy Reese!" Helen yelled after us. "Don't make me hunt you down!"

Chapter Twelve

STORYTELLING

"Tommy Reese? You look so . . . upside-down."

"Thanks?" he said like a question, and we both laughed. "I go by Thomas now."

He grasped my outstretched hand and pulled himself up in one smooth move, bringing me in for a hug. His chest smelled like clothes fresh out of the dryer, and his embrace was remarkably gentle for a person his size.

"I'm thrilled to see you," he said like he meant it, holding me out in front of him and inspecting me from head to toe. "I may look different, but you sure as heck don't."

"I still look like a twelve-year-old girl?" I frowned, pretending to be offended.

Thomas threw his head back and laughed. "Now, you don't look anything even close to twelve. It is amazing how much you favor Helen. I couldn't believe it when I saw you going inside yesterday. The two of you look more like mother and daughter.

You sound like her too. Minus that heavy drawl of hers that non-Southerners either find charming or grating."

"I'm hearing that a lot," I replied, thinking it sounded like something a normal person would say. Or a clone that watches how others act, attempting to blend in, hoping no one will realize it was only pretending to be the real thing.

My mind raced with questions as it flooded with half memories. "Do you have a few minutes to catch up?"

He smiled. "I got nothing but time."

"So," I paused, unsure of where to start. "What have you been doing for the last eighteen years?"

"Wow," he said, holding his hands apart as if measuring a very large fish. "Eighteen years, huh? Let's see. I moved back to Augusta full-time the year after you disappeared and broke my heart. I graduated from Emory University, stayed in Atlanta, and went into law enforcement. I got married and divorced. Married the same woman again. Got shot and divorced again, but those two things weren't necessarily related. And, sadly, that is what the last eighteen years were like for me. Southern gothic, right?"

I laughed along with him, but I realized my mistake. He would ask the same question I had, and telling him the truth was not a possibility. The truth sounded insane, more so even than divorcing twice and getting shot. My truth *was* insane. I ran the playlist in my head to hear what it would sound like if I said it.

> *My mother walked out of a locked facility in New York, flew to Savannah, and made me leave right then for a remote village in southern France. She then told me I couldn't ever use my real name again because the people who killed my father would find us if I did. I couldn't go to school for the same reason. We moved around France and Italy because my mother was convinced*

moving was the only way for us to stay safe. I wasn't allowed to have friends or attend any type of social event.

I asked questions about Helen all the time, and when I turned fourteen my mother told me that Helen had died in a car accident. I fell into a pit of utter despair because of her death and was admitted to a psychiatric hospital, where I was given massive amounts of medication and electric shock treatments that destroyed much of my memory and what was left of my soul.

I became a ghostwriter so I could do what I loved without anyone knowing. I had my mother committed to the best psychiatric facility in all of Europe. I also destroyed the only romantic relationship I'd ever had. Oh, and I almost forgot. Three days ago, I got a phone call from Daniel Grant that made me realize everything about my entire life was a big fat lie.

"That is my pitiful eighteen-year list, August. So what's yours?"

"Can we walk?" I deflected. A technique Helen used on me all the time. "I've been sitting all day."

"Sure," he said, his stride catching up with mine.

"My list?"

One tree, crazy mother. Two trees, crazy daughter. Three trees, failed relationship. Four trees, five, six, seven, eight . . . Exhale.

"Let's see. My mother was from a small village near Avignon, France, so we moved near her family since she didn't have anyone here. I had excellent schooling. Traveled a lot. Rebelled as a teenager, you know, the usual stuff. I moved to Paris a few years ago and bought an apartment. So grown-up. I was engaged, but that ended. And, other than doing some writing, that is my sad, boring list."

I was good at this lying business. Like creating fiction without paper.

"Kids?"

I slowed to a stop and shuddered. "Not a chance." I'd decided long ago that parenting was not in the cards for me.

"France, huh?" He seemed disappointed at how banal my life sounded, which meant I'd succeeded in throwing him off the trail. "And here I thought you'd gone into the witness protection program or something. One day you're here, and the next you're gone."

On an impulse, I decided to share a truth that hadn't been spun from a lie. "I'm sorry about that. I'm sure you didn't know this, but my father's murder was never solved, and my mother had reason to believe it was too dangerous to stay in America."

"You're right, I didn't know anything about your dad." His face looked like a bright sun that had disappeared behind a cloud. "It's not something we talked about as kids, and your aunt was tight-lipped about your sudden departure. I was only half kidding about the witness protection thing because no matter how many times I asked, she told me she didn't know where you were."

"I guess technically it was witness protection. She didn't know our whereabouts. I'm sure she would have told you if she had."

We reached the border of the property and stopped for a moment before turning back toward the house.

"Sounds like your mom did the right thing," he said. "We see a lot of cases where the wrong thing doesn't end up so pretty."

This was a compliment, wrapped in a morbid observation.

"She did," I said, not fully meaning it. I'd stopped believing most of my mother's paranoid rantings a while back; there wasn't anyone chasing us, or out to kidnap me. It was just as likely a random shooting as anything, or surely one of us would be dead.

I had long since realized her lies were created to explain our nomadic, solitary lifestyle and to gain control of me, especially those times she came into my bedroom in the middle of the night, shook me awake, and shoved a note at me saying, *Allons-y, on part maintenant.*

Thinking about Maman was souring my mood. Time to change the subject. I wanted to enjoy this moment with Thomas and to apologize. I was embarrassed that I hadn't immediately recognized him, so I wanted him to know I remembered a ton of things about him, even though they were fragments.

"Can I ask you a strange question?" I said, beginning the walk back to the house.

"If you're going to ask what I'm doing for the *next* eighteen years," he said, grinning, "I don't have that figured out just yet."

I laughed. "This isn't a question about the future. It's about the past."

"Ask away."

"Do you remember riding over to Bonaventure Cemetery a few days after you taught me how to ride your sister's bike? Which, by the way, I would like to thank you for doing. I probably still wouldn't be able to ride a bike if we hadn't met, and it's an important skill in the places I've lived. So, thank you."

"You're welcome, and I sort of remember us doing that."

"We were out riding, and when we got to the straight stretch out by Bonaventure, you yelled, 'Race you to the gate!'"

"Sounds a little more familiar," he said, waving his hand like he sort of remembered and sort of didn't.

"Well, I won."

Thomas stopped and pretended to be surprised. "What, you're gloating now? I have to say it's not your best quality."

"I'm not gloating." I punched him lightly in the arm, which was more muscular than it had been when we were kids. I blushed. "I just want to know why you let me win."

"Why I let you win?!" He rubbed his bicep in mock injury.

"I did not *let* you win, Miss August. If you won, you must have done it fair and square."

"Trust me, Tommy." I stopped both the joking and the walking. "Sorry. I mean *Thomas*. You most certainly did let me win. I was a weak, scrawny kid, and I'd only learned how to ride a few days earlier."

"You *were* scrawny?" He grabbed me by the arms and lifted me swiftly off the ground, putting me back just as effortlessly. "By the heft of you, you're still scrawny. Don't you ever eat?"

"Occasionally," I said, the wind knocked out of me by the swirl of emotions his physical contact had kicked up. "Don't you dare change the subject."

He turned his face to hide a grin, but he wasn't quick enough. "You got me."

"I knew it!"

"There's that gloating again," he chided, catching up and standing over me. His cheeks were as pink as mine felt.

"So, tell me, what twelve-year-old boy lets a skinny eleven-year-old girl from the big city beat him like that?"

He arched an eyebrow and smiled like there was some big secret between us. "Are you kidding?"

"No."

"Seriously?"

"Yes."

"All right." He took his sunglasses off and looked me squarely in the eyes. "True confession. I let you win for the same reason any twelve-year-old boy with an ounce of smarts would."

"Which would be . . . ?"

His giant smile turned into a shy grin that changed him back into a twelve-year-old boy right before my eyes.

"Because when I was that age, I already knew that getting a girl like you to like me," he said, "was way better than winning some stupid race."

Chapter Thirteen

WHEN IN THE SOUTH

It wasn't a bugle that jarred me awake the next morning; it was the hollow ring of a pan hitting the kitchen floor. A long string of swear words came after this (the likes of which I'd never heard before), immediately followed by the sound of the pan getting shoved back into a cabinet. I moved my sore body slowly and did an inventory: five bruises, six scratches, ten blisters, two splinters, one blood blister, a million mosquito bites. My first day with Tommy had been packed with the kinds of activities foreign to a city girl, and my enthusiasm had far outpaced my abilities.

The prospect of a breakfast like the one from the day before eased my worry that I had broken every bone in my body, and I rolled out of bed and made a jerky beeline downstairs—even my knees hurt—only to find a bland-looking basket of toast, a jar of red jelly, and two containers of low-fat yogurt. The sight of it brought a pang of disappointment. I groaned loud enough to make Helen turn from the sink, where she'd stood gazing out the window, her arms tightly crossed as though preparing for a battle.

"Look who decided to join us!" Her arms dropped and her face brightened. "I thought you could go without the bugle this morning."

"I appreciate it," I said, "but what happened to 'when in the South, eat like you're in the South'? I thought that was some sort of unwritten rule."

Helen arched an eyebrow at me and waved her hand over her torso. "Oh, those were splurge foods yesterday. You can't keep a body looking this damn good if you eat cathead biscuits and gravy every day."

"Humph. Anyway, what's on the agenda?" I peeled back a yogurt lid.

Helen handed me a spoon and reached for a slice of toast. "Do you have any experience picking blackberries?"

"Not unless you count choosing a specific container of them from Alberto at the corner fruit stand. I'm good at that. I seldom pick moldy ones."

She laughed and shook her head. "Good," she said. "I can introduce you to something else new. We'll make blackberry jam this afternoon. You ever done that?"

"Nope. Two things new!"

"There you go then," she said, smiling widely. "We'll be picking and jamming."

After cleaning up after breakfast, we collected two buckets of berries from a patch behind the carriage house, which took a lot longer than I would have thought, due to the thorns on the bushes and my need to run away every time I saw a wasp, which was pretty much constantly. Helen would bat them away with her gloved hand, but I knew better; I'd read books. Her bucket filled at twice the rate of mine, and after we swapped and she filled the second, we emerged victorious, and Helen did a little victory jog. Her steps slowed and smile faded though, as we neared the house. Something dangled from the front door. Helen squinted at it, and her face froze.

"What is that?" I asked, moving closer. Something was taped to the lion-head door knocker. Something small, gray, and furry. I thought it was a tiny stuffed animal, but when I looked closer, I saw dried blood. It was a dead field mouse. I gasped and felt my eyes welling with tears.

Helen put her arm in front of me. "Go around to the other door."

"Who would do something so cruel?" I asked as she handed me the buckets.

"I'm sure one of the kids down the road is playing a prank," she said, her voice hoarse, as though she'd seen this sort of thing before. She looked at the blackberries and blinked hard. "No way those will be enough. Put them in the kitchen and meet me at the car. I'll take care of this."

We drove in silence to a farmers market on the outskirts of town, with the top down and radio blasting songs from the fifties. I'd done the math: Helen was born after this decade of music, but it seemed to be her favorite nonetheless. We bought two more baskets of blackberries, a dozen fuzzy little nectarines, and a full crate of what Helen dubbed "the best peaches in the world."

By the time we got home, either Helen's spirits were high again or she was good at pretending they were. We cooked and smashed berries, stirred in cups of sugar, and spooned the deep purple jam into small jars. Though I had doubted her need for more berries, I was shocked to see that it all simmered down into a mere dozen containers.

"This was a lot of work for so little output," I moaned, blowing out a loud breath. "My arms and hands ache."

"Well, ole Achy Arms," my aunt joked while handing me a roll of tags, "we're not finished yet. Those jars are naked as a jaybird until you smack a label on them."

I pulled one from the roll. It said AUGUST CAINE'S FAMOUS BLACKBERRY JAM.

I laughed and held one out for her to see. "Where did you get these?"

"A shop downtown," she laughed. "I ordered them yesterday while you were out with Tommy Reese. The shop owner dropped them off before you got out of bed."

"That is really neat," I said, my vision blurry. I'd never seen my name printed on anything. "I don't know what to say, except thank you so much."

My aunt threw back her head and laughed. "Well, like my favorite bathroom print says, 'We aim to please. You aim too, please.'"

Her comment made absolutely no sense, but she seemed amused by it, so I laughed along with her as if it were the funniest thing in the world.

"What are we going to do now?"

"The day's still young," she laughed, grabbing two jars and her keys. "Let's go for a drive!"

By late morning, the heat index had tipped ninety degrees. We drove into town to tour from inside the car.

"I have a little trick." Helen buzzed the top down and cranked up the air. "It's hell on the gas mileage, but on a day like today, I want the wind in my hair, but my hot flashes to be in control."

"I don't mind a bit," I said. With my windblown hair and the oversized sunglasses Helen had loaned me, I felt like a movie star. It would get this hot in New York City, but on those days, I didn't leave the brownstone.

Helen looped around the town squares, same as the day before. I took notes whenever she pointed out a monument or a historic site with a ghost story attached to it, of which there were many. She showed me the Andrew Low House, where the founder of the Girl Scouts, Juliette Gordon, once lived. We drove past the Green-Meldrim House, where General Sherman wrote to President Lincoln, telling him he had spared Savannah from his destructive March to the Sea.

"Do you have a favorite story, Aunt Helen?"

She made a sudden right turn, pulled the car to the curb next to a NO PARKING sign, and pointed to a manicured square with a towering monument in the center. "Alice Riley," she said.

I sat up straight and turned to a fresh sheet of paper.

"When the city was first founded," my aunt explained, "Wright Square was used for different things. A courthouse. A post office. A place for hangings. It's one of the most historically significant spaces in the whole city, and one of the most haunted. A lot of people were executed here, but Alice Riley was the first." Helen crossed herself twice as she said this.

"What happened to her?"

"She came to Savannah from Ireland as an indentured servant in 1733 and had the misfortune of going to work for a horrible, abusive man named William Wise," she explained. "When he was found next to his bed with his face submerged in a bucket of water, Alice was charged with his murder and sentenced to death." Helen glanced over at me. "Here's the real kicker. Alice had been assaulted by William Wise in the worst way, and she was with child because of it. Her execution was delayed until she had the baby. That poor girl was only eighteen years old when they tore that baby out of her arms and strung her up right over there. They left her hanging for three days before burying her in a plot right across the street. Not only was it the first female execution in Georgia, it was the first recorded hanging in this square."

I put a star next to Alice's story and clipped my pen to the notebook. This was one worth looking up in the library.

"Caramel apple?" Aunt Helen asked as she pulled the car away from the curb. She was well cut out for these terrible tales, as they seemed to barely affect her. Maybe that's what it was to grow up with a legacy of so much death, destruction, and sadness surrounding you: You're left with no choice but to shelve your empathy for when you really needed it.

I sank my teeth into the thick caramel coating of a huge apple as we sat on a bench along River Street and watched a variety of boats and ships along the docks.

My aunt closed her eyes after finishing her apple and said, "Here's another sad fact. Over twenty thousand abducted Africans were brought here and sold like cattle. Right on this street. This beautiful, terrible street."

My jaw dropped, and Helen looked at me.

"What? You don't think we should talk about these things?"

"I don't know what to think," I whispered. "I was just trying hard to imagine twenty thousand people."

"The city had a nine-story warehouse built right up the street." She pointed to her left. "They forced the slaves to build it, and then they used it to quarantine newly abducted men, women, and children in conditions your heart would break to imagine."

I set aside my half-eaten apple and used the towelette to wash off the stickiness. It was cool against my clammy palms, and I pressed it flat there for a moment. She was right: My heart ached from the images.

Helen stood and dusted off her shorts. "Let's drive over to Tybee Island," she said, smiling and waving to the crew on a ship coming into port from Holland. "I haven't taken any groups there yet, but I've been thinking about adding it too. Tybee is full of history and mystery. Plus, my friend lives there. I'll call and ask her to lunch, if you don't mind the extra company. I should probably feed you something decent." She walked briskly ahead of me, dialing, and pressing her cell phone to her ear. I hung back for a moment, looking out at the distant horizon, seeing the shape of a small sailboat and shuddering at the thought of it being crammed with people.

"We'll take the Islands Expressway," Helen explained as we looped around Bay Street and turned onto East President. "You need to learn the names of places. It's good for your brain. Like putting a giant puzzle in the shape of America together, one tiny piece at a time."

"I know all the capitals," I shouted over the wind, realizing that probably wasn't too impressive for an eleven-year-old. "And the governors of each state." That felt better.

"Well, that doesn't surprise me at all," Helen said. "But did you know that the creek we are crossing is called the Lazaretto? Do you know what that word means?"

"Italian?" I thought for a minute, went through my knowledge of Latin roots and came up empty. "I don't honestly know."

"It is Italian, for 'quarantine.' This was another place that slaves and indentured servants like Alice Riley were held to make sure they weren't carrying some mysterious disease. But really, if they did have anything, they most likely got it from the ships that brought them here."

I looked at the marshes surrounding the creek, with no buildings or graveyards in sight. The high summer sun glistened in the reeds, and the air smelled both salty and damp.

"Tybee is as full of ghosts as the rest of Savannah. It's another place that at certain points, when people died here, they just threw them in mass, unmarked graves. Now it's a sleepy little village with beautiful beaches."

We came into a residential area that quickly opened into the commercial strip with a couple of resort hotels, souvenir shops, and fried fish shacks. After three laps around the parking lot, Helen finally found a space. She dropped coins in the meter, then we pushed our way through a blast of furnace-level heat that felt like it had the power to melt me. We went out to the end of a long pier and watched the ocean churn for a few minutes, the breeze drying the sweat in patches on my lips that I could taste.

"Salty," I said, brushing more fine grains from my brow.

"That's what *Tybee* means." Helen laughed and tousled my hair. "It's the Euchee word for salt. They were the original tribe who hunted here before the Conquistadors came and, well, I probably don't need to spell it out for someone with a membership at the New York City Natural History Museum. Anyway, want to take off your shoes and walk on the beach?"

"Are there sharks?"

"I've heard tell of the occasional shark, yes."

"Then I will pass, thank you." Besides a healthy fear of being drowned or mauled, I also could not tolerate sand on my feet. The thought of the needlelike texture gave me goose bumps. "Maybe some other time."

"That's fine by me," she said while looking at her watch. "I hate having sand on my feet. Let's go see my friend."

We drove to a flamingo-pink cottage on the south end of the island and parked in the driveway. Waving wildly and smiling at us, a woman came running out from the house. She pulled me into a tight hug before Helen introduced her as Laney. I tried to tell her it was nice to meet her, but she squeezed the air from my lungs before I had the chance.

Helen motioned for me to follow her. "We're eating at that place across the street," she said, walking toward a small, shack-like restaurant on the corner.

We sat outside on the deck next to a giant fan with a mister. It was hard to hear over the roar of it, but Helen and Laney didn't seem to mind. They gossiped that much louder. They also occasionally seemed to be talking in code, and it left me feeling a little awkward. Like a third wheel. Helen's gaze drifted toward Laney's house. I wasn't sure, but I thought I saw her nod toward the house right before she asked Laney if "she was sure she'd gone out of town."

After lunch we puttered around the island and took a tour of the Tybee Lighthouse. My legs were weak by the time we pulled into Helen's driveway that evening. I could barely drag myself from the car. Helen, on the other hand, bounced out like she was ready to run a marathon.

Later that evening, we sat on the porch, drinking grape soda from glass bottles and nibbling on cold ham sandwiches and potato salad. I read a couple of the stories from *The Unrested Spirits of Savannah* and jotted down a few interesting things to use on the tours. I went to bed that night weighed down by a million thoughts. As strange as my life had been at home, it'd gotten a lot stranger since Helen showed up at our apartment. She'd unsettled things. I stared at my father's stars for a long time that night and wished I could tell him everything about my day. I knew this was impossible, so I changed it to wishing I could tell my mother instead. My words would be wasted, though, so I stopped wishing for anything and settled for listening to the sound of the shutters tapping from the wind. And later, when I got up to go to the bathroom, from down the hall, the soft sighs of my aunt crying.

Chapter Fourteen

EVENING LIGHT

Thomas and I fell into a comfortable rhythm in no time. My memory of him had all but gone dormant, but within minutes, all the miles and years between us disappeared. Something tugged at my stomach again when I thought about how my mother's lies had taken everything from me, including his friendship.

I'm sure I didn't think much of it at the time, but Tommy . . . Thomas had been kind and polite and well-mannered at a time when it wasn't always expected for children to be that way. The "beginning of the end of civility," as Helen had called it. How had I repressed so many essential things about my life but could remember Helen complaining about parenting styles going to hell in a handbasket?

We traipsed around Helen's property and talked for an hour. Thomas explained how his grandmother's house had caught on fire a few years earlier and that she'd had the new house built on the opposite end of her property. Something about better drainage.

This cleared things up for me, for I recalled a much different-looking house. It was a relief to know years of being overmedicated hadn't damaged every aspect of my memory.

Thomas glanced at the tan line from a watch that had been on his wrist. "Speaking of," he said, "I need to meet with an electrician. Grams has decided at the age of eighty-seven she needs a bigger kitchen."

He turned and gave a casual wave when he got to his grandmother's front door. I returned the gesture and gave him a smile like all was right with the world.

I drove into town for dinner and ended up at a restaurant Helen had taken me to a couple of times. It was more upscale than I remembered. People were elbow to elbow, and it took nearly an hour to be seated.

It had never bothered me to eat alone. I'd done it most of my life. I'd done most things alone. For some reason it was awkward this time. Sets of eyes lingered too long when they drifted my way, and I wondered if they pitied me because they thought I was meeting someone who had ditched me. Or maybe the disquiet of my mind had revealed itself on my face. In all fairness to my fellow diners, my eyes tended to linger too long as well. Which, of course, is how I could tell they were staring at me in the first place.

I ordered an oversized salad with fried oysters and then fiddled with my phone so I could avoid eye contact altogether. I should have waited for Thomas to finish with the electrician and asked him to join me for dinner. Having some company would have been nice. Thinking about my hour-long visit with him made me realize I hadn't talked to anyone that long since the day I left Savannah on my twelfth birthday.

I had talked to Helen and Thomas more than I had all other people combined the three years before I came to Savannah, and all years since I'd left. I drew a conversation pie chart with my finger: At least 80 percent of the pie included Thomas and Helen. The man I was supposed to have married only occupied a tiny sliver, because I'd been distant and too wrapped up in my mother's issues to give him the time he needed and deserved.

Time to flip my focus outward. I'd spent a lot of my life watching others from afar, so I studied the faces of my fellow diners as they shared secrets and bored conversation. While they talked of the past, gossiped, planned, and gave each other life-changing news, I then moved on to guessing who was on a first date and who had been together for years. Which partner was happy in the relationship, which one wanted it to be over.

After I ran out of real faces, I moved on to studying the framed ones hanging on the wall. I wondered if the people who took those pictures ever thought that someday the moments they were so desperately trying to capture would be nothing more than distant memories on a square of yellowed paper. Probably not. I wondered if my father ever thought about this when he was behind the lens. He'd done it for a living, so he likely had. Did capturing a moment in time, expressing its truth through its image, satisfy a longing in him?

The evening light fell and ricocheted across the Savannah River onto small shops lining the cobblestone street. I finished picking at my dinner and headed in that direction. I still needed something to wear for Helen's service. I had a black sundress paid for and bagged in no time. A pair of sandals and a jacket that gave the dress a more formal look came three shops later.

I wandered into a tourist store stuffed full of T-shirts. I couldn't remember a time I had ever worn anything with sayings or graphics of any kind. I tarried a minute longer, reading the shirts. Some were funny. Some struck me as hilarious. One in particular—I CAN'T KEEP CALM, MY FAMILY IS NUTS—made me laugh so hard I burst into tears, a reaction that happened to me before, but not in the middle of a crowded store. I put on my sunglasses and hurried back to where I'd parked, sobbing onto the steering wheel in a way that made me spin out of control of what I was feeling: a collapse of my ability to restrain my anger toward my mother over all she had taken from me. What she had done to me.

When I was younger, I worried each person had a limited amount of sanity. Like sand in an hourglass, sanity slipped away until it was gone. The mystery was why some people's sanity slipped away quickly and others slowly. But the result was always going to be the same. As I got older, I stopped believing this. I understood my mother was the exception, not the rule. At my lowest point, I never thought I would lose a grip on reality as my mother had. My earlier fears had been replaced by a sadness so bottomless I eventually stopped trying to crawl out. It began when I thought Helen didn't want me in her life, and it took a final bow a year later, when I thought she'd died. Thinking about those years and my mother's role in the hopelessness of them brought so much anger it could tear my soul in half if I let it.

The words that often centered me now did little to tamp the rage in my heart. *She did not choose mental illness. It chose her.* This thought turned into something darker. It was something I'd never allowed myself to form into words. Would it have been better had I never met Helen? I had accepted my life was going to be a certain way before Helen came to our house that day in New York. Everything changed at that exact moment. She offered me a glimpse of a better life, but at what price? The 365 days I had with her made every single one of the days that followed that much harder. I should have either never come to Savannah or never left.

Helen had not been obliged to love and care for me, but she had all the same. My mother had been obliged, but hadn't. A pang of guilt hit me when I realized that had I been able to choose, I would have stayed, even if it meant never seeing my mother again.

Knowing this about myself was awful, so I tucked these thoughts away and pulled out of the parking lot, as unsure where I was going as where I had been for the last eighteen years.

I drove around the historic district in what at first I thought was a random pattern. I soon realized, though, that my route was the same as Helen's ghost tour. It had stayed with me. I recited her words as best as I could from memory, but for fear someone would see me and think I had a serious problem, I stopped myself short of making the same dramatic gestures she had.

I eventually made my way to Wright Square, the place where Alice Riley was hanged. I thought about the way Helen had first told me that story, and the time that I had then spent in the library researching the facts. Alice had come to America from Ireland on a boat where the conditions were terrible and many people died having gained passage in return for a job in the colonies. Little did they know that they would never be able to earn back the money they owed for the journey, and that their indentured situation gave them no choice in their lives and even less freedom. Alice had been traveling with Richard White, to whom she was not married, and they kept their relationship a secret from William Wise, the cattle farmer who "employed" them. Beyond working all day in the marshes, they were also tasked with Wise's physical care, which included bathing him and combing his long hair. Wise was a notorious letch, and before long, Alice and Richard drowned him in his own bath bucket and ran off to the Isle of Hope to hide.

I always liked the notion of them never being found, that the Isle of Hope had lived up to its name and their story had a much different ending. But no, Richard was hanged first, and then six weeks later, after a stillbirth, Alice was hanged.

The child was not Wise's, as Helen had told me, and though he was by all accounts a horrible human being, there was no real proof he had raped her. Even though I had dug up all these interesting details in an old book of colonial letters, I never corrected Helen's way of telling her favorite ghost story. What did the truth matter when the facts were so ugly?

I sat in the car and looked at the empty space where Alice once dangled, the air beneath her feet, the roar of the surrounding crowd eager to see a woman hang. I imagined the swell of her stomach where there had recently been a child and how lucky it was for that baby that it never drew breath in a world that would have shunned it.

She did not choose indentured servitude. It chose her.

Was Alice really all that different from my mother, from any of us? How much do we choose, I thought, *and how much chooses us?*

It was pitch-black when I got back to Helen's. The flashlight feature on my phone gave off a lot of light, but I still managed to stumble over a rock on the driveway. I put my things away and settled into Helen's favorite porch chair. Paper lanterns were swinging from the trees next door. Someone turned lights off and on as they moved room to room. I watched the windows, hoping to get a peek of Grams. I'm a curious person in general, but in her case, it was because I couldn't remember a single thing about her.

The inconsistencies in my ability to recall things hadn't worried me all that much before, but it was starting to wear on me. I could remember minute details from random, meaningless things, yet I couldn't pull up much of the major stuff.

When it seemed likely all the lights would stay off, I went back to watching the paper lanterns stir in the breeze. A mosquito buzzed in my ear and snapped me out of the trance I'd fallen into. Helen had taught me that mosquitoes can't land in moving air, so you should always keep a fan going when you're outdoors. I turned on a tabletop fan and then stared at the sky while wondering if everyone had this level of strangeness in their family. The odds seemed against it.

Helen's grandfather clock chimed eleven times. I'd run out of steam, and my brain hurt from the effort of prying things loose. I locked up, took a quick shower, and thought about what I'd learned so far. I'd come back to Savannah determined to find out why my mother had lied to me about Helen's death.

I was also determined, though, to make it through the next few days without falling apart. Helen's funeral service would be filled with people who loved her, including me. What if I discovered something about her that changed my feelings? How could I talk about her life if she wasn't the compassionate, wonderful person I had always believed her to be?

If my mother had a legitimate reason for keeping me away from Helen, I still wanted to remember her as the person who had dropped everything to come to New York to save a lost and lonely eleven-year-old girl she barely knew. The person who made sure I laughed every day and who did everything in her power to make my life into something more than just bearable.

I couldn't leave Savannah until I understood what had happened all those years ago. I couldn't ask my mother. I could never again believe her. I was left with getting to the bottom of things on my own.

For a reason I couldn't pinpoint, I didn't want to sleep in my father's old room that night. I made my way to Helen's bedroom, closed the hurricane shutters, pulled the curtains tight, and crawled into bed. I caught a faint whiff of her perfume on the quilt. I'd hoped for a deep, dreamless sleep, but hours later I was still staring into a night so dark it hurt my eyes, with thoughts so dark they hurt my heart.

Chapter Fifteen

A WILLING STUDENT

Tommy was one of those kids who could do just about anything; I was not. Sure, I'd taken swimming lessons at the YMCA when I was five or six, so there was that, but as far as riding a bike or a skateboard or climbing trees, I was a novice. Most of my preteen outdoors years had been spent on a Central Park bench, reading a book while watching other children play endless rounds of monster tag. I had gotten very proficient at swinging, though, but never risked doing anything that would draw attention to my solitary state. More than once I had to quickly leave the park when asked by a concerned mother or nanny when my parent was coming to pick me up. Being on the small side, I'm sure I didn't escape their notice or their cautious side-eyed protection. If there was ever a kid who would be easy to snatch, it would have been me.

Under Tommy's guidance, before too long I had an impressive collection of bruises, scrapes, and probably light sprains. Tommy was an impatient instructor, and after three days of his intense outdoor skills training program, I could wobble on most things with wheels and decently climb a very small tree. A week later, we were racing our bikes on backroads.

As the summer melted into mid-July, Tommy spent weekends at Isle of Palms over in Charleston with his family, and Helen and I spent them the same way we passed most weekdays—exploring downtown, street by street, and giving three tours a night. Helen seemed to have the backstory of nearly every house and building down to the smallest details.

Saturday night was my favorite ghost-tour time. We'd roll into town in that clunky old hearse, Helen at the wheel in a goofy-looking chauffer's hat and me handing out maps to the eight wide-eyed passengers we picked up at the visitor center.

Helen was a great entertainer, and by summer's end she had built up a following. She did three tours every Friday and Saturday night, each one more elaborate and animated than the last.

Though she had occasionally tried to cheerlead me into participating in her performances, I was most happy with the writing part, mainly because it required me to spend hours at a time at the library researching what Helen had called "well-known sightings and verified haunted places." I had laughed at this only to later find myself digging through stacks of dusty books, looking for the smallest details she might have overlooked. Information that would scare the daylights out of her customers.

There were several libraries in Savannah, but the one that made me feel the most at home was the Bull Street Library, due to the way its imposing facade with Ionic columns reminded me of the best of New York City architecture. Helen would drop me at the steps after breakfast, and I'd first read the words etched on the capstones: THE ETERNAL COURT IS OPEN TO YOU WITH ITS SOCIETY WIDE AS THE WORLD, THE CHOSEN AND THE MIGHTY OF EVERY PLACE AND TIME.

These words inspired and comforted me. Walking through the doors was like traveling through time and back to the place that felt more and more like it had never existed. My new reality was akin to Dorothy opening the door post-twister and seeing the world in color for the very first time.

By early August it became apparent that I wasn't going to go back to the world of sepia-colored survival, even though Helen hadn't mentioned when or where I would be going to school. I turned my library hours to studying up on Georgia's educational expectations and benchmarks for a child my age, and quickly discovered that I was well ahead of the pack. A decision would have to be made on my part: tank entrance exams to be with my age level, and therefore excel at academics, or shock everyone with my precociousness. Either way, a good problem to have.

I took my lunch, as usual, across the street in Thomas Square. It had rained since the morning, breaking the weeklong swelter that had settled over the city. Helen liked packing a paper bag with delicious reconstructions of the previous night's meals, and I was pleased to unwrap a roast beef sandwich with homemade pickles and peach relish. One of the things I liked about this tiny park tucked into a neighborhood thick with Queen Anne and restoration architecture was its simplicity.

I lifted the sandwich to my mouth, but before I could take a bite my eyes landed on a scrap of paper taped to the first slat of the bench. I reached for it. The note only had two words written on it. *August Caine.*

I looked around but saw no one who would have a reason to place it there. I studied the note again. It hadn't been written by my mother. I'd seen her handwriting enough times over the last three years to be certain of this. Nor did it match Helen's penmanship. I'd not seen anything Tommy had written, but I could tell this had been done by an adult. And a woman.

I sat frozen until Helen's convertible appeared at the appointed time, a good thirty minutes later. Shoving the uneaten lunch into my backpack, I jogged to the car and swung into the passenger seat.

"You look like you've seen a ghost!" Helen yelled as I got settled. "I hope that means you've written us some new material—a repeat group just booked us for next week!"

I decided not to mention the scrap of paper until I could mull it over and hopefully come up with a reasonable explanation for it. I shifted to what I'd learned in the library instead. "I came across a story that I'm sure you're already familiar with about a man named Rene Rondolier."

"I am familiar but refresh my memory. It's been a minute."

I took a deep breath. "According to local lore, Rene Rondolier was born in the early 1800s, and by the time he was fifteen, he was seven feet tall and weighed over three hundred pounds. He was delayed, couldn't talk, and was always accidently killing animals that he loved because he hugged them too hard. Anyway, he was eventually accused of murdering a young girl in the alley close to where he lived with his mother, and to make things worse, her body was found with her heart cut out."

"Yes, I remember this story now," Helen said, tapping the steering wheel in time with Buddy Holly on the radio. "What else?"

"He was eventually hanged for her murder," I told her. "But when more young girls—about my age—were found in the following years with their hearts missing, rather than admit they got the wrong guy, the police claimed he had somehow cheated death. Anyway, all these years later, Rondolier has been seen wandering Foley Alley, where the first girl was found, blood dripping from his mouth, and a small, beating heart in his very large hand."

Helen pulled the car to the curb and lifted her sunglasses to look directly at me. "You're making that last part up, aren't you?"

"Yes, ma'am," I replied. "But there are a lot of versions of this story. We tell this one and follow up by telling our customers that it's not true. You gotta debunk the fiction if you want to sound legit."

"Well aren't you the professional con artist!" she exclaimed while swerving back into traffic. "I got us some ice cream to eat at home. We better get there before it melts."

I'd written to my mother a few weeks after arriving in Savannah, but hadn't heard anything back. As we turned onto our street, I worked up the nerve to ask Helen if she'd heard anything from the hospital. Her answer surprised me, mostly because I didn't fully understand it.

"I'm not your mother's next of kin or appointed legal representative, August," she explained, slowing the car for the turn into the driveway. "I filed the mental hygiene application, but my involvement ended there. I've called to see how she's doing, but they won't tell me anything other than I can leave a message for her."

"That doesn't make any sense, if you were able to commit her," I said quietly. "I mean, you did sign the papers, didn't you?"

"Look!" Helen exclaimed, a bit too enthusiastically. "Tommy and Liz are here!"

Sitting on a wrought iron bench next to the front door were Tommy and a girl I'd never met before but had heard a lot about. Liz was always away at some sort of camp, the most recent one lasting four weeks. On one hand, I found it hard to imagine being away from home for that long. On the other, I realized that was exactly what I had done as well.

"About time!" Tommy yelled as we pulled up and I got out of the car. "Did you forget our date?"

My face instantly got warm. "I sure did," I said. "I'm sorry."

"This is the famous Liz," he said with a flourish. Though she was only two years older, Liz was even taller and lankier than Tommy. Her dark hair was pulled back into a high ponytail and bangs covered her eyebrows, giving her face a serious look.

"Thank you for letting me use your bike, Liz."

"Not like I had a choice since I didn't even know you had been," Liz said, holding out her right hand to shake mine. Under her left arm was a bulky Trivial Pursuit game box. "Let's find out how dumb Tommy is, shall we?"

Helen shooed us around the house, and we sat cross-legged on a blanket under the giant oak in the backyard. An hour later, Tommy grumbled, "This game stinks."

"Says the boy with zero wedges," Liz said while reaching for another card from the pile. She handed it to me. "Here you go. Read the brown question real slow or he won't understand."

Something about the way Liz looked at me as if she were examining me like a bug under a microscope made me nervous. "Sure," I said, before turning back toward Tommy.

"Whose final novel was entitled *The Mystery of Edwin Drood*?" Before he had a chance to answer, I repeated "Edwin Drood" like a professional TV game host, slow and dramatic. My wheel was only missing the sports wedge, since so much of my three years of raising myself had been filled with books, television, the internet, and museums. There really wasn't much trivia I didn't know. Except sports.

Tommy still hadn't answered his question. I repeated, "Edwin Drood."

"What is this crap?" he groaned. "I get this, and you get who wrote *Harry Potter*?"

"Edwin Drood . . ." I said for the third time in case he'd forgotten the question.

Tommy smirked a little. "Charles Dickens."

"Correct! Go ahead and get yourself a brown wedge," I said into my pretend microphone. "A brown wedge."

Liz stood and dusted off her designer shorts. "This is boring as all get out. I'm gonna go watch Gram's stories with her. Peace out, loser."

"No idea what her problem is," Tommy said after she disappeared.

"She was about to win, and I don't think she wanted to do that," I said, lying down on the blanket to stretch out my back while he packed up the game.

"Now *that's* stupid." Tommy lay down on his side of the blanket. A light breeze moved the oak's branches and speckled us with bits of sunshine.

"Not to someone who's a lot younger. That's worse than losing."

"Wrong again," he said, smiling and slow-shaking his head. "She'd crawl over the back of a newborn to win if she had to. Want to play twenty questions?"

"I guess." Tommy didn't follow the usual rules of twenty questions. He just liked asking a bunch of unrelated questions that had no theme or end point, rather than trying to guess a person, place, or thing. He had also made up this random rule that we had to answer questions within five seconds of being asked. He stated this kept a person honest. Just when I thought I had it down, he added one more random stipulation: We couldn't both use the same answer.

"Favorite TV show?" I went first.

"It's *24*. What's your favorite TV show?"

"*Friends*."

"I did not see that one coming." Tommy sounded disappointed.

I was offended without understanding why. "What do you mean?"

"Nothing. It's just, you're not one for all that primping and hanging around a bunch of other people. You're more of a lone wolf. Plus, you're a tomboy. But like in a good way because you like doing guy stuff even though you look like a girl." Tommy sat up, suddenly looking terribly uncomfortable.

"Okay," I said, still offended. "I guess there's a compliment in there somewhere?"

"Someday you won't be a tomboy at all," Tommy blurted, apparently realizing he'd upset me. "You'll be all girl. I mean woman. Definitely woman."

Something about Tommy's awkward stammering caused a sudden warmth to spread across my body. When I took in the miserable look on his face, my heart ticked a little faster.

I sat up and pretended to look for a blade of grass thick enough to make a whistle, like he'd taught me to do. I caught a whiff of soap on the breeze and rubbed my nose, thinking about how much nicer clothes smell when they've been dried outside. Tommy smelled like the wind on a hot summer day, and I liked it.

"My turn," I said, shaking my head of Tommy thoughts and wishing Helen would appear with cookies and lemonade.

"Okay," he stalled. "But, new rule for this lightning round: Questions need to have yes-or-no answers." It was my turn, but he held up his hand and asked, "Do you like Savannah?"

"Yes." I wedged the grass between my thumbs and blew a low note. "Do you wish you lived here full-time instead of Augusta?"

"Yes. Have you, August Caine, ever liked a boy?"

"No," I blurted out, caught completely unawares. When I saw his face fall, I quickly added, "I mean yes. I mean, I don't know? Do you mean *liked* liked, or just plain liked?" He ran his hand through his hair and looked me in the eyes.

"Don't you know?" he asked.

"It's my turn," I replied, but before I could ask him if he'd ever liked a girl, the kitchen screen door whined open and the refreshments I had been hoping for appeared at exactly the wrong time.

Later that night I lay in bed and thought about Tommy, especially about how shy and awkward he had seemed. I wondered what he was doing right then.

My room was hot and stuffy, and the air conditioner didn't seem to lower the temperature one bit. I tried flopping one leg on top of the sheet and one under it. I twisted my hair high on my head and flipped the pillow over a dozen times. Helen was banging around in the kitchen again, which made sleep seem impossible. *What the hell is she doing?*

I climbed out of bed, opened a window, and hung my head out, hoping to get some air, but there wasn't even a hint of a breeze. My gaze drifted to the oak tree where we'd spent the afternoon, wishing I'd simply answered yes to Tommy's question.

I imagined I saw him there, standing still and looking back up at me—my own personal Romeo. The night sky's clouds shifted, and I was startled to see there *was* someone standing there.

I dropped to the floor, measuring my breath, considering the options. It couldn't be Helen; she was still clanking around in the kitchen. It wasn't Tommy; he had a very strict curfew. Maybe Liz? I inched back to the window and looked again. The person was still there, but I couldn't make out if it was a man or a woman. A young, middle-aged, or older person. The only thing I could see was a motionless silhouette, one I imagined was staring right back at me.

When my eyes adjusted to the darkness, the woman who'd cornered me in Helen's kitchen that first day filtered into focus. I heard myself gasp when she gave me a slow, terrifying wave.

I ran to the kitchen so fast I nearly missed the bottom step. When I got there, I found Helen surrounded by pots and pans and her head engulfed by the bottom cabinet. She crawled out when I yelled her name and the smile slipped from her face when she saw mine.

"What's wrong, August?"

I couldn't tell her right away. I stood there chugging air and shaking all over while my mind sorted through her possible reactions. Helen might say it was a dream or that I had an overactive imagination.

"I saw"—I took a deep breath—"your friend in the yard. That angry lady who was here the first day I came to live with you."

Helen's expression immediately turned from concerned to angry as she hurried outside.

I wasn't sure if I should follow or stay put. If I should tell her about the scrap of paper with my name on it or stay quiet. Before I had to choose, Helen returned, locked the door, and avoided my eyes as she moved the pile of cookware from the floor to the counter.

"Nobody's out there." The lids clanked from her hands, shaking.

"But I know it was her." I intended to hold firm, but in that moment, I suddenly understood. Helen was struggling with a decision: To tell me everything or nothing. To tell the truth, make up a story, or avoid the subject. When I saw a tear slip down her face, I decided to make things easy for her. I made a slow move toward the stairs.

"I'm sure you're right," I said. "Maybe I nodded off and was dreaming."

Helen gave the smallest nod, but no eye contact. I heard her sigh out a small sob as I left the kitchen.

I hurried upstairs. I crawled back in bed and studied my father's stars while thinking about how weird and unsettled things were. Helen didn't want to tell me what the deal was with that woman. The most likely explanation was it had something to do with me. I couldn't imagine what I could have done to earn that woman's anger or why she wanted to scare me, but the realization that she *wanted* me to be afraid of her led me to a decision. Unless she directly threatened me in some way, I was never going to mention her to Helen again. I didn't want to put Helen in an awkward position, as I'd just done, but more crucially, I didn't want Helen to confront her. I didn't want to give that woman the satisfaction of knowing she'd succeeded in making me afraid.

I pulled the sheet up to my eyes. Late into the night, I tried to convince myself I wasn't scared of her or anyone else. Not the least little bit.

Chapter Sixteen

TIME CAPSULES

Someone pounded on the kitchen door early the next morning. Thomas was standing on the front step, as though he had grown there like one of the oaks. The polo shirt and sneakers he wore probably meant he wasn't working. The badge and gun clipped to his belt probably meant he wasn't ever *not* working.

"Morning," he said, his hair damp and tousled. One small lock fell lower than his hairline.

"Good morning, Thomas," I answered, happy to see him. "Are you holding a pie?"

"Yes, ma'am," he answered with a small bow.

I unlatched the screen door, and he slid right past me. His clothes smelled hot out of the dryer, and freshly pressed. I leaned forward and inhaled more deeply. He stopped short of the kitchen door, and my nose nearly bumped into his spine.

"Anywhere on the counter is fine." I pushed past him, ignoring our near collision. "I already had breakfast. I could force myself to eat some pie, though, depending on the flavor."

"Peach," he said, while pretending to be stunned. "Is there any other kind?"

"There are rumors to that effect, but frankly, I'm skeptical," I said in my best Southern belle voice, and batted my eyes.

He laughed, and I smiled.

"Want some coffee?"

"That would be terrific."

He gathered dessert plates, a knife, and two forks.

"Cream? Sugar?" I asked, while noticing that he opened the silverware drawer like he knew his way around this kitchen.

"Black is fine. You look terrible. Did you sleep?"

I laughed at his bluntness. "You are as subtle as ever, Tommy. Sorry. Thomas."

"About that," he said, slicing and plating the pie. "I've been thinking that I like it when you call me Tommy. Never really liked Thomas, but my ex thought it made me sound more grown-up."

"Are you working today, *Tommy*?"

I laughed, and he smiled.

"I'm off for the next four days, but I might have to go to Macon."

"I just realized I didn't ask what you do." I took a bite of pie. "You mentioned you went into law enforcement, but what agency specifically?"

"GBI," he said. "Sorry, Georgia Bureau of Investigation. I forgot you live in a foreign country. You couldn't possibly know the initials for every American agency."

"Did you make this, Special Agent Reese?" I took a larger bite and talked around the explosion of peach juice. "It's delicious."

He smiled at my juvenile behavior and scooped a bite with a spoon. "Grams made it. She can't remember where she left her shoes, but she still bakes like a pro."

"Did you tell her about Helen?"

Tommy sighed and shook his head. "Carly, my niece, did. She's staying with Grams this week. She didn't realize my sister and I had decided not to tell her. She didn't realize it even though I told her twice not to mention it."

"Kids," I said, although I understood very little about children. Kids were never a consideration for me, so I'd never bothered to learn much about their phases and stages. Their quirks and weird rituals.

"Helen was great with Grams," Tommy added.

I nodded, unsure what to say. "Were they close?"

"They always got along as neighbors, but within the last three or four years, Grams really started failing. I can't tell you how much Helen keeping an eye on her helped us. I live in Atlanta. Liz, in Charleston. We couldn't have managed without Helen."

I tried to ask what he would do now that Helen was gone, but everything felt so, so sad. The past. The future. This moment. *I will not cry. I will not cry.* I shook my head, hoping to trick my brain into believing things were fine. But they weren't and never would be. The cruel, casual way my mother had lied to me about Helen's death was something I would never get past.

Tommy's hand froze with the cup at his lips. "I didn't mean to upset you," he said. "I just wanted to tell you how much I appreciated Helen. I should have waited until after the service. I sometimes don't read the room like I should."

I waved a frantic hand at him. "It's okay. I want to know everything about Helen, but every time I hear her name, I feel this overwhelming guilt."

He slid around the table so close it left me no choice but to meet his eyes.

"Why would you feel guilty? You were a kid when you came

here, and you were a kid when you left. You had no control over anything."

"I'm almost thirty-one years old," I croaked, unable to stop the tears. "I could have come back years ago. My mother told me terrible lies about Helen, but I shouldn't have listened. I shouldn't have let myself become like one of those birds that has spent so much time in a cage, it never tries to escape. But that's exactly what I am now. A bird that's too afraid or too stupid to leave, even when the door gets left open."

Tommy touched my arm. I expected him to try to convince me I shouldn't feel the way I did. Instead, he did something much kinder. He said nothing. He didn't ask me to explain or offer me trite, generic words of wisdom. He just let me ramble.

I realized my mistake seconds later. No, not a mistake. A major slip. He would start to wonder what I meant about my mother lying to me about Helen. He may or may not ask me about it, but he would wonder. I decided to try something new—telling the truth.

"Tommy, do you remember the things I told you yesterday about my life?"

He nodded and tapped his watch. "Sure," he said. "We only had that conversation twenty hours ago. I'm not senile just yet."

I smiled at his attempt to infuse some humor into the situation. "Most of it was a lie. I didn't go to fancy private schools or college. I wasn't even allowed to go in person to high school. I didn't have friends or travel for the sake of traveling. I only ever traveled when my mother made us move because she believed we were in danger."

"You don't owe me an explanation," he said. "It doesn't matter what was true and what wasn't. You're my friend, so whatever it is, it is. Families are weird."

"My mother is more than weird. She has a severe mental illness."

"Okay," Tommy said, and leaned in. I looked past him at the floor.

One tile, I tell him about Maman. Two tiles, I tell him about the hospital. Three tiles, I tell him about Cort. Four tiles, I tell him about the awful secret I've kept for twenty-three years . . .

His phone buzzed and shook on the table next to my unfinished pie.

"I'm sorry," he said, one finger in the air. "Hold that thought, or those thoughts, because you look like you're working on a mighty big puzzle in there." He tapped the middle of my forehead and looked at his texts. "I'm sorry, August. They need me in Macon after all. Can we pick this up where we left off when I get back?"

"Sure," I said, an equal amount of disappointed and relieved. "It's not like I don't have plenty to do, you know. Write a eulogy, organize the silverware drawer . . ."

I stared out the window for a long time after Tommy left for Macon. I wasn't sure what to do with myself post-meltdown. I cleaned up the dishes and put the pie in the fridge, nestling its roundness amongst the many untouched square foil pans of hot dishes and lasagnas that kept appearing at my door. If I'd never had an eating disorder, I certainly would have acquired one amidst all that soggy pasta and cream sauce. My anorexic brain kicked in, and I went upstairs and pulled a pair of running shoes from Helen's closet and headed east. Within five blocks of near-sprinting, my side caught and the afternoon breeze died.

Helen's feet were not like mine at all, and her shoes were already blistering my little toes. In my haste to get out of the house, I had forgotten my earbuds, and without music, this whole experience turned into a nightmare.

I slowed to a stop on a road in the middle of nowhere and turned back. Cutting through the side yard and the blackberry patch, I leaned against the carriage house to catch my breath and retie my right shoe—for the third time, even though I'd double-tied it when I first set out. I realized I'd never been in this small building overgrown with wisteria and couldn't see anything through the side window. I went around to the front and examined the door. It looked freshly painted, with new hinges and a number lock over the antique doorknob. I punched in 2004, as that was the year that Helen first discovered push-button locks, and was not at all surprised when the bolt withdrew and the door swung open.

If time itself had a scent, this would be it: damp and earthy. I turned a slow circle in a room meticulously crammed full of curiosities. Shelves lined two of the walls, stacked with vases and knickknacks that should have been sold to an antique dealer decades earlier. Helen clearly liked to collect a random assortment of things—one shelf was dedicated to salt and pepper shakers in the shape of fruits and vegetables, another to a complete flock of painted wooden duck decoys from different eras. In the middle of the room was a large purple velvet wingback chair and a small side table that could have been plucked from the pages of Lewis Carroll. A perfect teacup rested on the marble top, with a residue of dried tea leaves at its bottom. It looked entirely out of place.

Staged even.

My body was sticky from cooled sweat, my calves cramped, and I was tired. I sat down in the chair, which faced away from the bric-a-brac, and tried to connect to Helen's reason for this room, when she had so many rooms in the house where she could have displayed her treasures.

This was high-end hoarding of a very unusual nature, hidden away and compulsively ordered in a way that must have given her some sense of control over her life. I let my eyes wander from one wall to the next, one completely covered in vintage tin signs, and another in a ghostly array of both cuckoo and Felix the Cat clocks. I suspected that she would come out here, wind them all, and listen to the ticking and chirping as a sort of hobby.

The carriage house at first appeared to be comprised of one large room because I hadn't noticed the seamless door cleverly hidden by the way the old tin signs were hung. I ran my fingers along the tiny crack, but no obvious catch revealed itself. Intrigued, I lifted the center picture of a rosy-cheeked Santa, and the door clicked. I heard a slight rustle behind it. *Please don't let a rat be behind that door. Don't let it be a serial killer either. If it has to be one of those things, though, let it be a serial killer.*

When I gave it a push, the door swung halfway open, and I pointed my phone's flashlight inside a small room filled with dusty white boxes stacked along the wall. Instinctively, I reached over my head and connected with a string pull that lit the stark space. For the most part, the white boxes looked identical and were meticulously ordered and labeled. One stack stood out for two reasons: They were heavily taped brown cardboard shipping boxes, and under closer inspection, bore my mother's unmistakable handwriting. *Property of Davis Caine.*

My mother had packed up all my father's belongings the week after he died. At first, I couldn't understand how she could remove all traces of him. I later came to accept that it was too much for her. Reminders were too painful. But she hadn't been able to completely get rid of his things either.

I hefted the boxes from the carriage house and directly into the screen porch, depositing them one by one next to the coffee table. Upon further inspection, I noticed that Helen had apparently opened the boxes, done an inventory, and then taped them shut again. She had labeled each of the boxes on the outside before stowing them away in a dark, hidden corner of the property.

The top box was marked LEGAL DOCUMENTS/TAX RETURNS. As good a place as any to dive in. The files were neatly organized and notated in my mother's distinct handwriting. Had they existed like this before my father's death, or did she work through her grief one manila folder at a time? The files were marked by date, the oldest from the year before I was born, and ended the year he died. I started with the most recent and worked backward.

The first few returns, from his time as a photojournalist, had my father listed as "self-employed." The attached income documents, consistent with this, were 1099s from dozens of different newspapers and magazines. My mother had never held a job that I knew of, and this narrative played out in her role as simply "dependent" along with me on his returns.

The oldest return was different from the others. My father had not listed himself as self-employed, and the income statement was a W-2. This wouldn't have struck me as all that strange except the name and tax ID number of his employer had been blacked out on the return and all the attachments, as had his income.

I flipped back to the first page. My father's home address was also redacted. Marital status: single. The other returns had our address in New York.

I held it up to the light, trying to see through the black squares. It didn't help. Why would my father have gone to the trouble of hiding his place of employment? The rest of the box was filled with invoices, pay stubs, and other work-life ephemera.

I sliced open the next box, marked NEGATIVES, and was surprised to find boxes of slides, each carefully numbered, named, and dated in black marker in a masculine script.

Before I could exam them, my phone dinged.

Mind if I swing by? Daniel Grant texted. *Need to finish up paperwork.*

Anytime, I texted, hoping it would be much later. I needed a break from everyone and everything. My mind swirled around and over all the motion of the day, the small victories, the large disappointments. There was no break. The detritus of death's aftermath was relentless, and what I really needed was a stiff shot of something and a long nap.

I'm in the neighborhood.

Of course, I thought, *no rest for the wicked.*

Two minutes later, Daniel knuckle-rapped the side door. I steered him to Helen's office, where the box he'd so kindly given me to sort through sat unmoved and mostly unread.

Daniel gave the office a long, admiring look while I opened the bottle of wine I had snagged from the kitchen. "I have never been in this room. It's amazing."

"It is, isn't it?" I took the kind of sip from my glass that looks small, but requires immediate refilling.

"It's like something you would see in an English castle." Daniel picked up his glass and moved to the window. "What a view. Clear sight line all the way down that row of trees."

"I always thought of this room as a museum. I loved coming in here, but I didn't want to bother Helen. She was in here a lot doing historical research. Writing articles. Catnapping." I laughed. "She spent about ninety percent of her time either in here, on the porch, or in the kitchen. I'm not sure she ever actually slept in her bed."

I smiled at another memory. "Sometimes I would sneak in here and sit behind her desk, pretending I was the head of the Smithsonian. Or a bank tycoon. Or a psychiatrist. I was indecisive back then."

"Didn't Helen have a computer?" Daniel moved back to the nearly empty desk and laid his hands on the top of the box. His nails were perfect, each with a tiny white moon at the cuticle, and no rings.

"I remember a laptop." I pulled the door open to an oak armoire in the corner. "Here we go. The only modern convenience she'd let out in the open was the toaster."

"A purist," he said, smiling. "My aunt was like that. She hid phones in drawers so no one would be offended." He tilted his head. "You doing all right?"

"I am." I blinked and took a long sip, feeling the warmth of the wine mixed with Daniel's concern in the middle of my chest. "It's just a lot to process. Sorry, I haven't gotten a chance to look at the documents. I keep getting distracted."

He gave me a don't-worry-about-it smile before opening his leather case and removing a file. "If now isn't a good time to do this," he said, "most of it can wait. There are a good number of documents for you to sign, though, so I thought we could get the legal end of things moving."

Seeing him pull those papers out was awful. It brought an image of Helen, weak and ill, spending her last few days trying to put her affairs in order. As a distraction, I silently counted the number of law books on each shelf.

"It seems insensitive to discuss these things right now, but I thought you might be leaving after the service tomorrow."

"I haven't made arrangements to return, but we can do this now."

He nodded and uncapped a fountain pen with his initials engraved on the side. "That's the great thing about what you do for a living," he said. "You can do what you do from anywhere. Me, I'm needed at specific places at specific times. There are strings attached to my strings."

"True. I'm a no-strings-attached type of person. No one depending on me," I added, while thinking about how I had spent my entire life entwined in my mother's problems.

"We'll go ahead and talk through this, but I've arranged for a notary to be here in twenty minutes. We'll need him to make everything official. Once that happens, I'll file everything with the probate court. It will take about ninety days, start to finish."

I opened the top drawer of the desk and picked a pen from the trough. Caine and Caine Ghost Tours. I stifled an urge to cry.

"Since the will is perfectly clear that all of her holdings, possessions, and accounts be transferred to your name, and there are no other living relatives, everything is fairly straightforward." He neatened a stack of papers with small colored tags decorating the right edge, each indicating another piece of Helen's life that was about to be mine.

"Here's another copy of the will." He laid it to the left of the pile. "You have copies of the deeds for both houses in the file box, but these are the originals. Have you gone over to Tybee to see it yet?"

I shook my head.

"This is more paperwork for checking, savings, and stock accounts, and this is the deed to the Montgomery Street office."

I skimmed the document. "The whole building?"

Daniel grinned and handed me a rental agreement. "Which," he said, "makes me your first official tenant, if you'll have me."

"I don't see why not." We signed our names, one over the other, his hand brushing mine in the transfer.

Daniel checked his bulky watch again. The notary was running late. He picked at invisible lint on his pants before he made his way over to a wall displaying two dozen postcard-size prints. Each one depicted a city Helen had visited during her naval career, when she'd had free time to explore as a tourist. The last time I had been in her office, twenty-seven prints had lined that section of wall. Two had since been added.

"These are beautiful," he said. "Is there a theme?"

"When Helen traveled, she liked to shop in open-air markets. Mom-and-pop shops with local artists. Those are scenes from places she vacationed. She did her own framing."

"Neat," he said while I counted them a second time. Twenty-nine.

"She always wrote the date of her visits on the back." I lifted one of my favorites from the wall hook and held it in front of him. "See here. She visited Rome on July 13, 1990."

I put the print back on the wall, and my eyes drifted to another one farther down the row. I froze when I recognized the location.

"Neat," Daniel repeated right before the door knocker thudded.

Daniel grabbed the stack of papers and made his way to the kitchen. I pulled myself away from the print and followed him. Because everything had already been signed, the notary—whose business card said his name was John—only needed me to initial each page. Everything was done in a matter of seconds, which reminded me of how fast a person's life can change. Or end. One minute a person is happy, surrounded by the things they cherish—the next someone is pushing a seal onto pieces of paper and erasing everything about them.

As soon as Daniel and John the notary left, I made a beeline back to Helen's office. My interest this time had nothing to do with fossils or old books or any of the artifacts in the display cases. It was the two extra prints that had grabbed my attention. The first was from a place I knew well. Better than well. I had lived behind the timeworn walls of Avignon off and on for the last eighteen years. I tugged the print from the hook and inspected it. The spot in the picture was the Pont d'Avignon—Avignon's famous bridge to nowhere. Seeing it brought a childhood song to mind.

Sur le Pont d'Avignon, l'on y danse, l'on y danse.
Sur le Pont d'Avignon, l'on y danse tous en rond.
On the bridge of Avignon, we all dance there,
we all dance there.
On the bridge of Avignon, we all dance there in a ring.

Twelve years earlier, Helen had written *July 2nd* on the back. I did the math in my head. I would have recently turned eighteen. Instead of finishing high school like most people my age, I had just gotten released from the psychiatric hospital, where I'd spent three years.

I read the date on the print again and worked the numbers backward so I could figure out how close or far apart we had been on that exact date.

Avignon becomes overrun with tourists every year in July for the Festival d'Avignon. Thousands come to attend the theater productions, concerts, and dance performances. I knew where I was on the date Helen had written on the back of that print. More so than any other year, I remember that one because I had wanted to stay in Avignon for the festivities, but my mother insisted we relocate for a few weeks. She had been nearly agoraphobic in New York, but once we got to France, she did a 180-degree turn. The longer we stayed in one place, the edgier she got. She wanted to be in constant motion.

"The crowds and noise and commotion of the festival would be too stressful for us both," she claimed. I should have insisted we stay. I desperately needed crowds and noise and commotion. I craved it. Silence and isolation had almost killed me.

But I didn't argue with her. I never did. I packed my luggage like every other time, and we left. Sometimes leaving Avignon meant staying gone for a few weeks, and sometimes it turned into months. Once it turned into two years.

She'd rented a house that summer for us in Bordeaux, and although I didn't want to leave Avignon, the Bordeaux countryside was one of the most incredible places imaginable. It was my first time there, and the experience of discovering a place I'd read so much about did wonders for my mood. I became enthralled with the public gardens, the curving river quays, and all the wonderful, preserved structures lining the streets. I would often walk the streets and hills for hours at a time.

Even our rental house turned out to be an amazing place to explore. It was an old stone warehouse that had been remodeled into a beautiful, quaint house full of antiques. It sat on isolated grounds, which offered wide, unobstructed views of the green, rolling hills.

We stayed at the Bordeaux cottage seven weeks before returning to Avignon, only to pack up and leave for Reims three days later. My mother had said she'd inherited a small farmhouse there when she was young. I didn't doubt her at the time, but it could have been another of her lies. Once we got there, she hadn't seemed all that familiar with the house or the area.

Thinking about her moving us all over the place brought up a question that had nagged me for years: How was my mother able to function when I was hospitalized?

At times we had housekeepers, and depending on her level of paranoia, we even had internet service. I'd always assumed we relocated to places familiar to her from childhood. She told me she had traveled around a lot as a young girl. Maybe that wasn't the case. Maybe she'd arranged everything online. That's how I'd taken care of things before and after my hospital stay.

She'd tell me where we were going, and I'd find a house or an apartment online.

I was sure money had never been an issue. I'd been helping with the bills and shopping even before I moved with Helen to Savannah. My mother had several bank accounts, and if Helen hadn't told me that first day in Savannah that my mother had come from old money, I might never have come to understand that she'd inherited it from her family. Still, financial security alone couldn't explain her ability to navigate the chaotic world she had created for us.

In any case, our leaving Avignon at the exact time Helen was there surely could not have been just a coincidence.

Our worlds had intersected without colliding. Had my mother insisted we leave because she'd somehow learned Helen was coming? And why had she gone to such extremes to keep us away from each other? It made no sense. My mother hadn't conveyed any hostile feelings toward Helen. Then again, she had never answered any of my questions about her either.

I put the print of Avignon back on the hook and took the second one down.

When I recognized another familiar location, I whispered, "No way." It was a small watercolor print of the dome of the Cathedral di Palermo in Italy, near Sicily. The date on the back of the picture was from October, six years earlier. No specific dates were listed. Only the month and year. We had rented a house in Palermo for nine months that same year, after my mother became insistent that things were no longer safe for us in France. Helen had been there in October. She had missed us by less than a month. Why had she come? Could that also have been just a coincidence?

Avignon and Palermo get tons of tourists, but neither is a place someone would visit before the major destinations. Helen had visited Rome many years earlier, but she'd not gone to Venice or Florence.

The same with France. She had never been to Lyon or Nice. These were much more likely destinations than Avignon. It didn't feel like a coincidence. I put the print back, still unsure of many things but now knowing three things for certain: One, my mother was either sadistic or more affected by mental illness than I had ever imagined. Two, she had to have had help, because she'd known Helen was coming. And three, Helen had known where to come looking for me long before I made the life insurance withdrawal that she had told Daniel Grant led her to me.

Chapter Seventeen

OLD AT ELEVEN

Summer wrapped up in a blur, with the start of school shocking me in the middle of August. Even as a homeschooled kid, I had been set in a New York rhythm of post–Labor Day soft slide back, and Helen hadn't thought to mention how rude an awakening being back in a classroom while the days were still long and lush would be. I'd already taken the required placement tests, but I'd just as quickly forgotten about it, or more likely blocked it with my fear of reentering adolescent society.

"You're going to love St. Michael's," she said as she pulled up to the multibuilding campus. "Are you sure you don't want me to escort you in?"

"Yup," I mumbled, still fuming from the weekend. Helen had sprung everything on me by laying out a green-and-blue-plaid jumper on my bed, along with a long dissertation on her glory days at "St. Mike's." I was pretty sure the uniform had been hers. She started to get out of the car, camera in hand. "That's okay," I said. "We took one at home."

"Gotcha!" She thrust two thumbs up. "I'll be right here at three fifteen, earlier if you need me."

As soon as I stepped into the middle school building, I realized I shouldn't have waved off her offers to come with me. I'd not been inside of a school for over three years. My thought going into it was that all schools were different, but they were also all the same. This school was nothing like my last one, though; it was ultramodern, with a lot of glass and shiny tiles—clearly the newest addition to a sprawling K–12 campus.

Kids swarmed in all directions. Their voices became so overwhelming and buzzlike I had to hide in the bathroom until I could pull myself together. Ten minutes later, I located the seventh-grade homeroom listed on the schedule Helen had laminated for me.

Ms. Branson's classroom was already filled with chattering students and freezer cold. My first realization was that the school's uniform had been modified to a green polo shirt and navy short or skort casual look. Strike one. I pulled on one of my tightly woven braids and slid into the only empty seat, next to a girl with *Sienna* written all over her notebook in every shape, color, and size. She'd drawn little hearts and the names of a dozen different boys next to them. I wasn't sure what to make of this.

Sienna caught me staring and covered the notebook with her arm, scowling at me.

"One," she snipped, holding up a finger. "What do you think you're looking at? Two, who the hell are you supposed to be? Pocahontas?"

Strike two. Strike three.

With my dark hair, I supposed I could have passed as an American Indian. Otherwise, I wasn't sure what she was talking about, and I wasn't about to ask. I looked away while she whispered to the girl on the other side of the aisle.

Ms. Branson looked about eleven years old herself, and stood barely taller than the seated students. She moved to the front of the room and clapped her hands briskly together three times. "Good morning!"

Crickets.

"I hope everyone enjoyed their summer!"

More crickets.

"I have an updated student list," she said, her voice too big for such a small room. "Superintendent James has erroneously assigned . . . August Caine to this class." She raked her finger down the list and scanned the room. I shrank down in my seat while my face heated to a sizzle.

Sienna giggled and whispered to the girl next to her, "She's probably in special classes."

I noticed her making air quotes.

"August Caine?"

I pulled myself up straight and half raised my hand. Thirty sets of eyes turned my way and slowly looked me up and down. My face burned hotter.

The teacher motioned to me.

I collected my backpack and shuffled to the front. She handed me a sheet of paper with my name on it.

"You're in advanced courses. You'll need to go to the high school campus," she said, loud enough for everyone to hear. "Mr. Cunningham's freshman homeroom. Two buildings over, just left of the cafeteria."

She turned her attention back to the room. "Can someone escort this young lady to B53?"

Everyone shot a hand into the air except Sienna and the mousy girl next to her. Sienna made a face at me instead. By the time I got to the correct room, the bell rang and I was nearly knocked over by a wave of much bigger children, and my back was soaked straight through my shirt and jumper.

Mr. Cunningham took pity on me and introduced me to a girl who shared my schedule, and she took me under her wing—at least for the first day. By the end of the week, I was finding my solitary way around, invisible once again. This made me strangely comfortable and was far better than the hell I saw coming had I stayed in Sienna's world.

That Sunday, Tommy's family came to visit his grandmother. When he found me reading my biology homework on the screen porch swing in the late afternoon, I was too exhausted to be mad at him for not warning me about the onset of school.

"Your aunt told me not to," he explained and shrugged, unfolding a PB&J from wax paper. "I figured she had her reasons. Adults usually do."

"Well, did she also tell you that I tested out of middle school? That made me instantly popular with Sienna and Mackenzie."

"Who?"

"Oh, just some hateful seventh graders I'd never met before but were mean to me anyways." I took half of the PB&J—my favorite snack due to Gram's homemade peach jam. He elbowed me in the ribs.

"Stop complaining," he laughed. "At least you know you're smart *and* pretty. Who cares about a couple stuck-up girls?"

Peanut butter stuck in my throat. *Pretty.* I took a swig of soda. "I wish you lived here," I mumbled as he stood up, making the swing wobble unevenly.

"I gotta go. We're headed home. School starts for me tomorrow." He handed me the uneaten portion of his half. "See ya Labor Day!"

As I watched him cross the yard I couldn't tell whether he'd heard me and was trying to get away, or if he'd heard me and felt the same. Or, as was most likely, he hadn't heard me at all.

"Oh, did Tommy leave?" Helen asked as she entered the screen porch from the house, pulling me from my thoughts.

"School starts for him in the morning," I replied.

"Well, *August*, this is a dumb question, but have you finished your homework for tomorrow?" I looked down at the bio book on my lap and noticed I had left it open to a dissection of the human heart. I blushed, thinking about Tommy saying I was smart *and* pretty.

"Why is that a dumb question?"

"Because you're eleven years old and more responsible and self-sufficient than I am at my age. I'm childlike. And you, well, you're old for your age, and clearly smarter than the average bear."

Helen eased down next to me and gave me a playful shove, making the swing wobble again, which only served to remind me of Tommy. I didn't respond.

"It's a dumb question, but I think adults are supposed to ask those sorts of things," she said. "I don't have kids. I'm learning as I go."

For some reason I was softened by her uncertainty. "You're doing a great job, Aunt Helen. And I did my homework. Most of it anyway." I pointed at a notebook on the side table. "I still have an assignment for creative writing. I meant to do it earlier, but I cleaned my room first. I can't concentrate when something is hanging over me."

"You do realize they make a pill for that?"

"For what?"

"For just about everything."

"Wait. What?"

"I'm teasing," Helen laughed, and shoved the swing off again. She planted her feet like she couldn't concentrate on swinging if talking. "Are you okay with going to school? I know I sprung it on you, but ripping off the Band-Aid seemed like the right course of action."

"It's okay," I said, suddenly fine with the idea of it. "I guess I just don't do well with sudden changes."

"I wish I could promise you that something else like that won't happen again, but you're smart enough to know that the world does what it wants, when it wants."

I shrugged. "School is fine so far. I try to make good use of the time."

Helen gave me a strange look and pushed the swing again. I was getting a little seasick with all the starts and stops. The wobbling.

"Have you met any new friends? Anyone you find interesting or nice?"

I shrugged. "I hang out with Tommy."

"Who else?"

"Tommy," I said again, and we both smiled.

"Tommy Reese is a fine young man," she said, twisting a tad closer.

"He's really smart too, but he pretends he's not."

She gave a dramatic eye roll. "Boys," she said. "And if you're going to hang around Tommy, I guess we better have the old you-know-what talk soon. Not tonight, but soon."

It took me a beat to figure out what she was talking about, and when it dawned on me my face heated up about a thousand degrees. If I had three wishes right then, I would have used one of them to disappear. I'd spent hundreds of hours in a library. Sex was a topic I was never going to need to discuss with her. At least from a textbook end, I was aware of the entire process.

"The kids at school are immature compared to you," she said, and I was beyond thankful she had moved on. "But don't write them off. You won't see what's under a person's surface if you don't spend time looking for it."

I nodded to be polite and to move the conversation in a different direction.

She dropped her eyes to my notebook. "So, what is your homework?"

"Write a short story using at least three words from this list." I showed Helen the SAT vocabulary attachment. "The story needs to somehow tie in with one I wrote in class, and it must include a metaphor and a simile. Piece of cake. That's a metaphor for how easy the assignment is."

"I guess you don't need me," Helen sighed, clearly disappointed by my independence.

"Well, I'd like it if you'd check it over for me?"

"Perfect," she said. "I guess I better go look up the word *simile* in a dictionary."

"This swing is like a boat—it's making me feel seasick. You see, the swing isn't *actually* a boat, it's *like* a boat."

"Okay, wise guy." She stilled the swing. "What's your story about?"

"The story I wrote yesterday was about Grace Riley, the daughter of Alice Riley, who was hanged in Wright Square for murdering William Wise. I made it so Grace survived, rather than dying at birth. A lot of awful things happened to her when she was a girl, but she grew up and fell in love with the apprentice at her adoptive father's tailor shop on the riverfront. They got married and couldn't have any children, so they adopted fourteen kids from a local orphanage and a cat named Sergeant F. E. Lines."

"Clever!" Helen clapped her hands.

"This next story has to stand alone but also relate to the first one," I continued. "It's about Grace being visited by Alice's spirit. At first, Grace is afraid of Alice because her neck is broken and the noose is still around it," I said, cocking my head for dramatic effect. "You can read the rest when it's done."

My aunt's eyes changed from narrow to wide. "Do you know the strange thing about you, August?"

"No. Well, yes, but you'll need to be more specific."

She chuckled. "The strange thing is that you don't believe in anything remotely mystical or supernatural. You don't believe in divine intervention or that God has a plan for us. You're all about science and hard evidence, and yet you're still creative. Your imagination is wonderful."

"I've never told you that I don't believe in those things," I said, feeling defensive. "But even if I don't, why is that strange?"

A shadow of sadness crossed her face. Her voice softened. "You don't always need to say what you believe or don't believe. Sometimes people understand things about a person without them ever saying a word. In a lot of ways, you're like an old skeptical person, but an eleven-year-old girl is still in there somewhere. A girl with an incredible imagination who wants to believe in something beyond what she can see or touch right now."

"Thanks," I said, although I was unsure if it was meant in a good way. It was one of those sorts of compliments (or not) that needed to be mulled over for a while.

She gave my shoulder a tiny squeeze. "You have a bright, wonderful future."

My face got hot from the good kind of embarrassment again, and I didn't need to think this over to understand Helen was proud of me and had a lot of faith in me. Sometimes adults try to build kids' confidence by throwing praise like confetti, but Helen was different.

"Let me know when you're ready for me to give it a look."

"Sure," I said, practically giddy from her interest and praise. "But try to remember, I'm just a kid."

Chapter Eighteen

LIES AND HALF-TRUTHS

I woke from a late afternoon nap and lingered in bed a bit, enjoying a small ripple of sun through the curtain. The house was quiet, my increasingly robust memory full of nostalgic sounds. Helen talking on the phone while she paced in the kitchen. Pots and pans clanking together. Helen humming or singing or filling the coffee pot. Loud sighs and feet on stairs.

Helen often used a phrase when she was flustered. She would half yell, "Hello, Bello." She would then move on to more standard curses, including some with vicious f-bombs. When riled up, she cussed like a sailor, which shouldn't have been surprising since technically she *was* a sailor.

Another sound that used to drift up from the kitchen was Helen opening the makeup case she kept in her purse. She wore subtle lipstick that she reapplied frequently. It made a distinct *click-clack* when she opened it, and *snap* when she closed it.

I missed these sounds. These beautiful, simple sounds. Much to Helen's disappointment, I never believed in ghosts. If I did believe, I imagine these would be the sounds they would bring with them. Not heavy chains dragging or spooky, throaty noises. Just the beautiful collision of day-to-day noises that hadn't been treasured until they were gone. The clicks and clacks. The hums and sighs. Squeaks and creaks.

When I let my mind flash back to our house after my father died, I realized everything I had heard was rote and methodical. High-heeled shoes clicking on marble tile. Forks gently clinking on plates. Classical music playing in the background at the same volume every time. No songs with words. The same lifeless music over and over.

The brownstone walls and windows filtered out noise, so even though we lived on Central Park West, our house had the dull quiet of a prairie. It was the same rotten solemnity that now pervaded Helen's empty house. An emptiness I simultaneously hated and sought.

I made my way to Helen's desk and worked on her eulogy. Every fifteen minutes or so, though, I was interrupted by one of Helen's friends showing up to drop off food. Each time someone knocked on the door or told me how sorry they were, I imagined myself as a movie character with amnesia. Only in this movie, the other characters didn't realize I had amnesia, so even though I had no frame of reference for any of it, they talked and asked questions and told me things like I'd been a part of it all along. Of course I vaguely recognized the many people who had graced Helen's parlor or card games, but I also suspected that more than a few of those people had preceded Helen to the graveyard, and so this day was hard on everyone who had the grace to show up for me.

No one asked me the type of questions I thought I would be asked, such as where I had been for the last two decades. Mercifully, Daniel had arranged for a couple of women to oversee

Operation Bury Helen, and I was able to pass well-wishers on with ease. He anticipated fifty or so people coming by the house for lunch after the funeral service; Helen's friends had already dropped off enough food for three times as many.

Just as I settled back into Helen's chair for the umpteenth time, someone texted from an unknown number.

> *Bringing you some things.*

A few minutes later, a soft knock came from the side door. Tommy held four plastic bags out for me. I slumped at the sight of them, then did a dramatic drop of my head as a follow-up. "No. More. Food."

"Don't blame me," he laughed. "This is from Liz. I'm just the delivery boy."

"I'm teasing." I waved him into the kitchen. "This is sweet of Liz. Of both of you."

"Geez, ole Pete," he whistled, surveying the counters. "Welcome to the South."

"Drinks over there." I pointed. "Desserts this way. Meat, fruit, and cheese trays go on this side of the fridge. Casseroles, this side. Paper products in this cabinet if you can find room."

Tommy gave me a salute while I jotted his and Liz's names down on the list for thank-you notes. He took the pen from me and crossed it off.

"Have you eaten?" he asked.

"Toast this morning. Plus some of that delicious pie you brought."

He laughed and eased into a chair. "I've been thinking about something. Can I ask you a personal question?"

"After all the things I told you yesterday, you're asking if you can ask me a personal question? Do you think I would divulge all that and then clam up?"

"That was situational." He shrugged. "This is about you. Not your situation. You."

I nodded, and he gave me a stern face.

"Do you still count stuff all the time?"

I covered my mouth and laughed. "I didn't realize I told you about that."

He smiled. "You didn't, but you were never subtle about it. Your lips and fingers move while you do it."

"That must have been very attractive." I shook my head. "I still do count things. But in a way that helps me organize my thoughts and calm my brain when it starts going in loops. A method I learned long before I was sent to a sleepaway camp for crazy teens."

He nodded, considering this. "So, it's not like every time you see a certain type of thing you have to count?"

"No. It can be anything at any time, and the next time, it might be something else. And occasionally I'll just zone out and find myself counting every book on a shelf. It's not a perfect science."

"Cool," he said.

"All right, then," I said back.

"Next topic. I was thinking about what you told me about your mom and all the moves. The not letting you go to school," he said. "Have you heard the saying 'Just because you're paranoid doesn't mean they aren't out to get you'?"

I shook my head. "No. But I'm quite familiar with folie à deux, or when paranoia is shared between two people, the first of which is completely insane, the second, an innocent bystander. Most often a child."

Tommy leaned closer. "What I'm saying is, your mother may have been paranoid, but it may not have been baseless. There may have been something to it. Maybe it's like the parable about the blind man and the elephant. If you can't see the whole thing, you can only go by the small part you have access to."

Before I had time to think about it, my eyes drifted to my phone, and I remembered Tommy's text. I replayed our conversations over the last two days and couldn't remember having given him my cell.

Tommy studied my face. "What is it?"

"You texted me a few minutes ago, yes?"

He gave me a Cheshire cat grin. "Guilty as charged."

"How did you get my number?"

Tommy got the look on his face people get when they're trying to decide whether to lie or tell the truth. He blew out a slow breath.

"Guilty as charged," he said again. No playful smile this time.

"Did Helen give it to you?"

Tommy shook his head and leaned closer. "No. I gave your number to her."

I waited for an explanation. Something flickered in my brain when he dropped his eyes away. I'd been lied to by someone else.

"Helen called me four or five months ago," he said softly. "She asked me to find you."

He brought his gaze back to meet mine, but only for a second. His mouth set into a tight, troubled line. "She told me about a website she suspected was yours, and she asked me if I could use it to locate you. I shouldn't have done it, but I gave the information to a guy I work with, and he tracked the IP address. Once he had that, he was able to access your physical address and your cell."

"Why didn't Helen just contact me through the website? Send me an email like a normal person? Why didn't you?"

Tommy shrugged. "I don't know," he said. "She asked me to

help, so I did. I didn't ask any questions. Like I said, I shouldn't have done it. But I'm glad I did."

I tried to keep the anger out of my voice, an anger that hadn't come from him breaking the law by tracking me down, but one that came from his pretense of acting surprised when I told him I'd been living in France all those years.

"So, the whole twenty-year thing yesterday was an act?"

"No," he said, shaking his head. "Helen asked for help, and I did it no questions asked. I was telling you the truth when I said she wouldn't tell me much about your situation. And I didn't do any other digging on you, I promise."

I couldn't look at Tommy, though his intentions must have been good. I almost laughed at the realization that I was angry because he'd lied about knowing I lied.

"I'm really sorry," he said, the words fading as though he was unsure about saying them. "In my experience, if a person doesn't want to be found, there's usually a good reason for it, but I couldn't say no to Helen."

"It's fine," I mumbled. I wanted to mean it. "It really is fine."

Tommy nodded and stared at the floor some more. "So," he said, "where do we go from here?"

"How about we just drop it? Like it never happened."

We made small talk, but things felt strained before he left. Standing alone on the porch in the dark, watching lightning in the distance, my thoughts were troubled. The more I learned about Helen's attempts to find me, the more convoluted my feelings. I'd left Daniel's office thinking she'd found me eleven or twelve months earlier. The framed prints in her office, though, made it seem she'd found me years earlier, not months.

Now, after talking with Tommy, the timeline had shifted again. She had tracked me down again just four or five months ago—long before she became ill.

How different might my life have been if only I'd questioned the things my mother had told me? If I'd taken an ounce of initiative rather than shutting myself off from the past, things wouldn't have come to this. Folie à deux or not, I must have had some autonomy at some point, or it wouldn't have been so easy for me to live in this house, away from the influence of my psychotic mother. Unless, of course, psychosis did run in the family.

I reached for my phone. "Siri, search Davis Caine photojournalist." I'd never thought to do this before, even though I research everything online. Like mother, like daughter. I'd shut him out of my life.

His picture appeared, and I studied his face for a minute before clicking a link about his career as a photojournalist, followed by the section about his personal life. He was in his late-forties when he married my much-younger mother, and had me quickly after. It had never occurred to me when I was little that he was that much older than her. To an eight-year-old, an adult is an adult. In hindsight, their age difference made me wonder more about how their paths had crossed.

I scrolled to the section dedicated to education. My father had started at Georgia State, but had graduated instead from the Massachusetts Institute of Technology. I found an article showing he had earned a bachelor of science in aerospace engineering and a master's in aeronautics and astronautics. Hardly the normal path of a photojournalist.

I clicked on one of his more famous pictures, starting with one he'd taken in Cambodia during the fall of Saigon in 1975. He'd graduated from college the year before that. The next was from the Soweto Riots in South Africa, in 1976. From there, I found some of his work from Egypt, Eastern Europe, and France.

"Siri, search Helen Caine, Savannah."

A few links from the local newspaper contained articles

she'd written about her beloved city. She'd done a monthly column that highlighted a current preservation project or featured something from Savannah long gone.

Helen had been obsessed with history and preservation, and that included our family. She had done lengthy genealogy studies on both sides. She'd collected historical documents for births, deaths, and marriages. She'd obtained copies of old deeds and tracked down artifacts and memorabilia including her grandmother's china and silverware. I'd gone with her a few times to the courthouse to research old records.

With her passion for such things, it seemed odd she'd had such limited contact with her own brother. There was no indication she'd gone out of her way to stay in touch with him.

I once asked Helen why she and my father had not stayed in touch. She answered by saying they simply drifted apart as siblings do. She'd hesitated, though, and then quickly changed the subject. Maybe something had happened between them, and she hadn't been honest with her answer. Or maybe Helen had been interested in family only as an academic exercise, wholly intellectual. Either way, it didn't add up.

I googled my mother. No results other than the same Wikipedia article listing her as my father's wife. Her former name wasn't mentioned, which I found unusual. Even more unusual, I realized I didn't know her maiden name. I'd never asked her.

We had lived in Avignon off and on all those years. She claimed to have been born and raised there, yet seemed unfamiliar with the area. At first, she couldn't find her way around. She didn't appear to recognize buildings, and even stranger, she never seemed worried about running into someone from her past. If we were hiding, why go back to the most likely place someone would look? I had picked up on this inconsistency years earlier and had chosen to ignore it.

Helen had told me that my mother came from a prominent family but wouldn't give me any details. My mother had never wanted to talk about Helen either. There must have been something between them, but neither of them had shared that information with me.

That I'd never been comfortable asking my own mother the most basic of questions was crazy. She likely wouldn't have answered, but I still should have asked. Maybe I had, but then given up trying after futile attempts?

The day my mother took me away from Helen was the day I started shutting myself off from the life I had been allowed to live for a single year. Later, when she lied to me about Helen's death, I surrendered any thoughts of connecting to family, or asking questions.

The grandfather clock in the hall struck eleven, shocking me out of my reverie. I needed to get some sleep, wake up early, and then bury the last person who could have helped me unravel my past.

Chapter Nineteen

WITH US ALWAYS

As summer moved rapidly into fall, I missed the dramatic changing of the leaves in Central Park and settled for the much cooler sleeping temperatures that mark the approach of winter in Georgia.

I woke up early one October morning with an urge to snoop through my father's childhood possessions. I'd claimed his bedroom closet as my own months earlier, but I'd only given the storage boxes a quick glance before moving them to a guest room.

I dragged everything out into the middle of the floor and started my search with a tote that had been tucked into the back corner. It held nothing but old copies of *National Geographic* and an eight-by-ten photo that had gotten stuck to the bottom. I pried it loose and went hunting for Helen, starting with her office. She'd been spending more time there, researching Savannah history and writing guest articles for the local newspaper.

I found her at her desk, with a pencil in her mouth. With that faraway look she sometimes got, she stared out the window.

While I waited for her to notice me, I looked the office over as if it were the first time I'd ever seen it. It was my favorite place in the entire house, probably because it had the essence of a library. Almost every inch of wall space was covered by old maps, historic documents, lawbooks, and a collection of Audubon bird prints. Heavy wood display cases covered an entire wall and held tons of interesting things, from antique writing instruments to pocket watches in glass domes. I'd noticed the watches weeks earlier and had memorized the exact time each one had stopped.

The only nonantique thing in the entire office was a collection of small framed postcards next to Helen's desk. When I'd asked her about them a few weeks earlier, she explained the prints were from places she'd vacationed over the years. To ensure she would remember the date of each trip, she'd written them on the back side.

Helen clutched her chest when she noticed me. "You scared me half to death! I'm going to hang a bell on your neck, like a cat."

"Sorry. I didn't mean to startle you."

She gave a nervous laugh and motioned to me.

I handed over the picture. "Is this your mother?"

She smiled at the glossy black-and-white print of a beautiful teenage girl with curls pinned all over her head. Helen's expression softened. "It is."

"Is that from her high school graduation?"

Helen flipped it over and looked at the back, which was blank. She handed it back to me. "If I'm not mistaken, this was taken at her debutante ball."

I hated to ask what a debutante ball was, but I was clueless. Helen bragged so much about how smart I was, I'd gotten it into my mind that I was letting her down when I didn't understand something. This was silly, but it didn't change things. This time all I could do was shrug.

"This is the South, August," she said, laughing. "A debutante ball is basically a high school prom for college-aged girls. It is a way of introducing high-society ladies to eligible bachelors. They parade around on a runway, hoping to find the best possible man to marry."

"That's pretty weird," I said. "Kind of like an old-fashioned horse sale."

"Exactly like that. Debutante balls are still around," she explained, "but not as much. Thankfully, they've fallen out of fashion." Her eyes dropped to the picture of her mother. "My mom was different from other girls. I'm surprised she ever participated in such nonsense."

I waited for her to explain.

Helen eased into the chair next to mine. "My grandparents owned timber mills all over North Carolina. Well-to-do women like my mother were expected to marry and stay home with the children. She had other plans, though, so she turned down several suitors and enrolled at Duke University." Helen smiled. "She met my father there. They got married at the start of her junior year. He came back without her to get his law practice going while she finished her accounting degree.

"She graduated, moved here with my father, and helped him run his law practice all those years. Her background was in accounting, but she was as well-versed in law as my father." She smiled and looked away. "When I first went away to college, I was so homesick I called her three times a day from my dorm. I will miss her forever."

I considered how different our lives and our mothers had been. A difference marked by speech and silence. Connection and distance.

Helen stared out the window for a long time before turning her face back to mine, her eyes damp. "I'm curious. Do you believe the people we love are always with us even when they're gone? I don't mean actual ghosts like in the stories we tell. I'm not exactly sure what I mean or what I'm asking."

"I don't believe in ghosts or an afterlife or anything like that," I said, regretting it but still talking. "I think when a person is gone, they're just gone. They don't hang around like we tell your customers. They just stop existing. There is nothing beyond right here, right now."

Helen's expression wilted. "I don't understand how you could think that way. Or how you could live your life believing in nothing. How you function day after day without hope of more."

There was no possible way to explain this to her. It was like asking a person why they didn't like zucchini or the color orange. Still, I could tell my words had hurt her, and although I was ashamed, I added, "I don't think any of us choose what to believe, Aunt Helen. It chooses us."

"Oh, to be young and foolish again," she said, her eyes closed tight. A few seconds later, she stood so abruptly, I flinched. "Let's go shopping and have a pumpkin carving party tonight!"

Random, but that's how Helen did things.

When Helen wasn't entertaining strangers with tours, she was hosting friends at her home. She was quite good at throwing instant theme parties, and there were always people who would change their plans and swing by her soirees.

"Do we have to?" I groaned while hiding a smile. I liked it better when it was just the two of us, but her odd, quirky mix of friends were fun, and they were very kind to me.

For some reason, rather than try to remember all their names, I mentally categorized them: hippies who didn't know that era was long gone, artists, do-gooders who talked more about doing good than doing it, professor types, socialites, and the yet to be determined.

"You know you love my friends," she chided. "And besides, until you're willing to bring around friends of your own, I give you no other choice. Pumpkin carving party it is!"

"As long as I don't have to read a book about pumpkins," I said. Helen's attempt at a book club fizzled out when one of the members fell and broke her hip and a week later another one had a stroke.

"I have younger friends now," she said. "Though I do miss Louise and Sadie."

"You know you sound like you're ninety when you talk like that?"

"I'm a *very* mature, middle-aged gal."

We were so comfortable with each other that we could joke like this, and Helen had stopped going overboard saying the things people say to convince you that you're wanted, the things that inevitably make you feel more of a bother than if nothing at all had been said, the "make yourself at home" and "holler if you need anything" statements.

I had also stopped filtering every word I said to her. When she asked me something, I almost always answered right away.

To my great surprise and delight, the pumpkin party was a complete bust, as a severe storm warning kept all of Helen's friends at bay. We still put out all the puff pastry and drank mocktails together out on the screen porch.

A bolt of lightning hit a power line, ironically in the Thunderbolt area of town. Everything turned pitch-black. The air crackled. Sirens wailed.

Helen fumbled for a small flashlight in the table by the swing. "I better go fire up the generator," she moaned. "Back in a flash. No pun intended."

As soon as the door clicked behind her, the phone rang—a phenomenon that Helen had tried to explain to me, something about phone wires not being electric so emergency calls could still be made in a blackout. I wasn't sure if I should answer. I'd never answered her phone before, but with the power out, the answering machine was useless.

I reached for the phone six rings later and said, "Hello."

Silence. For a second, I thought the storm had done something to the phone. That a line had gotten fried, or a pole knocked down. But nothing I thought of could explain the faint breathing I heard on the other end.

"Maman?" I whispered. "Is that you?" My heart beat quickly and my palms went damp. I waited for a response, but all that came was a click and a dead line. It had to be her. I was sure of it. Who else would call and say nothing?

I hit *69 and jotted the number of the last caller on a scrap of paper, surprised to hear a local area code. The generator kicked in and the lights sputtered back to life. A few seconds later, Helen appeared. With plans to put the paper in a little metal box I kept hidden in my father's desk, I shoved it in my pocket.

"That should do for a while," she said, smiling like she was pleased with herself. "You look like you've seen a ghost! But of course, you don't believe in them, so how could you have seen one, right?"

"My pupils must have dilated in the dark," I said. I didn't mention the call to Helen.

"I thought I heard the phone," Helen replied. "Another ghost?"

"I think the storm did something weird to the phone," I lied after turning away so she couldn't see my eyes. "It seems to work fine now."

Chapter Twenty

GRAMS

The image in the full-length mirror next to the front door could easily be mistaken for Helen, though my hair was longer and not yet gray, and the black sundress I had bought was something she wouldn't be caught dead in. I smiled at my reflection, knowing that was exactly the kind of joke that Helen would have appreciated on the day of her funeral.

I took a deep breath and opened the door to find Tommy wearing a navy blue suit, which made him look somber and handsome. A heaviness lifted from my chest when I saw his awkward grin.

He glanced back toward his Tahoe. "Would you like to ride to the cemetery with me? Grams is in the car."

"Sure," I said, tilting my head and smiling gently. "Let me grab my things."

He nodded and looked away. "I'm sorry about lying to you," he mumbled. "If you'd prefer not to have my company, I'd understand."

"I appreciate the company, and I'm not mad," I said, snapping Helen's small makeup bag, which I was using as a clutch. The sound brought me a sliver of peace. "I'm the one who should apologize."

He smiled but didn't look convinced. "What for?"

"For not trusting you," I said, before letting some silence settle between us. "You dress up rather nicely, Mr. Reese."

"Thank you, ma'am," he said, a faint blush surging to his cheeks. "And you look stunning as usual."

Grams had gotten out of the Tahoe and was standing next to it, quite a feat for someone so petite. I hadn't seen her in many years, and had forgotten everything about her, but as soon as I saw her silver bob and piercing violet eyes, it was like I'd never left. Her skin was still smoother than most women half her age.

Tommy rushed over and folded his arm into hers. "You're going to fall, Grams. Don't scare me like that."

She shooed him with her hand and beckoned to me.

"Good morning, Miss Ida," I said, taking her white-gloved hand in mine. In her slim black dress, aubergine fascinator, and bulky pearl necklace, Grams was the quintessential elderly lady from the South. An old-fashioned brooch of a hummingbird sparkled from her shoulder, catching the light in its deep purple wings.

"Grams, do you remember August?" Tommy asked.

Grams inspected me from top to bottom with the sweetest smile on her face the whole time. "Why would I not remember August? It comes after July and before September."

Tommy rolled his eyes. "Seriously, Grams?"

"I got a good mind," she said directly to me.

My face heated up. Hopefully she understood I'd not implied anything about her mental state.

Tommy swept his hand through his hair. "You do have a good mind, Grams. It's just been a long time, and August is all grown-up."

Her scowl changed to something murky.

"Let me ask you something," she said, waving me even closer so that she could whisper. "Whatever happened to that niece of yours?"

"My niece?"

"You know, that sad wisp of a girl with the big green eyes that Tommy was all gaga about?"

"Grams," Tommy loudly interrupted her, and she refocused her gaze on his words. "Grams, this *is* Helen's niece, August."

I smiled, amused that someone who seemed as hardened as Thomas could be so easily humiliated by a grandmother's tattling.

"Well, we'd better make room for Helen," she said, looking directly at me again.

"Would you mind if I sat next to you, Miss Ida?" I asked, stopping Tommy from explaining why Helen wouldn't be joining us. "Miss Helen is gone now."

"If Helen's gone, where's car?" she asked me, her voice suddenly frail.

Tommy shrugged. I wasn't sure how well she could hear, so I spoke a little louder. "Helen's car is in the garage."

Grams shook her head. "I didn't say car," she informed us. "*K-A-T*. Not *C-A-R*."

Tommy moved between us and leaned into the car. "Helen gave her cat to one of her friends."

"Gave to a friend?" Grams shook her head. "No, that doesn't make any sense."

"She had a friend take care of him when she went into the hospital."

"*She*, not *he*," she said, looking more confused. "She's been very sick. Cancer, I suppose."

"Yes, ma'am," Tommy answered in a practiced, soothing tone while giving me a shrug. "She was very sick."

Grams nodded, though her expression said she still struggled.

Tommy gently closed her door and turned to me. "Depending on how this goes, Carly or Liz may leave with Grams before the service starts."

"Depending how this goes," I echoed, "I may leave with Grams before the service starts."

My beloved aunt would be laid to rest near her parents in Bonaventure Cemetery. As we turned onto Greenwich Road and began our slow crawl past the graves and monuments, I realized that Helen had never taken me here, nor did she ever suggest I explore on my own. It would have been prime ghost story territory, and yet she had avoided it. We'd gone to other cemeteries. Why not this one? We wound past tourist groups stopped at various points and eventually parked in a long line of cars near the Wilmington River.

"It's just over there," Tommy said, pointing across the parking lot. "Between Johnny Mercer and Conrad Aiken." He helped Grams out as I stepped out into the warm, clear day.

"You've been here before?" I asked, taking Grams's purse and offering her my arm to steady her gait.

"More times than I can count," Tommy said over her head. "The summer after you disappeared, I spent a lot of time here, reading tombstones in case you came back and needed material for your tours."

We quietly made our way to the spot where honor guards stood next to my aunt's flag-draped coffin. Grams pulled a handkerchief from her purse and handed it to me before my eyes had even begun to sting. The family plot was cleanly delineated by a marble border, with a large O'CATHAINE capstone decorated with Celtic carvings and a large ornate marble cross. In our many ancestry discussions not once had Helen mentioned this Irish connection. There were a few dozen flat stones on the far side of Helen's casket, and a couple upright headstones marked CAINE. On the dirt road that fronted the plot were fifty seated people, all eyes trained on me.

Daniel Grant rushed over and guided us to six chairs marked by a ribbon that read FAMILY. Six chairs when only one was needed. I had a sudden memory of Helen telling me that she and I were the end of the line for my father's people. I was relieved when Tommy and Grams joined me without being asked. In so many ways they were more family than anything else I'd known.

While Helen's priest spoke of her wonderful life on this earth, and a much more glorious one in the next, I imagined her standing here, burying her parents, inheriting from them everything that I now owned. The magnitude of unearned possessions felt crushing in the slow, creeping heat, and I pushed away thoughts of what I would do to live up to a responsibility I had never imagined.

Tommy nudged me. It was time for me to speak of Helen's life. To bend and shape and reduce her beautiful existence into a few meager words. I kept my eyes hidden with sunglasses so no one would know I could speak of Helen only with my eyes closed tight.

"Good morning," I began. "I'm Helen's niece, and I want to thank each of you for being here today to honor, remember, and celebrate her amazing life.

"I've never had the privilege of speaking at a memorial service before, so I spent some time online, searching for suggestions of appropriate things to say. Several articles advised that I should open with one of her favorite quotes. Maybe a poem or a Bible verse. Other articles recommended that I focus on the things that were important to her. Her good works.

"I can't quote Helen's favorite words, and except for what some of you have shared with me, I can't tell you much about how she spent her time these last few years, because I don't know these things about her. I was a child when Helen was in my life, and we had not been in touch for a very long time. So, I'm left with telling you about the Helen I knew then.

"It's impossible for anyone to know all the versions of their life story that might have been. We can't know the impact of every variable or decision. We can't know what would have been set in motion if we'd turned left instead of right on a given day. If we'd met or not met a certain person, been thrown into a different set of circumstances, or had our genetic map etched another way.

"We don't have these powers of divination, yet we intuitively know that even one small change can change everything. A choice, a person, a single act has the power to set, or alter, our course in ways we can't imagine.

"Sometimes, though, we can imagine it. We know exactly how one link in a chain led to another and another after that. We understand what shaped us. Steered us. One of those sometimes for me was the day Helen came into my life.

"I met Helen for the first time on my eleventh birthday when I came home and found her standing at our kitchen sink. I didn't know of her existence until then. She introduced herself and, in her take-charge way, promptly informed me I needed to pack a bag. I was coming with her to live in Savannah.

"I didn't know Helen before that day, but I also knew I had no one else. Still, her words devasted me. My life wasn't great, but it was all I knew, and in my mind Helen's sudden existence meant mine was just as suddenly over.

"Now, all these years later, I'm certain it's what saved me. The gift of history is like that. It brings a light that lets us see things we couldn't see before.

"Helen was many things. We each knew her in a different

way. I only lived with her for a single year, and even though both of us wanted it to be much longer, it became the most significant, pivotal point of my life. During that year, Helen became my friend. My teacher. My anchor. She was the best unofficial therapist imaginable, her methods more creative and subtle than those of the best trained professionals. More than anything else, though, the Helen I knew, the version I was blessed to have in my life, was a harbinger of hope at a time when I didn't have an ounce of it left. A hope I thought I'd lost again but now realize has been with me all this time. That's the power of her gift.

"Most of you knew Helen much better than I, so there is little I can tell you about her. You already know she was funny and had an amazing sense of humor. She was an eternal optimist who not only looked for good in the world but set out to do as much of it as she could. Everything about her was contagious. Her smile. Her overly loud laughter. Her undying love for this amazing city and its preservation.

"So, enough of this. Helen would be furious with me for getting what she would certainly deem as too sentimental. Mushy. Let's talk about her epic parties instead . . ."

A few minutes later, I drifted back to my chair. Time and more words passed in a blur. An honor guard presented me with Helen's flag, but I felt like a fraud with it in my hands. It had been given to me by default, but it should have gone to someone in her life. Her entire life. The trumpet played "Taps," the coffin was lowered, and people lined up to place flowers on Helen's casket.

The service lasted a little over forty minutes, but something told me the people who had come would have stood under that Georgia sun all day if that's what it had taken to honor Helen. Their faces told her story better than I ever could. I asked Tommy to take Grams home, as I wanted a moment alone with my aunt.

I've never believed the departed can see or hear us. They can't share our experiences or communicate with us in some mysterious, unspoken way. If I did believe these things were possible, I would have wanted Helen to understand how sorry I was things had turned out the way they had. When my mother told me to stay away from Helen because I put her new family at risk, I had blamed and hated them for standing between us. Even Helen's supposed death did not lessen my resentment. I had not reached out to them or tried to learn anything about them. If I had, I would have discovered the truth, and things would have turned out differently.

The thing I wanted Helen to know more than anything else, though, was that I meant every word I had said a few minutes earlier. Especially that I would be forever grateful for the 365 days that I got to be a part of her world.

The word *needless* looped through my head. While trying to remember the last time I had seen Helen's face, desperately wanting to recall the exactness of it, so much like my own, I closed my eyes and listened to a tired lawn mower buzzing in the distance.

Something she told me that first day in her beloved city came to mind instead: *Savannah will let you leave, but she'll never let you go.*

I grinned. "I'm here, so as usual, you were right."

I worked my way around her plot barrier, nearly tripping over a granite stone splattered with grass and dirt. I cleared off the words and took a step back to confirm what I already knew. It was impossible, and yet there it was: DAVIS DRYDEN CAINE.

I suppose there are many things I should have felt when I saw my father's name. Sadness. Surprise. The only thing I felt, though, was rage. My chest got so tight I could hardly get a breath. This was yet another cruel lie.

When my father died, there was no funeral, no burial, no body. My mother told me that the police needed to keep the body for evidence, and later that he had been cremated, as he had wished. Yet here he was, in Savannah, under my feet. But why had she lied? What possible harm could have come from my knowing my father's final resting place? And why had Helen never told me he was here or brought me to his grave?

There was no point trying to calm my grief and anger by counting headstones or taking deeper breaths. Grief tends to reveal us. It strips away layer after layer until our rawest, truest feelings are exposed. When most people lose a person they love, they hang on to everything associated with that person. They don't erase them like ink on a whiteboard, but my mother had done just that. She had erased all three of us.

Had my mother hated my father? Did she hate or resent me?

She did not choose mental illness. It chose her.

These words had gotten me through so much, and now all I could think through my fury was that *she chose it.* All these years wasted, destroyed, in a pretense that she was doing what was best for *me.*

I would never understand how my mother could have been so cruel, but after a few minutes more I finally understood the logic behind her insane equation. Every horrible lie she had told, plus each of her cruel actions, equaled one terrible purpose—to keep me from ever returning to Savannah.

But why?

Chapter Twenty-One

THE HOLIDAYS

Summer simmered into fall. Fall faded to winter. There'd been no more encounters with the mysterious lady. When the house was quiet and there was nothing but painted stars to distract me, though, I thought about her. Sometimes, just to make sure she wasn't lurking under my bedroom window, I got out of bed to check.

Just before the holidays, there was an evening I noticed an unfamiliar scent hovering through the house. I became convinced it was somehow related to her. That it was her perfume or lotion. Maybe a hair product. Whatever the source, it had the cloying essence of rotting fruit. I never mentioned it to Helen, but I watched her face for any indication she'd noticed the smell too. Nothing. I waited until she'd gone to bed that night and then looked through every room except hers, trying to track down the source of it. That scent was everywhere and nowhere.

Helen was big on celebrating, and with some help she had enlisted from me, she went overboard on Christmas decorating. We spent the entire Thanksgiving weekend decking the house out with pine roping, a giant Fraser fir, and wreaths we'd made earlier in the year from dried magnolia clippings. There wasn't a room that didn't have something festive. Helen wanted more, though, and so sent me to the attic to dig through boxes.

This was the one part of the house I had never entered—I hadn't even known that the door at the end of the hall led anywhere but another dusty closet. I mounted the steep stairs with fantasies of finding hidden treasure, but quickly realized that all the treasures were downstairs, and the attic was reserved for the junk of generations. Helen was a hoarder. A neat, organized one, but a hoarder nonetheless.

I was about to give up on finding anything when, in the back corner by a small window, I saw an old steamer trunk. The hinges were so stiff I had to use a screwdriver to pry it open. I found old clothes and a box of ornaments fragile as butterfly wings. I later learned they had been fashioned from mercury glass. The box was labeled Jules Dryden Caine—Purchased in Macon, Georgia, December 1874. My great-great-grandmother and the origin of my middle name. When I handed them to Helen, she cried and hugged me first, then the box.

She had signed us up to be Secret Santa for the people staying at the city's largest shelter, so we started shopping on Black Friday. We piled so much stuff into Helen's office it took on the look of a department store. I wrapped boxes until my fingertips bled from paper cuts and tape cutters, but it was the best time I'd ever had, and I felt a moment of triumph each time Helen applied a fresh Band-Aid. Christmas and other holidays had disappeared in the wake of my father's death, so this overabundance was almost more than I could handle. Almost.

The Sunday before Christmas, Tommy showed up on Helen's doorstep. He had a cheesy look on his face, and his hands behind his back.

"Promise me you won't open it until the twenty-fifth," he said, producing a small blue velvet box in the space between us.

"I promise," I replied, but my fingers were crossed, and I opened the box before Tommy even rounded the corner. It was a bracelet with two pewter charms: a petite pen and book. I rolled it over my hand and found any excuse I could to jangle it from my wrist. *Need help getting that bowl? Here, allow me.*

New York winters are cold, so when the temperature soared to sixty-three degrees on Christmas Eve, my spirit melted. I missed the snow. I missed crisp, frosty air and the elaborate holiday displays in department store windows. I missed hearing sleigh bells in Central Park.

The temperature dropped by only a few degrees that evening, but Helen had come in with her arms full of logs, singing carols and informing me that a fire on Christmas Eve was mandatory—heat be damned. To counter the swelter she'd created, she cracked open a few windows and turned on the air conditioner.

Several of Helen's friends trickled in for dinner that night. When the last of them left around eleven, I started toward the stairs, but Helen stopped me and explained that her family had always exchanged gifts on Christmas Eve instead of waiting until morning.

I ran upstairs and grabbed the hardcover reissue copy of *Turn of the Screw* that I'd bought for her weeks earlier. I hurried back downstairs and found her piling more logs on the fire. Her face glistened with sweat. Old-time Christmas music blared from the kitchen, and the whole scene looked like something from the fifties. The stack of presents next to my chair had even been wrapped in vintage-looking foil paper.

Helen poked at the logs and smiled at me. "It doesn't happen often," she said, "but maybe we'll get snow next year."

I smiled back. A tight sensation wrapped my throat. "That would be something to see." There was something surreal about sitting in front of that fire, on a night far too warm for it, with Helen desperately trying to create a Christmas experience for me like the ones from her own childhood.

I stared at the flames a long time that night, afraid to look Helen in the eye because I knew if I had, she would have seen that I understood what she'd been trying to do. That I understood how hard she'd worked to make things perfect because my happiness was important to her. *I will not cry.*

Christmas Day was uneventful and so low-key I later realized this must have been by design. Without Helen saying it, I knew she understood I missed my mother and worried about her. I kept thinking if she could only come live with us, everything would be easier. She would love Savannah as much as I did, and it would help her get better, as it had me. When I tried to bring it up to Helen, though, something stopped me. I was sure she wouldn't be angry with me, but I didn't want to put her on the spot. Plus, I wasn't even sure how something like that would work. Helen had explained that my mother had a legal representative, but I didn't know who that might be or what their role was in deciding where my mother lived.

We spent most of Christmas Day watching old black-and-white movies and playing gin rummy, but by late afternoon my butt hurt from sitting so much, and I went outside to ride my new pink beachcomber bike. I'd only pedaled around on it for a few minutes before Helen yelled for me to come back inside. She informed me we had tours that night, starting at eight.

I couldn't believe anyone would be interested in riding around in that old hearse listening to Helen's nonsense on Christmas, of all days, until she explained ghost stories on Christmas were an old Southern tradition, based on an even older English tradition dating back centuries. Had I never read *A Christmas Carol* by Charles Dickens?

I was exhausted by the time we got home that night, and based on the way Helen had flopped down on the couch and stayed there until the next morning, I would guess she was too.

It rained nonstop for the next two days, so we stayed inside and watched more old movies. We also both spent a lot of time reading. I curled up on the porch swing with a Stephen King novel and a fruit basket someone had sent as a gift. I tried not to be too judgmental when Helen came out carrying a stack of Harlequin romances and a supersized box of Little Debbie cakes.

We had a New Year's Eve party that year. Tommy's parents dropped him off at his grandmother's house on their way to a weeklong couples retreat. He and a dozen of Helen's friends gathered around the backyard firepit with us for an oyster and shrimp roast. Things were going great until around ten, when the wind turned vicious and hot ashes blew all over everyone.

Helen herded us inside. The adults played cards and drank cocktails in the library while Tommy and I watched scary movies in the front parlor. We ate popcorn and drank sparkling grape juice from wine glasses. The glasses were small and the popcorn too salty, so we had to get several refills. Each glass required a new toast, so we took turns making up rhyming ones such as "Here's to you and a Happy New Year. May you never fall in a field full of steer."

Helen's friend Gene yelled from the library, "Come on, everybody! The ball is about to drop!" Helen's friend Katie yelled back, "Your balls are about to drop!"

Everyone roared, and we gathered in a tight group around the TV while Helen handed out noisemakers and Gene started a chorus of "Auld Lang Syne."

"May old acquaintances be forgotten. Especially Gene!" Katie yelled at the top of her lungs, and everyone laughed again. Gene honked his noisemaker at her, and the sound of it triggered a memory of standing in Times Square with my parents when I was small.

"Stay awake, my love," my mother had whispered when my father handed me to her.

"I'm trying," I had mumbled as I snuggled my head into the softness of her neck.

"Five, four, three, two, one . . . Happy New Year!" We all hugged and kissed each other on both cheeks, as if we were European. "Auld Lang Syne" blared from the TV as Helen pulled me tight and kissed the top of my head. I tried to pretend I didn't notice she was crying.

I hugged Tommy last.

"Happy New Year, August Caine," he said soft as a pillow, his lips brushing my cheek. "Make a wish, but don't tell anybody what you wished for, or it won't come true."

"Happy New Year, Tommy Reese," I whispered back. "You make a wish, but don't tell anybody what you wished for either."

"Deal," he said.

"Deal," I parroted.

My stomach twisted when we shook on it, because I noticed the bracelet Tommy had gotten me was gone. I hadn't even thanked him for it yet, and I'd already lost it.

I was sure it had been on my wrist earlier by the firepit. I made an excuse about needing to go to the bathroom because we'd had so much to drink, and when I was sure Tommy wasn't looking, I slipped out the back door to search for it.

The night sky was black as coal, and the fire had burned down to embers. While my eyes adjusted to the darkness, I felt around on the ground for that bracelet, and just as I wrapped my fingers around it, the sound of tires crunching over gravel drifted up from the driveway.

I stood, curious to see if someone was coming to the party or leaving, but it ended up being neither. No one had left, and no one was arriving. Instead, a car with no headlights was idling halfway down Helen's driveway. A few seconds later, the driver moved forward a few feet and then back. I wrapped my arms around myself and watched them repeat this five times.

That someone would barely move without headlights was creepy enough, but it felt like someone had thrown an entire tub of ice on me when I realized the car didn't have tail or brake lights either. They must have been disconnected, but why?

I ran to the door, unsure if I should get Helen or Tommy. I ended up doing neither, because when I turned to take another look at that car, it had disappeared into thin air.

Chapter Twenty-Two

CHOOSE TO BELIEVE

When I got back from the cemetery that afternoon, twenty-nine cars lined Helen's driveway. I slid in through the kitchen and snuck up the back stairs so I could wash up and change into some fresh clothes. I glanced at my phone while changing and noticed I had a text from Cort. *Call when you can.*

Interesting. I'd not seen him or heard a word from him in weeks. No time to think about it, I shoved the phone in my pocket and headed down to face the crowd.

Buffet tables had magically taken over the downstairs. Everything was well-organized, with people milling about, nibbling from small plates, and sipping drinks from plastic glasses.

An older lady who'd come by the house the day before to offer her condolences approached me first. I couldn't recall her name.

"I hope you don't mind that we started without you," she said much louder than the people around her, who were speaking in hushed tones. "Funerals give me a terrible appetite."

Before I had time to say anything, she grabbed me into a tight hug. Her perfume was overdone but still didn't mask the smell of alcohol. Apparently, funerals gave her a terrible thirst as well.

Tommy raised an eyebrow at me from across the room before pretending to take a swig. I pushed back a laugh. He moved on to a woman I'd seen him talking with earlier at the cemetery, just as Daniel appeared holding out a glass of wine for me.

"I wasn't sure what you wanted," he said. "I guessed you preferred white wine since that's what you had yesterday when I was here."

"I prefer gin, myself, Mr. Grant," the woman at my elbow said, her words slow and slightly slurred. "Two fingers. Neat. Helen kept the good stuff in the pantry."

"I'll see what I can do, Miss Lilly."

Tommy approached after Lilly wandered over to another lady. "Can I get you something to eat?"

"I feel like you're always trying to feed me."

He nodded. "I am. I've even hatched this elaborate, evil plot to fatten you up. It involves this stuff called food." He pantomimed eating with a spoon.

I laughed. "I swear, I eat. That fried chicken didn't disappear on its own."

The woman I'd seen Tommy talking with earlier moved next to him and put her hand on his shoulder.

"Speaking of too thin and evil, you remember Liz?"

She smirked at Tommy in that playful way that involves scrunching your eyes tight and your lips tighter. She pulled me into a hug. "It's wonderful to see you again, August."

"It's good to see you too, Liz."

Liz had been a pretty teenager who had morphed into a stunning woman, with the features of a hand-painted China doll.

I was surprised to find that I now towered over her, when she seemed so much bigger when I was eleven.

We talked for a few minutes about Grams and Helen. I gave her a watered-down version of my life in Paris, and she filled me in on her life as an obstetrician in Charleston, South Carolina.

"It's pretty status quo," she said. "Charity balls, lunches with the ladies, sailboat races. Do you ride?"

"Sailboats?" I said, lost in the swirl of the Southern lady lifestyle.

"Ha! You were always so *funny*," she said. "I'm referring to *horses*."

"I'm allergic," I said, though I had no idea whether I was or not. Horses scared me, and it seemed the fastest way out of an invitation if that was what she intended.

I was glad for her company. It kept me from thinking about my father lying a mile away in the cemetery. I kept telling myself that it didn't matter that he had been here all this time, that it didn't change anything, that he was as gone now as he had been twenty-three years ago. But that was denial trying to smooth the rough edges. It did matter. It mattered a lot.

The mystery of why my mother had gone to such extremes to keep me away from Savannah gnawed at me. I'm by nature both a curious and a skeptical person, yet I never questioned anything she ever told me. She'd float into my room, a beautifully scripted note in her hand, informing me that we had to leave because she had a "feeling" the nameless, faceless people who had killed my father were about to find us. I never did anything but comply and in doing so became part of her madness. I had jumped up and relocated on a moment's notice. I'd triple-locked doors, taken four trains to places when one would have done the job, and used a dozen different names. Folie à deux.

A soft touch on my shoulder rescued me from myself. I turned to find a woman who looked to be in her sixties. She wore a gold-copper headwrap that matched her eyes. She smiled and tilted her head while she studied my face.

"I'm sure you don't remember me . . ."

Another domino fell in my head. "Laney Jenkins," I interrupted. "You were Helen's friend we ate lunch with on Tybee and the one book club member who didn't break a hip."

Liz mouthed, "We'll talk later," before disappearing into the crowd.

"Well, I've broken one since!" Laney laughed and hugged me tightly. When she pulled away, she kept one hand on each of my shoulders and studied my face like a road map. "My gosh if you don't look just like her," she said, still smiling and studying me.

"Thank you," I said. "It means a lot to me when people say that. Refresh my memory. Didn't you know Helen in high school?"

"I sure did," she beamed. "Lifelong friends."

"This has nothing to do with that, but do you happen to know what Helen did about the house when she was gone for work months on end? A house shouldn't sit empty, so I'm not sure how to handle that myself. Did someone check on things for her, or . . ."

Laney Jenkins's face took on an uneasy expression. "Why don't we grab lunch before you go back to Paris? I'll be glad to tell you everything I can," she said.

A strange answer to such a simple question.

"Sure."

She leaned in for another hug and then moved toward the food table. "Oh, by the way," she said as an afterthought, "Helen's cat is with me now. He's adjusting fine, so don't worry about him one bit. My other cats don't care for him, but they'll work it out."

"Him?" I remembered Grams saying Helen's cat was a female. "I thought it was a girl."

"Well," she said, looking thoughtful, "I assumed it was a boy.

The name sounds masculine to me, but you never know these days."

"Why? What's the cat's name?"

She reached across me and plucked some olives from a small bowl. "Sergeant F. E. Lines, if you can believe that."

"Well, whattya know," I said to myself, amazed that Helen would remember something so insignificant as the name of the cat in the short story I'd been assigned and had her proofread.

There was a light pressure on my elbow, and I turned to see Daniel Grant.

"Do you mind if I borrow August," he said without letting go of my arm.

"Not at all!"

"I have something for you," he said as we moved out of the main room and into Helen's office. "I wanted to wait until everyone had cleared out, but I need to get going. Helen instructed me to give you this after her service." He handed me an envelope that felt heavier than the paper it contained.

"Should I open it now?"

He shrugged. "You have a houseful of people. I'm not sure what it contains, but it might be better if you look at it after everyone has gone."

I laid the packet on the center of the blotter. "I'll wait."

By seven o'clock I had taken a nap and a shower and pulled on pajamas, avoiding the kind women who had stayed behind to set everything in the house right again. They had even taken away most of the food, for which I was grateful.

I poured a large glass of wine and made a small plate of fruit and vegetables before fetching Helen's letter from her office. I took it to the screen porch, where we had spent the most time together. I eased into her favorite chair and pulled the document from the folder. It was a handwritten letter from Helen.

My Wonderful Niece,

Where do I begin? I would say the beginning, but that would take far too much time, and I don't know how much of that I have left. I left a letter for you a while back in my safety deposit box at the bank, and while it explains a lot more than I can say now, it also leaves out things I wish to add.

This is many years too late, but I want to start with an apology that it took me so long to come for you after your father died. I kicked myself many times over the years knowing if I would have only come sooner, Claire would have gotten help and things might not have turned out the way they did. You would still be here. If not that, we'd at least still be in contact with each other.

It was her right to take you, but I cannot tell you how frantic and depressed I was for the longest time. It was as though you had disappeared off the face of the earth. Claire did give me the courtesy of leaving a note at the Savannah airport. She paid a skycap to call and tell me that a note was waiting for me after your flight had left for France. In the note, she asked that I not try to contact you and explained it would be a long time before she contacted me. I waited to hear from her, but six months later, I began to lose hope.

Letting that much time lapse made finding you impossible. But as much as I missed you, I knew you were all right. You don't believe in such things, but I felt in my heart you were doing fine.

I came to Europe twice looking for you. It's a long story why I came to France and Italy searching for you, but it doesn't matter, because I couldn't find you. I never stopped trying.

According to my doctors, I'm very ill. Please know that if my next procedure or recovery doesn't go as planned, I'm not afraid to die. I stopped fearing death a long time ago.

The only thing that has always bothered me about the thought of dying is that I don't get to see how things turn out. Even things as simple as who will be elected the next president or which team will win the next World Series. Or how many children my wonderful niece will have. Whom she will spend her life with, and how she will fill the years and the walls of our house if she ever comes back here to live. That, sweetness, is what bothers me most.

I remember hearing you quote someone once and you said, "You don't choose what to believe. It chooses you." I believe the opposite. I think we can choose how we feel and what we believe.

If I am to leave this world, I will leave it believing certain things. People can write their own stories, so I'm writing the beginning, the ending, and everything in between the way I want it to be. So, I choose to believe you've made a wonderful life for yourself. You're with the person you love most, and you will someday have two beautiful children.

After all these years, I choose to believe you will come back to Savannah and become one of those old women who sits on the porch at dusk, listening to the spring peepers for hours while feeling the hope they bring.

You'll watch the sunrise each morning from that same spot and the sunset at night. As the light and moments slip away faster than you thought possible, you will feel the warmth of God's promise on your face. You will be humbled by the grace that has been with you always, and you will realize how much you are loved by the people lucky enough to be in your life.

I also choose to believe you've not been dealt a minute more of sadness. Of tragedy. Of loneliness.

Please always know that having you here for that year was the best year of my life. The BEST! My life was wonderful before you came into it, and it eventually became wonderful again. But, after I lost you, it took a while for me to get there. A long while. I missed you every single day, but I've been happy and not a day goes by that I don't know how blessed I am. To grow up when and where I did, surrounded by so many incredible people. Asking for more than what I've been given in this life would simply be asking for too much.

I love you,
Aunt Helen

I set the letter aside and listened to the crickets, peepers, and cicadas make their crazy symphony around me as I sipped my wine and contemplated how easy it would be to become Helen. *Two deeds, car, stocks . . .* There was so much of her left, while so little of me ever existed. Helen's letter had cleared up a lot, but there was still so much to learn. The one thing I now knew for sure, though, was it was time to set aside my newly found rage, collect more evidence, and for once, make some choices based on truth.

Chapter Twenty-Three

MY TWELFTH BIRTHDAY

An entire year flew by faster than seemed possible. The temperature had not fallen below fifty all year, so the transition from winter to spring, and then full summer, was swift and subtle.

Two weeks before my twelfth birthday I wrote to my mother, even though she'd not answered the other letter I'd sent her months earlier. I had no idea if she was capable of caring about my life, but I guess I wanted to believe she was. I wrote to her about Tommy and school and all the things Helen had taught me about Savannah.

I'd made some decisions about my future. I shared with her that I wanted to go to medical school, but because I felt it would be disrespectful to her, left out the part about wanting to specialize in psychiatry. I wrote that my favorite bands were Dixie Chicks and Pearl Jam, and that Destiny's Child had been my favorite but I'd outgrown them. I listed the things I'd learned to cook and do, but I was careful not to make it sound like I was having too much fun.

I woke up early on my twelfth birthday and lounged in bed for a long while, pondering the past and wondering what the future might hold. I thought about how my father had been gone for four whole years, yet I didn't miss him one bit less.

Helen had a surprise party for me up her sleeve. I knew this because I'd heard her on the phone the day before, her voice soft and low, ordering a cake and inviting her friends over for, as she called it, a "birthaversary" party. She'd said, "Any time after five is fine." I smiled thinking that she had come up with a way to celebrate me and our first year together on the same day, with one festive, thoughtful word.

Tommy's baseball team was playing the team from my school that afternoon, and he'd called the night before to see if I could come to the game. I figured this was all part of the secret plan to get me out of the house for the surprise party. I told him I'd be there. I made sure I said it loud enough for Helen to hear.

I wanted to stay in bed with my eyes closed and the smell of wisteria and honeysuckle trickling in the window. School had been officially over for more than a week, and I had managed to keep my grades right where they needed to be.

Wondering what the day would hold, I crawled out of bed and found Helen in the kitchen fixing my favorite breakfast: biscuits and cooked apples.

"Morning, glory," she said in a dry tone, and I smiled. Helen loved nicknames. She had a different one for me each day, and I always looked forward to hearing what she'd come up with. "Big plans today?"

"Not really," I said, paging through one of the three newspapers on the table: *The Savannah Morning News.* Today's forecast was just what I expected: *Periods of light clouds followed by periods of sunshine. High eight-seven, low seventy-one.*

"Maybe I'll spend the day at the library until Tommy's game," I said, changing my plans on the spot. "It looks like it's gonna be a scorcher."

"That sounds about right," she laughed. "Only you would want to spend your first full week out of school studying. Back in my day we would have called you a nerd."

We lingered for a while at the table over coffee, reading the obituaries and making up stories to entertain each other about how people *really* died. Helen didn't mention one word about my birthday, which confirmed my suspicions about the party. The phone rang, and I ran upstairs to get my backpack while Helen took the call.

She was waiting for me in the car with a brown bag lunch when I came back down. I shoved it into my backpack and waited for what came next.

"Buckle up," she said, like she did every single time I got into the car.

"Was planning on it," I said, like I did every time she reminded me.

Helen was unusually quiet on the way to the library. She drove one-handed and chewed her thumbnail the whole time, her expression flat and faraway.

"I'll just walk over to the game this afternoon," I told her as she pulled up to let me out. "It should be over between four and four thirty."

"Call from the pay phone if it's over earlier." She handed me a coin purse. Though many kids my age already had flip phones, we'd never seen the need for me to have one. Helen was always there when I needed her to be.

I jumped out, took the steps two at a time, and turned to wave when I got to the top. Something was different, though. Helen had gotten out of her car, was standing next to it, watching me go. She'd never done that before. Something prickled on the back of my neck, but for the life of me I didn't know the reason. I tried to take a step, but my legs wouldn't move. Helen then waved at me, got back in her car, and drove away. I watched her taillights disappear.

I left the library later that afternoon for the baseball field, and although I was certainly no athlete and the day was blazing hot, I made it there in about twelve minutes—and much to my relief, the home team was already warming up. The stands were filling up with parents and siblings of kids I didn't know, which made getting lost amongst them very easy. I'd played this same trick often enough at playgrounds in Central Park: If you look like you're with someone else, no one will question why you are always alone. This was no longer a necessity, but it's hard sometimes to turn habits loose.

Tommy's bus pulled up to the side of the field, and I counted the players as they emerged from the bus until his familiar cowlick emerged. His face lit up as our eyes met, and he tipped his hat in my direction before securing it tightly to his head. I fought the urge to run to him, to warn him that something about the day didn't feel right and that we should call Helen to come pick us up right then. But I didn't do that. I merely sat, frozen to the bleachers, while his team began to warm up in the outfield, first throwing balls back and forth, and then the coach popping a ball high into the air for the outfielders to find in the midday sun of June.

Maybe if Tommy had been wearing sunglasses, maybe if he hadn't been glancing over at me every other minute. Maybe if it hadn't been one of the longest days of the year, or a cloud had miraculously appeared to help him find the ball. Maybe if I hadn't run out onto the field when his body hit the ground with no arm thrown back to break his fall, or if he hadn't looked up at me and said what he said—five little words that I couldn't believe he would say at a time like this.

Maybe if one of those things hadn't have happened, in the exact order they had happened, then I wouldn't have burst into tears—of relief? Joy? Fear?—and I wouldn't have run away from Tommy, away from the people who had encircled him to help, away from my embarrassment, my loneliness, and the shame at being so unloved for so long.

Maybe if I hadn't written that letter to Maman, if I hadn't let it slip that I was happy with Helen, I wouldn't have run past the bleachers and right into my mother, her hands hard on my upper arms, her face solid but stern. She shook me once to bring my blurry vision into focus as she handed me the familiar square of paper, a large Post-it the color of lemonade.

It's not safe here.

We must go NOW!

My eyes went from that note to hers, our height now nearly the same. Time skidded to a halt. The earth moved, but we didn't. It was eighty-six degrees, but a wave of cold, needlelike chills paralyzed me. My eyes stayed locked on hers while my heart thumped in uneven beats, and my mouth dried to a taste I imagined similar to copper and ashes. Breathing became difficult before it turned impossible.

When I think back on my twelfth birthday, I realize it was the first time I had one of the full-blown panic attacks I would later become so familiar with. It was also the first time I ever allowed myself to wish my mother would disappear for good and that I could stay with Helen in Savannah forever.

That was my birthday wish.

What I got instead was my life torn apart all over again.

Chapter Twenty-Four

HEALING WATERS

"Would you want to go out on the boat with me?" Tommy asked the morning after Helen's funeral. He stood at the kitchen door with his arms held down by his waist with a ragged ball cap folded in his hands. I wondered if it was the same one he'd worn the day he got hit in the head. Of course it wasn't, but my mind was full of memories now, and every detail nudged a smaller one.

I thought back to the letter Helen had left me. When I had first come to Savannah with Helen, I wished that I could be like her, because she was the most positive, optimistic person imaginable. She found joy in almost everything, and I envied her that because no matter how hard I tried or how much I wanted to be like that too, I couldn't. Reading what she'd written to me had confirmed this. Her rosy view of the world would never be mine.

All that aside, Helen's letter had lifted a tremendous weight as well, because I now believed she'd not been part of my mother's deception. Helen wasn't at the park that day; she was home, planning my birthaversary. She hadn't known my mother was taking me to France. She hadn't purposefully avoided me or cut me from her life, but gave me the space she thought I had needed to rebuild with my mother. Or at least that's what I thought as I stood there watching Thomas pull at his hat like he was making taffy, studying it rather than looking at me.

"Go out on your boat? What for?" I said playfully.

"Um . . . to fish?"

"Well, I never learned how to fish," I said, which wasn't at all accurate, but I had to stay true to our conversation as it was. I added a dramatic sigh. "So, I guess it would be pointless."

"We don't have to fish. We can just ride around."

"Could we read? That's what I do for fun."

"Um, sure."

"That's not what you're supposed to say. You're supposed to ask if I mean read as in books."

Tommy scrunched his right eye, as if trying to remember something. "Okay. I see what we're doing. Let me think," he said. "I'm supposed to ask you what else you do for fun."

"You are," I answered. "And I'm supposed to tell you I write."

"Then I'm supposed to say something like . . . Hell, I can't remember that far back."

"Come on in." I laughed and motioned to him. "I planned on sorting through some of Helen's things, but if you'll give me a minute to dress boat-appropriate, I'll go out with you."

"No hurry. I'm at your disposal," Tommy said while standing next to the switch for the garbage disposal. Of course, he was pointing to it to make sure I caught the double entendre. I shook my head and smiled at him.

"Gonna be here all week, folks!" He mimicked a cigar.

"If you plan on staying out there all day, Groucho, I'll drive myself over. I need to stop at the bank at some point." What I didn't tell Tommy was that I was so obsessed with what Helen's other letter might say, I wasn't going to be very good company.

"Still at your disposal." Tommy grinned. "Oh, and August? It's Sunday."

I mentally smacked myself on the forehead. "Every day feels like a Sunday right now," I said. I wouldn't be able to get into Helen's safety deposit box until the following day. Spending the afternoon on the water with Tommy would be a perfect distraction. "Oh, and since we're going to Tybee, this might be a good time for me to drop by this mysterious house of Helen's I didn't know existed. Why don't you make us some sandwiches out of the funeral food that got left here, and I'll pull myself together. There's beer and soda in the back fridge."

The drive to Tybee was shorter than it had been in my imagination, and before I knew it, we were already high up on the bridge.

My mind took a random turn. "Do GBI agents work with partners?"

Tommy glanced over at me. "You writing a new book, or contemplating a career change?"

"Neither," I said, amazed by how comfortable I felt in his truck. I had literally never been in a personal vehicle so big. "I'm a curious person."

He seesawed his head. "Well then, curious person . . . we aren't assigned partners like detectives, but a second agent is present during interviews." He smiled. "It's weird you asked that because about ten seconds earlier I was thinking about a guy I get paired with a lot."

"Why were you thinking about him? Did something happen?"

"No," he said, taking a sharp right turn onto a dirt road. "It was a random thing. Cal was on my mind because I hate getting stuck with him. And I hate that I hate it. He's the nicest, most annoying person you could ever be around."

"In what way? The annoying part, I mean."

Tommy tapped his hands on the steering wheel in rhythm with the low-volume bluegrass music on the radio. "This is a stupid example, but he talks too much in general, and he's always saying stuff that people stopped saying years ago. It's like he didn't get the memo that he's using these tired, worn-out phrases."

"You mean like saying he didn't get the memo?"

Tommy pointed a finger at me. "Exactly."

I shook my head slowly and scowled when he looked over at me.

He laughed. "What?"

"Nothing," I said, hiding a smile. "I was just thinking it would be rough to partner with you. You sound a little on the persnickety side."

The road got increasingly bumpy and was edged with high marsh grasses. If I hadn't seen the marina from the bridge, and hadn't known Tommy so well, I would have thought he was taking me somewhere to kill me and dump the body. Georgia can give you that feeling sometimes.

"Hey! Getting me as a partner isn't terrible."

"Uh-huh."

He glanced over at me as we pulled into the marina and he swung his truck into the only open spot, which had the number 44 on a sign. His expression changed, and he turned his body toward me. "Speaking of not being someone's partner," he said, "I have a confession. Remember when we did the twenty-year catch-up thing?"

"It was less than forty-eight hours ago, so sure, I remember. I'm not senile yet."

"Right. Well, remember when I said I married and divorced the same woman twice?"

"I do."

"That's not exactly true. Don't judge me, but I actually married and divorced the same woman three times." He held up three fingers to make certain I'd heard him correctly.

I held back a laugh. "Why did you say it was two times?"

He shrugged like a little kid in big trouble. "I guess I didn't want you to think I was a nut. Or indecisive. Or someone with either a fear of commitment or a fear of not being committed, because I could see that going either way."

I let the laugh ease out. "No judgment here. I've made up so many stories I can't keep them straight."

He smiled, and I smiled because I'd made his smile happen.

We gathered our things and headed for the dock. It was only a little after ten, and I was already drenched in sweat.

I'm not comfortable prying into a person's life, old friend or not. Still, I asked, "What happened between you and your ex?"

"I guess I could say it was complicated, but it really wasn't. Problems aren't complicated," he mused as we headed down a long skinny dock with boats tethered on each side. "Solutions are complicated, but problems aren't. Anyway, the long and short of it—opioids. It started with a legitimate injury—skiing accident. A year later, and she's buying off the street. She nearly lost her law license because of it."

"I'm sorry. How long have you been divorced this time?"

We came to slip 44, where a shiny blue boat named *Jawsome* waited. Tommy jumped on board and reached for my hand. "A little over a year."

"Do you see a round four in the future?"

Tommy tugged the cooler he'd packed at Helen's house from the dock and repositioned our bags before glancing over at me. He studied my face a second before turning back to organize his fishing gear. "I'm not the sharpest tool in the shed, but even I eventually figure out when it's time to fold," he said.

"Truth," I said, and for good measure added another worn-out expression. "Word."

"Alright now," he said, laughing.

His laugh made me happier than his smile had, especially since the topic wasn't the most pleasant one in the world. I couldn't recall too many times I'd made someone laugh. My interaction with other people had always been so limited. Mechanical. Basic transactions and minimal chitchat.

"Marrying the same person three times doesn't make you anything other than a hopeless romantic."

He half grinned and shook his head, deftly untying the boat and looping the ropes back on the deck. His movements struck me as extraconfident: easy, practiced, and not at all show-offy. He'd become the man I always imagined he would be. "Then what does getting a divorce from the same person three times make me?"

"I suppose we all eventually reach the limits of hope," I said. "It makes you sad but practical."

"That would be me, August Caine," he said while sliding his sunglasses back on, but not before holding my eyes with his. "Sad but practical."

We puttered out of the marina, and I told him about the letter I'd found from Helen and about the one still waiting for me in her safety deposit box.

"That's interesting," he said. "Weird but interesting."

Something I'd read in Helen's letter had bothered me all day. I didn't want to ask Tommy about it, because our last conversation about him tracking me down in France didn't go so well, but it was something only he could answer.

"I need to ask you something about Helen's letter, but I don't want you to think I'm harping on the phone number thing."

"Weird but interesting," he repeated.

"You said you gave Helen my number three or four months ago, but the letter she left makes it sound like she was still looking for me. Are you sure you gave her the correct information?"

"It had to be right," Tommy pointed out. "I didn't give it to her attorney, and he called you to let you know she'd passed. Helen must have given it to him."

"So, she had my number," I said, even more confused than before, "but she didn't use it, and instead handed it off to her attorney. We would have had time. I would have dropped everything and gotten on the first flight here had she called."

He nodded as if unsure what to say.

"Hopefully, her letter in the safety deposit box will clear things up," I shouted into the wind. "I'm going first thing in the morning to get it."

"You're not an American anymore, so you may not realize this," he shouted back, "but the banks are closed tomorrow for Memorial Day."

"That explains this crowd. I'll go first thing Tuesday." We fell silent for a bit as Tommy steered us past the edge of Tybee and out a good ways before killing the engine and dropping anchor in proximity to a couple of other small boats. He picked up the conversation where it had stopped earlier.

"The letter you found last night doesn't hint at what the second one might be about?" he asked and got to work on setting up the fishing gear.

"No," I said, while my stomach rolled at the thought of reading it. "The whole thing is so bizarre and overwhelming I'm not sure what to think."

The sun had climbed directly overhead, and my scalp was on fire. I pulled one of Helen's straw hats from my bag and adjusted it for maximum shade. Luckily, there was a soft breeze picking up the cooler temps of the ocean, and I took the fishing pole that Tommy had baited for me.

"Ever ocean cast?" he asked. I pursed my lips and tilted my head. "Never fished, I'm guessing?"

"Correct." I handed the pole back for Tommy to cast, and once our hooks were in the water and sodas were opened, I leaned back in my deck chair and let the rocking of the water settle me into the world's soft rhythm.

"I hope that letter gives you the answers you're looking for."

I smiled at him, knowing it was time to dial back the emotion. I'd managed to hold it together this long. I told myself it would be a shame to lose it now. "Let's fist-bump and make our hands do the exploding thing. People still do that, right?"

"Nope," he said. "You must have missed the memo. They sure don't."

We fished for a while, but not with any success. The quiet little spot Tommy had picked out was turning into a highway for holiday-weekend party boats.

Tommy stood and stretched. "I give up," he said. "Too much commotion for the fish to bite."

I reeled in my line. "I give up too," I said. "I've never seen such a bad fishing hole." I did my best to mock both his voice and his posture, which caused us both to laugh as we packed up the gear and led to more back-and-forth ribbing.

We spent the next hour tagging along behind a shrimping boat so we could watch gulls and dolphins chase after it and then dropped anchor to eat our leftovers. I stretched out on the bench seat to read the book I brought with me while Tommy sorted through his email on an iPad. About a page in, my eyes got heavy and I drifted off, but I could still hear laughter and kids squealing from the shore.

The sound of the waves lapping against the boat rendered me powerless to move. I tried to paddle through my thoughts but kept coming up against blankness and gulls shrieking high overhead.

At some point I heard Tommy say, "I'm jumping in to cool down." His voice sounded miles away.

I managed to crack my right eye open and watched as he peeled off his shirt. A scar the size of a grapefruit puckered a few inches from his rib cage. A larger scar zigzagged across his back. He said he'd been shot in the line of duty. If those scars were from that, his survival had to have been miraculous.

Without much of a splash, he dove over the edge. I rolled onto my stomach and folded my arms under my head to better spy on him. He swam out about fifty yards, his strokes smooth and strong, his head barely coming up for air. For me, a woman who had never set foot in anything other than a swimming pool, this was no different than watching the dolphins—pure amazement that any creature could achieve such effortless beauty. I sat up as he swam back, and when he climbed into the boat our eyes locked for a long moment, caught in sunshine.

"Did you have a good nap?" He grabbed a towel to pull around his torso, half hiding his scars.

"Is that where you got shot?" I asked. He nodded but didn't elaborate.

"Want to go check out your aunt's house now?" he asked instead, pulling a fresh T-shirt the color of the ocean over his damp body. "It's close to a nice little dockside restaurant where I know the bartender."

"That sounds great." I put on my shoes and attempted to get my fingers through the thicket my hair had become in the humid air. Tommy raised the anchor and put the boat in gear, his hand absentmindedly rubbing his scar. He caught me staring, so I quickly looked away.

"Grams wanted me to invite you over for a cookout this evening," he said. "Liz, Carly, and a couple of their friends are coming. Liz's husband, Sam, might make it if he can get away from work."

"Sounds good. What time?"

"Any time after seven is fine," Tommy said, his face and tone off. There was a reluctance in the way he had asked me to come. Like he expected or hoped I would say I couldn't make it.

"If you're only asking because Grams told you to, I don't have to come."

"It's not that," he said, sounding sort of miserable. "It's just that I don't ever know what Grams is going to say. She doesn't have much of a filter left with her dementia. I didn't bring her over yesterday after the service because I was on pins and needles, worried she would say something about Helen she shouldn't."

When he glanced at me again, his eyes found a smile that was intended to make him squirm. "You know I'm coming for sure now, right?"

Tommy grinned and shook his head before slowing down the engine as we approached the eastern edge of Tybee, dotted with small but expensive houses, each with a private dock. Tommy exhaled loudly, as though he needed to expel enough air to get to the bottom of something, or to finish filling a balloon.

"So, what exactly are you afraid Grams is going to say?"

"That's just it," he said, tying the boat to the dock. "She knew Helen better than I did, so there's no telling what she's going to share. Or gossip about."

"But you have something specific in mind." I wouldn't relent. "What is it?"

"Geez," he moaned. "Stick me in an interrogation room with the worst criminal, and I still wouldn't be half as nervous as I am around you. I'm sweating bullets over here."

I laughed. "Confession is good for the soul. What are you afraid she is going to tell me?"

"Okay. You win. I told Liz I thought Gram's dementia was getting worse because she was starting to spell things in a weird way. The example I used was when she was in the car with us yesterday and asked about Helen's cat. She'd spelled it out with a *K*. Liz laughed at me and told me Grams was fine and that she'd used the correct spelling."

His words didn't register. And then, they did. "Ah, I see. Grams was talking about a person. Not a feline, right?"

He nodded, and I waited for more.

"Looks like this is the place," he said, pointing to a house on the corner that looked the way a classic Tybee cottage should. Small and gorgeous, with beautiful landscaping and a screened-in porch.

I visually checked the place over before letting my eyes drift to the one right next to it. A flamingo-pink cottage. My brain hummed with memories. "This is strange."

"Her house is strange?"

"No. Not Helen's house," I said. "The one next to it."

His eyes followed mine. "Do you remember me telling you about coming over to Tybee to visit Helen's friend when I first moved here?"

"I do."

"Helen's friend is Laney Jenkins. She was at the house yesterday, and oddly enough she's the one who took Helen's cat."

Thomas nodded. "I remember Laney from years ago. I didn't recognize her at first when I saw her yesterday. She's lost a bunch of weight."

"Well, unless I'm crazy again, her house is right next to Helen's. I remember it because I'd never seen a house that color. It made a lasting impression."

I took a slow step. I still didn't know if I was going to knock on Laney Jenkins's door or check out Helen's house first. "Kat and cat," I said. "This place is six degrees of Kevin Bacon. A lot of things seem to be connected."

Thomas nodded without adding anything. His eyes bounced from one house to the other. I kept my eyes on him.

I wasn't done pestering him just yet. "Who is Kat, Thomas? And don't say you don't know because clearly you do. That sheepish look on your face gave you away just like it did when we were kids."

He swiped at his damp hair and blew out a breath. "Kat was Helen's girlfriend," he said. "For a long time, they lived together in Helen's house as a couple. A long time as in decades." He held up a finger. "Well, off and on for a long time, according to Liz. Rumor has it, they broke up and made up a bunch of times."

"Do you know this person?"

"I do not."

"Wouldn't you have seen her at Helen's when you visited Grams?"

Thomas shrugged. "I might have seen her at some point," he said, "but there was always a ton of people at Helen's house, and I didn't know about her until yesterday. Liz speculated that Kat wasn't entirely out of the closet, so they were low-key about their relationship. They didn't exactly hide it, but they didn't announce it either."

This triggered a memory of the woman who'd been in Helen's kitchen my first day in Savannah. I had more than a sneaking suspicion we were talking about the same person.

I told Thomas about it. "When I first came to Savannah with Helen, this woman showed up at her house. Helen was upstairs, so I was wandering around checking out the kitchen." I paused, trying to remember all the details. "She said only a few words to me, but she radiated this pure hatred. It was like nothing I'd ever experienced. When Helen came back downstairs, it was the most awkward thirty seconds of silence imaginable. They stood there glaring at each other. Even then, I knew it was a lover's quarrel."

I told him about the other things I suspected she'd done: the note with my name left on my favorite park bench, the dead mouse on the door, staring up at me from the yard.

Thomas shook his head like he couldn't comprehend such petty behavior.

I considered telling him more but decided against it. My eyes drifted to a pair of windsurfers soaring in the distance. I smiled at the thought of all that glorious, weightless freedom.

"Let's go check this place out," I said, suddenly feeling the need to stretch my legs. "It's not every day you become the proud owner of a beachfront cottage on Tybee Island."

Chapter Twenty-Five

KAT

After Thomas dropped me back at Helen's house, I took a shower and changed into fresh clothes for the cookout. After that, I spent some time looking through the file cabinets in Helen's office. Each folder had been labeled by topic and year. Helen had kept copies of everything: receipts, warranties, canceled checks. There were even packets with information for the lawn care and cleaning services, dating back fifteen years.

The second cabinet contained copies of the articles she'd written for the newspaper, along with her research notes.

I found the third cabinet more interesting because it was full of pictures and a stack of my old homework assignments. "What in the world?" I laughed. "Why would she keep this stuff?" Touching those pages was confirmation that without her ever saying such a thing, she thought of herself more as a parent than an aunt. Aunts don't keep folders of your homework. Parents do.

My phone buzzed.

"I need to run to City Market," Thomas grumbled. "Carly wants to be a chef someday, so she is doing the cooking tonight, and I've been given a list longer than my arm of things she needs. You want anything while I'm out?"

"Nothing comes to mind, but I was getting ready to call you."

I heard Thomas blow out a loud breath. "You're not backing out, are you? I swear, it was the thing about Grams saying stuff. There was nothing else to it."

"No. I have a question. When you told me about Helen and Kat, it stunned me, and I forgot to ask something important. If Kat lived with Helen, where is she now? If she was still living here, she can stay. There's no reason for her to move. If she and Helen shared this home, it belongs to her now."

Thomas moaned. "I don't bring anything except crappy news," he said. "You'll eventually stop talking to me if I don't get some better material."

"What do you mean?"

"I asked Liz that same question as soon as we got back."

"Did she know?"

"She did. Liz knows everything about everybody's business. She gets that from Grams."

"What did she say?"

"Kat was diagnosed with cancer last year and died almost four months ago. Liz also said Helen took it pretty hard."

An overwhelming sadness came over me when Thomas said this. I hadn't even known of her existence until a few hours earlier, but that didn't matter because if she'd been Helen's partner, she would have been an aunt to me as well.

Helen had lost her parents when she was little more than a teenager. Her only brother had been taken from her. Her relationship with Kat would have been the longest one in her life, and she'd lost her too.

"You still there?"

"I'm here." I thought about my earlier search of the house. "After you told me about Kat, I went through every room, and I can't tell that anyone other than Helen lived here. You'd think there would be an old prescription bottle. An extra toothbrush or a piece of mail for her. Something."

"Liz said Kat was over there a lot, but she thinks Kat mostly stayed at the Tybee house, and she worked out of town a lot. Helen stayed at the beach house a lot too."

"Did she say what Kat did or where she worked?"

"Didn't think to ask."

"What was Kat's last name?"

"I'm not sure. I'll text Liz," he said.

My brain shifted. "When are you heading to the market?"

"Now, I guess. Might as well get it over with."

"Give me five minutes. I'll ride with you."

"Huh," Thomas said slowly. "I need to think about how to interpret that."

I swatted at him over the phone and returned to the files. A folder marked PASSPORTS caught my attention. There were four inside. My eyes dropped to Helen's face. The air left my lungs when I saw her. She would have been sixty-one when it was made. Her dark hair had turned a glossy silver, but she otherwise looked the same as the last time I had seen her. She was still beautiful.

She'd kept her expired passport with the new one.

The third passport belonged to Katraine Evander. It had been issued nine years earlier. I studied her face. I'd only looked into her pale eyes for a few seconds that day in Helen's kitchen, but I recognized her. I would never forget those ice-blue, piercing eyes.

Katraine, also known as Kat, had kept her expired passport as well.

Katraine Evander's death certificate, dated just a few months earlier, was in the next folder. The cause of death had been listed as metastatic cancer of the brain. A pamphlet in the same folder provided information about a rare, aggressive brain tumor called anaplastic astrocytoma.

I didn't know what to make of these things other than they made me even sadder. I had a strong suspicion Helen had bought the Tybee house because of me. She was coming for me in New York and didn't want me to know about her relationship with this woman. She'd gotten a place for her nearby. My limited interaction with Kat had been negative to say the least. She'd scared me on purpose, and while I would never understand why an adult would do that to a child, I at least now understood the nature of her anger. I'd come into Helen's life, and she'd been pushed out because of it.

Chapter Twenty-Six

MEMORIAL DAY AND MEMORIES

By the time we finished the shopping, unloaded it all into Grams's kitchen, helped Carly create a vegan-Mexican taco bar, grilled hamburgers for the nonvegans, ate, cleaned up, and found our way back into the garden for s'mores over the firepit, I was beyond exhausted and could barely make conversation, much less think about how long the day had been.

Tommy slowly lowered himself into the lawn chair next to mine—clearly as done with the day as I was—and gestured to Carly. "So, what do you think? Future Top Chef material?"

I smiled up at the girl who stood between us. At the funeral the day before, her hair had been an unkempt, mousy brown. It was now strawberry-blonde and had been expertly cut into sharp edges and blunted ends.

"Indeed," I said. "I'd never had a tofu taquito before. It was delicious."

"Thanks." Carly returned a nervous smile. "I like to make up my own recipes."

"So, you want to do it as a career?"

Carly shrugged and touched her hair like she was still getting used to it. "I like the *concept* of working as a chef," she said as though apologizing for something, "but I don't like getting sweaty or standing for long periods of time, because it hurts my ankles. I don't like cleaning up dirty dishes either, especially if there's stuff like lettuce floating in the sink." She shivered and pretended to gag for effect. "I just want to create, you know? Be known for my creativity, or like, an influencer or something in the vegan foodverse. Maybe write cookbooks or do podcasts."

Thomas sipped his beer and stared at her like she was speaking a language he'd never heard. He shook his head and held out a beer toward her. She reached for it, and he yanked it away.

"That," he said, "was a test, and you failed it big-time."

"You don't need to be an asshole about everything all the time," she snapped, though somewhat playfully.

Liz's husband, Sam, emerged from the house and flopped down in the chair on the other side of me. "Hey, Carls. Can you get me a beer?"

"You were like, literally just in the house," she snipped. "And you damn well know I don't like being called Carls." She turned, sauntered to the house, and yelled through the screen door, "Mom! Your husband needs a beer. Get on that, would you?"

"So, August," he said, "we don't know much about you. Liz said you live in Paris now, so we were wondering how that came about. Did you end up there because of college?"

I'd determined during dinner that Sam was the kind of man who measured people against an imaginary frat stick by asking status-related questions that were none of his business, which made it perfectly fine for me to lie.

"I did," I replied, throwing a glance to Thomas, who had

been clearly enjoying my fictitious responses. "I got a scholarship to the Sorbonne, and after I finished, I never left."

"Well that's a weird coincidence," he said. "My first wife, Karen Dells, went there on her study abroad from Harvard seven years ago. Maybe you knew her?"

"Not likely," I smiled. "Last I checked, enrollment is at fifty-five thousand."

Liz appeared with four beers. "I figured I may as well take care of all you at once." She slid into the same chaise as Sam and snuggled her back up against his chest, and a bolt of envy zapped me. It was a rare moment when I felt how alone I really was, but seeing people effortlessly couple up always gave me a sharp pang. It was self-inflicted misery, though, so no point wallowing in it.

The popping and whining of cheap fireworks sounded in the distance. The unofficial start to summer was off and running.

Liz sat up and pulled her knees to her chest. "We don't know much about you, August," Liz repeated, which let me know I'd been the topic of discussion between her and Sam. "Tell us something about yourself."

"Not much to tell. I'm as boring as I appear." I shrugged, uncomfortable having three sets of eyes on me.

"Oh, I doubt that," she said. "From the little I know, your life sounds sort of nontraditional. There must be something interesting you've done in the past twenty years." She threw a strange glance at Thomas. "For instance, how many times have you been married? Don't be shy, the three of us have five marriages between us—seven if you count all of his."

"Zero for me." I laughed. "Guess I'm an underachiever."

She twisted the delicate chain on her neck and narrowed her eyes. "Never even came close?"

I glanced at my phone, just then remembering Cort's text from earlier, asking me to call him. I filed it in the back of my mind and pulled my eyes back to Liz. After a long day of secrets revealed and lies told, I said, "I called it off two days before the wedding."

Liz leaned closer and smiled seductively. "Now you *have* to give us details."

I looked over at Tommy, who grinned at me as though I were about to tell a lie. I wasn't.

"Six months before the Paris shutdown I got a new neighbor," I began. "I rarely saw him, but knew that he was a violinist with the Orchestre de Paris, and that he practiced almost constantly when he wasn't at rehearsals or on the road."

"Was he cute?" Liz interrupted.

I ignored the question, but Tommy mumbled, "Geez."

"I usually enjoyed the music he played, but I was under a deadline one night and couldn't concentrate because he kept working on the same dirgelike passage over and over. I needed to drown him out to get my work done, so I randomly picked something from my playlist—which turned out to be a song from an American group called the Red Clay Strays. When the song ended, he played it back note for note. It's embarrassing to admit, but it became a thing for a while, and then when the shutdown happened, it became my only source of interaction.

"After a while, I found myself trying to trick him. I would crank up anything from the Bee Gees to Metallica, but he always played it back exactly right."

"Like Fiddler in the Wall instead of on the roof," Tommy said, and we all laughed thanks to too much alcohol.

"How long did this go on, and do you have a picture of him?" Liz said.

I pulled up a shot of us together in front of Sacré-Cœur and handed her my phone. I didn't need to look at it to remember that day: The first time post-COVID we could walk freely in the streets of Paris, hand in hand, in love. Perhaps.

"It went on for a few weeks. But by then we were also leaving little gifts outside each other's door—a roll of paper towels, masks, cleaning products. You know. Romantic stuff like that."

"He is gorgeous," Liz said loudly, like she was surprised. "Maybe you can patch things up with him. If you need advice on how to do that, just ask my brother. He knows a lot about that sort of thing."

Tommy made a *humph* noise and stood. "Anybody want a bottle of water? I'm dehydrated. Heat and alcohol are not a good mix."

I nodded, and he disappeared.

"We have a long drive tomorrow," Sam said as he worked his way from behind Liz and out of the lawn chair. He held his hand out to give her a pull. "It's past bedtime for us old folks."

Liz stood and gestured at Tommy as he returned with our drinks. "Have him tell you about how his ex-wife got him arrested last month. It's a great story. And with that, I bid you goodnight!"

"Here you go," he said, either not hearing her or choosing to ignore her cryptic comment. He added some twigs to the firepit and sat on the edge of the chair they had vacated, his shoulders squared off to mine.

"Let's do the twenty-question thing like we used to do as kids." He smiled wide, the fresh crackle of pine needles reflected in his eyes. "Same rules."

"Oh, I think I've had enough questions for tonight," I said, even though I had a ton of questions I wanted to ask him.

"Okay, then, how about six questions?"

"Seems random, but sure."

"This is my fault for starting this, but I'm nervous again." He fumbled with the label on his bottle. "Not as bad as I was earlier today but still—"

"I'll try to take it easy on you," I said, quickly thinking of something seemingly mild. "Who is the first girl you ever kissed?"

"I've been saving myself for you," he said, and we both laughed at his stupidity. "My turn."

"Great. Now I'm nervous."

"I hope so," he said, smiling. "So, who is the first girl you ever kissed?"

"I don't kiss and tell," I said. His set his water on the ground and gripped the edge of the chair, squeezing his eyes shut in mock preparation for my next question. "What is your favorite song of all time?"

"Phew," he said on a long exhale. "I can't remember the exact name, but it's a song from Verdi's *Rigoletto*. What's your favorite song?"

I glanced over at him and frowned. "I was going to say 'Free Bird,' *but* since you picked something from an opera, I feel like a rube."

"Too late!" He snapped his fingers. "Already out. Rule are rules."

"Did you lie when you said your favorite song was from *Rigoletto*?"

"I said that to impress you," he said. "My favorite song is actually 'Free Bird.'"

"I thought so," I said, shaking my head. "Your turn, you little weasel."

"Are you still in love with this Cort feller?" All lightness had left his voice, and he looked at me in a way that made me look away.

"I don't know how to answer that," I said, matching his demeanor. "I'm not sure why we started seeing each other in the first place, or why I ended it. He's the only person I've ever had a relationship with. I guess I'm conflicted."

This earned me a long, silent look.

"Anyway, my turn," I replied. He'd opened this door. "Are you still in love with your ex-wife?" He moved his face so close to mine I could see the evening stubble. So very different than when we were kids.

"I, unlike you, am not conflicted. I am one hundred percent sure that I am not in love with my ex-wife. Fool me once, shame on you and all that. Well. I guess in this case it would be fool me three times, shame on you. Or me. Not sure how that would work."

His turn. "Favorite city you have visited or lived in?"

"Savannah," I said without giving it any thought. "Next question. What is your favorite movie of all time and why?"

"That is a hard one," he said a long moment later. "There are so many great ones, but I guess if I had to pick one it would be *Forrest Gump*. It has it all. Romance. History. Poignant relationships. The South. A slightly mystical twist. The message that amazing things can be achieved by anyone with the right support and some luck. Plus, the scene with Forrest sitting on the bench was filmed in Savannah, so that nudges it in the direction of making it my favorite. So, *Forrest Gump* is mine. What's your favorite movie and why?"

"Geez, Thomas."

"What?"

"I was going to say *Lethal Weapon*, but you keep making me sound sort of shallow and lame. A meathead."

"Too late. You said it. But you left out the reason a decades-old, lowbrow movie like that would be your favorite."

"I like the way Mel Gibson shoots a gun sideways."

"Oh my God!" he said, and we both laughed even though it was an honest answer.

Time for another ambush question. "Why haven't you ever had any children?"

"Same as you," he said. "It wasn't in the cards."

"Okay, by my count you can ask me one more question."

"I saved the best for last," he said, twisting in his lawn chair to face me. A wicked grin spread across his face.

I twisted my head at him and waited. Something twanged in my stomach that was close to nervous anticipation. My heart trotted a little. Then a lot.

Thomas leaned closer and whispered his last question next to my ear. A question that brought my face to a red-hot sizzle. A question that I could never, in a million years, answer out loud.

Chapter Twenty-Seven

AUGUST MISC.

The next morning, despite the misery of a hangover, I sorted through stacks of pictures in Helen's file cabinets. Because I battle migraines, I normally avoid more than a few ounces of alcohol, but throw in a temporary lapse of judgment, and there it was, pounding behind my left eye.

I massaged my temple and kept sorting. Helen had a ton of pictures in folders labeled by year, event, and person. One folder had been labeled Just August. Another said August and Me. The third was August Misc. The third folder seemed like a good place to start. It held pictures of me with groups of people in various places. Lancy was the only person I recognized in any of them.

Helen had taken pictures at the airport when she came for me in New York. She didn't have a camera with her, so she had bought a disposable one. She had tried hard that day to convince me we were going on some big adventure and that we needed to treat it as such. She said, "Smile like you mean it this time!" As sullen as I was, I apparently tried to do what she asked, but the look on my face could best be compared to that of a distressed monkey.

Staring at that forced smile almost made me sob. Sometimes you're lucky enough to forget how miserable you were, and then something like a picture comes along to remind you.

Those folders made me wonder if Helen had any idea when she came for me that it would last for a whole year. When I spoke at her service, I said she had intended for me to stay longer, but I wasn't sure this was true. It wasn't an intentional lie. More like wishful thinking.

If Helen hadn't planned on me staying, though, why buy the house on Tybee? Unless she planned on doing that anyway. The whole thing could be a coincidence. That's the problem with theories—one piece of misinformation can lead you down the wrong path.

I still didn't know if Helen had maintained her relationship with Kat during the year I was with her. If they were still a couple, why hadn't I ever seen them together? I had no recollection of Helen leaving me alone for an extended period. I'd seen Kat only twice: that first day in Helen's kitchen, and later when I looked out my bedroom window and saw her standing in the yard. Once I started school, Helen always dropped me off and always came to get me. It was the same with Thomas's baseball games: She was always back right on time to pick me up, every day—except the day my mother showed up at the stadium instead of her.

Ruminating about it was not getting me anywhere. The pounding behind my eye had gotten worse. I needed to take a break.

As I made my way to the kitchen for coffee, my phone dinged with a text message. It said, *Knock, knock.*

Who's there? I texted back and waited.

Ima.

Ima who?

Ima standing at your kitchen door.

I opened the door and found Thomas there holding giant Styrofoam cups. "Thought you might need something with some kick to it," he said with a sheepish grin. He held a cup toward me.

"Latte?"

"Yes, ma'am. Triple shot of espresso with skim milk and three hard shakes of vanilla."

"Bless you, my child. What are you drinking?"

"Something that's not that. Can we sit down a second?"

"Sure. Let's go out on the porch."

"Listen. I want to apologize for last night," he said before looking away once we were settled. "Liz has zero tolerance for alcohol, and she gets nosy and snarky when she's been drinking. You might not have picked up on it, but I know her. I should have intervened the second she started prying into your love life."

"Not a problem."

"And if I upset you by teasing you about that Fiddler in the Wall thing . . ." He stopped himself. "I'm sorry. It was rude of me," he said. "Even ruder was that last question I asked you. I don't even know what to say about that, except Liz wasn't the only one who drank too much."

I processed bits and pieces of what he was saying, but my mind was elsewhere. It wasn't four thousand miles away. It was nineteen years in the past.

"I sort of want to explain what Liz meant about my ex-wife getting me arrested, but it's a long story, and I'd rather wait to tell you about it some other time. If you're even interested, that is."

I nodded again.

"I want to wait to tell you, but I don't want you to think I'm a horrible person in the meantime." Thomas sipped his coffee and studied my face. "So, do you think I'm horrible?"

"Do I think what?"

"That I'm a horrible person?"

"Why would I think you're horrible?"

Thomas smiled and shook his head. "Did you hear a word I said?"

"Uh-huh." My mind drifted back to the stacks and stacks of pictures in Helen's office. I have an excellent memory for faces. It could be an inherent ability from my father. He was, after all, a Pulitzer Prize–winning photojournalist who had an incredible eye for faces.

Or maybe my memory for faces came from years of watching other people while I tried to navigate our wordless life. It began with my eyes staying glued to my mother's face. Trying to read her moods. Anticipating her needs.

This evolved into spending thousands of hours staring at people from the window in our apartment. Trying to decipher what normal people did with their lives. From there it turned to surveying faces for signs of danger. I was told year after year the person who killed my father was trying to find us too. That tends to make one a little more alert. So, while Thomas talked, my brain sorted through the hundreds of faces in those pictures.

"I want you to look at something. I'll be right back." I scooped up the folders from Helen's office and took them to the porch. I spread them out as much as the table space would allow and started sorting through them again.

"What are we looking at here, August?"

"When Helen came for me in New York, it upset her that there was nothing personal in our house. My mother had gotten rid of everything, including all our family pictures. Helen tried to make up for this. She took at least one picture of me every day I was here. Sometimes she took fifteen or twenty. It bored me, but I didn't want to hurt her feelings, so I smiled and tried to act flattered."

"And that's what these are?" he asked, pointing.

"Yes. But I must have subconsciously picked up something strange when I searched through them."

"Okay," he said warily. "What is it?"

I placed a picture in front of him.

"This is at LaGuardia. I'm hard to find in this one," I said while pointing to myself in a crowd of at least fifty people. "I'm right here."

"Okay," he repeated, and waited for me to pick four more from the stack. The urge to count them caused a buzzing in my ear.

"So, start with the airport in New York the day Helen brought me here. Then check out the picture a few days later, on the riverfront. The next one is the Fourth of July parade downtown. The one after that is my first day of school."

"And this one?" he said, pointing with his index finger.

"I'm not sure. I don't recognize any of those buildings in the background."

Nothing in the crowd offered any clues. People of all different ages were standing around waiting for the same thing we were.

"I don't recognize it either," Thomas commented.

"I know where and when the others were taken, but I don't have a recollection of this. Since neither of us recognize the buildings in the background, it was probably somewhere other than Savannah."

"All right," he said as though he already knew those five pictures held something important. He pulled his chair up to the table and picked them up one at a time. His eyes searched all five from top to bottom. He leaned back in his chair.

It had taken the seasoned investigator less than a minute to find what I hoped he would.

"And you don't know him?" he asked.

I wasn't crazy. He'd seen him too. The same thin, pale man in all five pictures.

"I have never seen that man in my life, Thomas."

He studied the pictures again. Helen and I had been followed.

"I can run his picture through our digital image system and see if it matches a driver's license anywhere in the country. There are other systems I can access if that doesn't work."

"Sounds like a good place to start," I said right before my mind drifted to the letter waiting for me in Helen's safety deposit box. "Meanwhile, I'll hit the bank first thing tomorrow."

Chapter Twenty-Eight

PANDORA'S BOX

Thomas dropped me at the bank the next morning. I went through the paces of setting up my own account and providing documents showing I had a right to access Helen's safety deposit box. She'd added me as an authorized person even before she'd been admitted for surgery. They just needed my signature and ID. An hour later, I was in possession of an ancient pocket watch with my grandfather's initials engraved on the case and a black jewelry box containing a dozen rings of various gem sizes and hues. There was also a necklace box that held a matching diamond choker and bracelet set that I instantly returned to the safety of lock and key. I couldn't think of an occasion that would require me to wear any of these objects. I also couldn't imagine Helen purchasing such lavish pieces, so I concluded she likely inherited them from her mother.

Lastly, the letter I had been promised lay folded in a half-sized manila envelope, with my name on the outside. I held it to my nose, somehow expecting it to smell like Helen—roses, lemon, or maybe jasmine. But of course it smelled like paper and tin.

I took the letter and handed the boxes back to the clerk for safekeeping, then walked to the library, found my favorite bench in the park, and opened the letter. The date at the top was two months earlier.

My Dearest Niece,

How do I begin?

I know by the time this letter finds you, I'll be cold in the ground, and though I'm in perfect health on this day, this won't always be the case. I'm working with my lawyer to set up the family estate for you, my beloved girl, as there is no one left for me to bequeath it all to. I hope it's not too big a burden; do with it what you wish.

I imagine you sitting outside of the library, on your favorite bench, where you would take your lunch on those long-ago hot summer days. When I first started dropping you off there, I would park nearby and wait in the car until you emerged, because I was too afraid to leave you alone. I should have stayed afraid, and I will never forgive myself for taking my eyes off you the day Claire snatched you away from me.

I know you have questions, or maybe Claire has finally given you answers to some of them. Others she could not know, and still others I do not know. I'm sure you must think that a postmortem missive is the worst way—the coward's way—to share information, and you're right, I suppose. I can only hope that by the end of this letter you will understand and forgive me for not being stronger. I did try to track you down in person twice in the past, but Claire was always somehow a jump ahead of me, and after Palermo, she had her lawyer send me a warning to leave you both alone. I am sorry I failed.

I want to tell you so many things. Part of me wants to omit certain facts, but the larger part wants to make sure you understand the series of events that altered the life that was intended for you. For all of us.

So, let me start the awful story I wish you never had to hear by telling you about your father. Everything starts with Davis . . .

I burst into tears and slid the letter back into its envelope. I thought I was ready to know things that would hurt me, but I wasn't. It was too much to process. Instead, I called Thomas. He answered without it ringing.

"Are you nearby?" I asked, my voice raspy.

"Fairly close, but I just started to call you. Are you okay?"

"I don't know," was all I could manage.

"Where are you?" I could hear him moving.

"In front of the Bull Street Library."

"I'm on my way now."

While I waited, I pulled myself together, mentally kicked myself for calling Thomas like some damsel in distress, and read more pages. Fifteen minutes later, Thomas eased to the curb.

"Can we drive somewhere for a few minutes? Anywhere is fine."

"Sure." He cruised around the city before pulling into a spot overlooking the Savannah River.

"What happened at the bank?"

"Let's talk about something else first. It doesn't matter what. Just start talking, and I'll jump in at some point."

He slow-nodded like he was thinking. "Before you called me, I was getting ready to call you, because we got a hit on your mystery stalker. Do you want me to tell you about it, or do you want to talk about something else? I can read you this week's weather report from my phone if you're interested."

I almost laughed. "I meant something not related to all this, but I can't look for answers and then hide when I find them, right? Who is he?"

Tommy handed me his phone. "His name is John Garner."

I studied the driver's license on the screen, pinching out to get a good look at his face. He was just as gaunt and pale, with thin hair and half-moon circles under his eyes. According to his license, he was seventy-one years old, which would have put him in his early fifties when he had followed me. He looked ninety. I repositioned the license to see his address, and when I did, air caught in my throat. It was impossible, and yet there it was: 355 Central Park West, New York, NY.

I looked away and then checked it again. My chest tightened when I saw nothing had changed. I heard the phone hit the floor.

"August? What's wrong?"

I thought I said, "The address," but he stared at me as if I'd said nothing. "The address is what's wrong."

Thomas retrieved his phone and gave it another long look. "355 Central Park West," he mumbled before shifting his eyes back to mine. "I don't understand. What is this place?"

"It's the place I used to live."

"When?"

"From the day I was born until the day I turned eleven. After Helen brought me to Savannah, I never went back. I was never given a chance to go back."

He studied the screen again. "Are you sure?" he asked before shaking his head. "Disregard that question. You're sure. You wouldn't have said it if you weren't. What do you think it means?"

I had no words to explain what I was seeing.

"Whatever it means," he said a few seconds later, "there is something else weird. Other than what you see on his license there, I can't find any information about him. He doesn't have any social media accounts. No tax records. In this day and age, that kind of anonymity doesn't exist."

"I don't know if Helen's letter offers any clues, but start with this." I handed him the pages I'd read so far. "I have no idea if he has anything to offer, but reach out to the detective in New York who investigated my father's case. His name is Hector Sanchez. I'll forward you his contact information. See if he knows anything about this man. If he's living in our old house, there must be a connection. This can't be a coincidence."

While Thomas read Helen's letter, I racked my brain some more. Why would this person have followed me from New York to Savannah all those years ago, and more importantly, what possible scenario would lead him to now be living in my childhood home?

I came up with nothing.

"Geez," Thomas said a few minutes later.

We went back to staring at the river for a few minutes without saying anything.

"I'm not going to take Helen's word on this. After all these years of being lied to, I have a new motto: Trust but verify."

Thomas pointed his phone at mine. "We can fact-check a lot of it."

So, for the next two hours, that's what we did. Here's what we learned.

Helen had said in her letter that everything started with my father, but she should have said everything started with my grandfather. My mother's father. My grandfather, Almon Albert Bernard, born in a small village just outside of Rouen, France, in

1922, had graduated from the Sorbonne with advanced degrees in physics and engineering. Post-graduation, he began a forty-year career that led to him being credited as one of the most important pioneers of France's nuclear program.

On a personal side, he was described as having been brilliant, driven, and domineering. By different newspaper accounts, he had been both eccentric and charismatic. On an even more personal side, he never married, but that hadn't gotten in the way of him having a large family. More accurately, two families. Concurrently. Almon had fathered five children with a woman from Rouen, whom he'd known since childhood. He later became involved with a chemical-fortune heiress he'd met at some point during his time at the Sorbonne. My mother was their only child.

Having two concurrent families would have been an uncommon arrangement, but in my grandfather's case it was more so, because he'd been completely open about it.

According to Helen's letter, even the children knew of each other's existence.

> *Your grandfather maintained two separate households, but he insisted from the beginning that the children from both mothers spend time with each other. The mothers were not expected to cross paths, but Bernard often arranged for all six of his children to travel and vacation together. Vacations he rarely attended himself.*
>
> *France was one of the last countries to develop a nuclear testing program, and by the late fifties, other countries were already starting to push for an end to nuclear proliferation. France faced worldwide criticism because as a member of NATO, they were assured protection in the event of an attack. They didn't need to develop their own weapons.*

The United States had taken an official policy of opposition to France becoming a nuclear nation, but the Nixon administration secretly reversed this policy and began providing technical assistance that would last for two decades, starting in the early seventies.

Your father was part of that technical assistance. Specifically, technical assistance relating to the safety features on ballistic missiles. Shortly after Davis graduated from MIT, he went to work for the Department of Defense. Soon afterward he was assigned to work directly with Almon Bernard and his group of scientists. A group that included two of Almon's own children, Almon Albert Bernard II and Katraine Bernard-Evander.

Katraine. My mother's half sister. The woman who had stood in Helen's kitchen and purposefully given me cold chills. The woman who I had begun to think of as a sort of aunt because she'd been Helen's partner was in fact my maternal aunt, living with my paternal aunt.

The crowds flowed around each other along the riverfront while Thomas flipped back and forth between something that had caught his attention online and Helen's letter.

Your father traveled back and forth from Washington, DC, to France dozens of times over a period of eleven years, starting in 1975, ostensibly as an adviser to the Bernard group. They likewise traveled from France to Washington and back.

A handful of the Bernard group eventually exchanged their visas for permanent citizenship, including Katraine and her twin, Albert. This was a difficult decision for Kat because she had a young daughter in France and her husband (who also worked with the group) refused to come with her. She filed for divorce within weeks of settling in DC.

Now the horrific, unimaginable part. Almon Bernard's family—his first family, including the mother of his children; the three children who had still been living in France; Albert's wife and sons; and Katraine's daughter, Alina—were on a flight from Rouen to Washington, DC, for a surprise visit when their charter plane collided with another small aircraft less than a minute after clearing the runway.

Your grandfather, Almon, was not on that flight. He was hosting a lavish party with your grandmother at her country estate, just outside Reims. Your mother, who was Almon's one daughter from his second family, wasn't on that flight either. By some odd, terrible coincidence, she was at a hospital in New York City, giving birth to you.

Chapter Twenty-Nine

MOONLIGHT AND TRAGEDY

I needed to clear my head, so I left Thomas in the car and walked along the riverfront for a few minutes before settling onto an unoccupied bench. I read more of Helen's letter.

> *I first met Katraine and Albert years earlier through your father when I visited him in Washington, DC, one weekend, then again in France several months later. The following year Davis asked if he could host a weekend retreat in Savannah. I was home on leave, so the timing was perfect. You know I love a good party, so I said yes. He showed up with six of the most interesting people I'd ever met. Something about Katraine was different this time, though—she simply glowed, and as the only woman in their group, she had five sets of eyes glued to her every move. To be bluntly honest, mine were glued the firmest. I had never spent much time pondering my sexuality, maybe because I was a daddy's girl who would never get over the grief of losing him*

early, or because no one had ever suggested that falling in love with a woman would be okay. And so, I fell pretty darn hard! We spent the final night of the weekend talking about everything. I couldn't help but feel that I had met my match. I decided that night if I never married it would be okay, because I had felt my soul crush up against another's.

As it turns out, Katraine was glowing because she was pregnant, and a few months later, I heard that she had given birth to Alina, a tiny duplicate that had stolen her heart. Nonetheless, she returned to work and left Alina in the care of her now ex-husband and her mother. She traveled back and forth to France every few weeks to see her.

Time passed, and I saw little of my brother nor really knew where he was most of the time. Then one day, years later, he called to tell me that he had fallen in love with Katraine's much younger half-sister, Claire, and that they had gotten married. They were moving to New York. He also said that he had left the defense department and was beginning a new career. Photojournalism is a great cover for a "retired" spy, if you ask me, but I never asked him about it.

One night, not long after that horrible accident, Katraine showed up at my door. I'd not seen her since the weekend Davis had brought her and the others for that visit years earlier. Katraine had left her job and life in Washington, DC, without telling anyone where she was going. She told me she didn't know where she was going. She'd just jumped in her car and started driving. I fumbled around for something to say. I knew the awfulness of losing my parents, but she'd lost her daughter, mother, siblings, nephews, and sister-in-law all at once. I couldn't comprehend that much pain. That much loss.

I assumed she would stay a few days and be on her way, but it didn't work out that way. Days turned to weeks. Weeks to months. Still, after all that time I still didn't know why she had decided to come to my house that night. I didn't know what her intentions were, or how she felt about me. If she felt anything at all. I was too afraid to ask.

When I was reassigned to a different city for work, Kat traveled with me. She trailed along behind me in the shadows. Lifeless and hopeless. She was drunk half the time and drugged up the other, but every time I looked at her or tried to get her to eat something or go outside into the sunlight, she reminded me of a beautiful, broken bird, and I wanted more than anything to fix her. I needed to fix her.

She had lost everything, but still, as broken as she was, I was infatuated with her. I couldn't get my words to come out right around her. I literally stuttered when I tried to say the simplest thing to her. I was afraid if I took my eyes away from her for a second, she would disappear. I was even more afraid that she would disappear if she knew how I felt about her. I told her none of these things.

I woke up one night and found Kat packing her things. I asked where she was going, and she said, "I don't know, but I don't belong here. I don't belong anywhere."

When I asked why she was leaving, she stopped folding clothes and turned to face me. She said she was leaving because she was ruining my life.

Her words stung, but they also gave me hope. It meant she felt something for me. I didn't know if those feelings were romantic or those of friendship, but it seemed like a start. This is a strange thing to remember, and an even stranger thing to share, especially with my niece of all people, but I remember racing through the house turning off every light because I thought it would be easier to ask her to stay if I couldn't see her face. If she couldn't see mine. I was suddenly a child who hides under a blanket because she thinks if she can't see the monster, the monster can't see her either.

I finally gathered the courage to go back to her room. I turned her lamp off last, and if she wondered what in the world was wrong with me, she didn't ask. She just sat there and listened while I begged her not to go. When I said all the things I could think of to say, she got up without saying a word and put more of her things into that small suitcase. She didn't turn the lamp back on. She kept packing in the darkness.

After what felt like an eternity, I summoned the courage to ask her again where she would go. It took a while for her to say anything, but when she answered, there was already something different about her. Something better. There was the slightest lilt to her voice when she said, "If we are going to be together as a couple, sharing the same room might be a good start. I'm moving across the hall with you." And she did. I still can't believe it, but she did.

Kat is gone now, and when I'm missing her the most my mind turns back to that night more than any other. The night I ran through the house like a crazy person turning off lights while she stood there, calm, silent, and broken, with nothing but all that moonlight and tragedy behind her.

Sometimes in life you can feel things slowly changing, and sometimes you don't know when or how or why the change was made. You only know that somehow everything is different. Everything is better. As it should be. My entire life shifted in that one moment.

Kat and I were together for over thirty years, and I'm not saying it wasn't without problems. How could there not be problems with that as our backstory? Kat struggled with severe depression. PTSD. She would sometimes disappear for weeks without so much as a phone call. She almost always traveled with me for work, but she would sometimes cancel at the last minute without telling me why.

Then those dark moments would pass, and she'd be back to her old self. Those dark moments came back, however, when I brought you to live with me. She acted terrible because I'd asked her to stay out of sight until I could explain things to you.

I thought it was a reasonable approach, but she stormed out and refused to talk to me for a year. I handled the situation terribly and ruined your chance to have a relationship with her. For that, I'm so very sorry.

My cell phone jarred me from Helen's words. I looked at the text: *You good?*

Yup.

Okay.

Kk

😊

I smiled at the ham-fisted emoji that followed. The quaintness of it made my cheeks burn, and I looked down the riverwalk, hoping I could still see him parked there. I wasn't sure if he could see me, but I waved to let him know I was fine. I had one more page left to read.

The only real conversation I ever had with your mother was the night she called me in Kuwait to tell me about what had happened to Davis. I'd been assigned there and had only arrived a few days earlier. Claire said there would be no funeral service and that she was having his body sent to

Savannah. We agreed that's what he would have wanted. She told me not to come, and I told her I would honor her wishes.

Kat was with me in Kuwait when I got that call. I begged her to reach out to Claire, but she refused. Kat always clung to her anger like a life raft.

Lastly, I can't help but think it was Kat's ex-husband, the father of her child, who ended Davis's life. The only thing I could ever get out of her was that he blamed Davis for convincing her to come to the United States. For his daughter being on that plane.

I know it's not enough for you, but it will never be enough. I just wish I could have done as much for you as I was able to do for Kat. I hope against hope that I did my best, and that the reason you never came back had to do with Claire and not the life I tried to give you.

Chapter Thirty

LOST, THEN FOUND

By the time Thomas dropped me back home, I was calm enough to extract myself from his truck, which was a good thing, as he'd been called back to Macon for a case.

"You sure you'll be okay without me?" he joked as we walked to the door. I stopped and gazed up at him, a look of genuine concern furrowing his forehead.

"I'll manage." I smiled and gave him a salute. "And duty calls."

"I'll be back tonight," he said, a worried tone back in his voice. "You call me if you need *anything*, got it?" I nodded and he pulled me into a tight hug, where we lingered for a moment. I gave a casual wave as he drove away in a cloud of dust.

My phone alerted me to a new voicemail. I recognized the number.

It was a message from Detective Sanchez. Thomas must have contacted him while I was out of the car on the riverfront. Just as I'd asked him to do. Efficient.

Hearing the detective's voice brought a surge of memories.

It also brought cold chills and a feeling of incredible gratitude for the kindness he had shown me years earlier. I found myself wishing I'd stayed in contact with him.

I closed my eyes and listened to the message again.

"Agent Reese sent me the information about the man who followed you. He was not a person of interest, but I'll look into it. Even if it doesn't pan out, I'm glad to hear from you. I've often wondered how you were doing. Anyway, when I pulled your father's file earlier, I noticed we still have some of his personal effects and those can be released to you if you would want them. There is one particular item that might interest you. Your father was carrying a birthday present home for you when he was . . ."

My breath caught in my throat a second time. Detective Sanchez's words brought an image of my father rushing home to surprise me, gift in hand, but never making it to the front door.

With that thought came the next—it was time for me to return to Paris. Staying longer would make leaving all that much harder. Plus, as much as I dreaded it, I needed to confront my mother about everything I'd learned since getting Daniel Grant's call. I had to get her side of the story even though it would be riddled with lies and half-truths.

I booked a flight and left a message for Detective Sanchez, telling him I'd very much appreciate him sending my father's things. I gave him Helen's address and thanked him for everything he'd done and everything he'd tried to do. I then texted Thomas to let him know I'd be leaving the next day. I added that I would appreciate him watching for the package Detective Sanchez was sending.

He sent back a frown emoji. And then, *When do you leave?*

Afternoon flight tomorrow.

Not sure I can make it back before midnight. If I don't make it back before you go to bed, see you in the morning?

Absolutely. And Thomas, I don't know how to thank you for everything. You're incredible. I'm beyond lucky to have you as a friend.

You won't leave without saying goodbye again, will you?

That was a onetime thing! It wasn't my fault! I won't do it again.

I'm holding you to that, August Caine.

I soaked in a hot bath for a long time and then went to bed. I was still staring at the ceiling when the grandfather clock chimed twelve times.

The house was quiet. Too quiet. The painted stars that had brought me comfort before were now a distraction. The clock chimed again to let me know another hour had passed. It felt like ten. I tossed and turned some more, with no hope of sleep. I decided to pack my one measly bag instead of waiting until morning.

I scooped up dirty clothes and headed for the laundry room. Before I got there, a faint glow drew me to the window. The paper lanterns in Grams's yard had been lit. In a lawn chair, Thomas was under the largest tree, his face buried in an electronic reader. The lanterns swayed in the breeze, and sheets of moss waved around him like old ghosts. I watched him fumble around for something next to the chair, and my pulse skittered when I imagined having to explain why I was standing in the shadows, spying on him.

It skittered more when I thought about how physically perfect he was. Especially that day on the boat when he had taken his shirt off. Scars and all, he was flawless.

I dropped my laundry and moved closer to the window.

Thomas swiped his hair with his free hand, and I imagined that one unruly lock tumbling forward. Something about that motion made me think about the way he looked at me sometimes when he thought I wouldn't notice.

I moved another step closer while hoping he wouldn't look up from that reader.

And then wishing he would.

I don't believe people possess a mystical sixth sense, but if I did, I would think Thomas did when he lifted his head and searched with his eyes until they landed on mine.

My face and neck got hot. I waved at him. He waved back, and even with all the darkness and distance between us, I imagined his eyes never leaving mine.

For a time, I must have blocked my memories and thoughts of Thomas, but I knew there had been a connection between us as kids, and within the last few days, that connection had turned into something electric.

"I'm tired of being alone," I whispered, even though there wasn't a soul to hear me. And then louder, "I'm tired of being alone."

My hands were steady when I dialed his number, but by the time he pulled the phone from his pocket, they were a quivering mess.

"August," he said, soft as a lullaby.

"Thomas," I managed to croak.

Things got quiet while he sat under wispy light and I stayed in the shadows. I smiled when I thought of the question he'd whispered in my ear the night before. His perfect balance of boldness and timidity.

I tucked the phone under my chin and waved at him again. I said, "Ugh," when I realized I was embarrassed by it.

Thomas pulled himself up from the chair.

I took a deep breath and had all the right words ready, but they froze in my throat the second I tried to say them. I tried again. No luck. This was insane. At my age, this should have been easy. My eyes went back to my phone. Sending him a text was absurd, but it was that or nothing. I gave up and wrote, *Do you want to come over?*

He stared at his phone for what felt like an eternity before bringing his eyes back to mine. He then did something unexpected. He pointed to himself and looked around while turning in a slow circle, pretending to be unsure if I meant him or someone else.

I laughed and imagined his smile.

"Turn the light on so I can see you."

So I did what he asked because I was powerless to do anything else.

Thomas took a sharp breath. "You know I want to come over. Are you sure that's what you want me do?"

I had the perfect answer in my mind, but I couldn't turn it into words. I gave up and texted him as fast as my concrete fingers would allow. *Very sure.*

His eyes went from mine to the phone and back again. He nodded and took a slow step toward the house. There was still a whole lot of space between us. Time was running out. At this pace, the sun would be up before he made it over.

So I did the only thing I could. I put the phone down, flew down twenty-four steps, and ran to him like a schoolgirl.

Chapter Thirty-One

PARTING

Rumbling across the ocean to Paris brought nothing but deep sleep and dreams of Thomas. My mind had already replayed every incredible moment of the past few hours before the plane had even taxied the runway. When the flight attendant gently pressed my arm to wake me, I was shocked to realize that I'd slept the entire journey.

The minute the wheels hit the tarmac, I texted Thomas.

Landed! ;)

My phone buzzed. "Bonjour," I said.

"August Caine," he said with a raspy voice that sounded sweet and exhausted. Just two simple words, but hearing him say them was wonderful.

"*C'est moi.*" I smiled. "You're up early."

"Did you sleep any on the flight?" he asked a long moment later.

"I might have dozed a few minutes. How about you?"

"Sleep has been the furthest thing from my mind." He laughed. "I'm fifteen minutes from my apartment. I'll try to grab a nap."

"*Tu me manques*, Thomas."

Another long round of silence. "I don't know what you just said, but I'm for sure not sleepy anymore," he said, laughing again. "This is nuts. I'm too old and way too manly to be this giddy!"

"I'll text you when I get to my apartment," I said, avoiding the word *home*. As long as I had lived in Paris, it had never been my home.

"Good luck today," he said. "Miss you." The words were said so easily but hit me so hard that I just sat there, staring at my phone, until my seatmate cleared his throat to announce that I was being rude for blocking his path. I gathered everything quickly and raced off the plane, through the airport, and to a taxi.

I gave the driver my address and studied the lights twinkling in the gray early morning drizzle. My phone lit up with another text as the cab arrived at my apartment.

You are missing from me too.

I smiled at his clumsy translation.

I contemplated unblocking my mother, but chose instead to not move that boundary now that I was back in France. I slipped through the front gate quietly in order to avoid my concierge—a kind old lady named Beatrice who was nonetheless the quintessential busybody that came with the job. We had seen each other through the doldrums of COVID, but I didn't have time to explain my whereabouts. I took the stairs, two at a time, hoping to also avoid Cort and his fiancée. Once I had broken the engagement, he quickly reunited with a cellist who was pretty and uncomplicated. The fact that I felt no jealousy comforted me that I had made the right decision to back out of the wedding. The past week with Thomas had helped me realize why I couldn't go through with it: My heart had always been elsewhere; I just needed to refind it.

I unpacked, read a stack of mail, and changed my outfit.

An hour later, I arrived at a boxy, nondescript building just north of the Champs-Élysées. The facade was classic 1860s marble baroque, built by one of the European banking families who had populated this posh part of town. I walked through a massive arched entryway that had once accommodated horse-drawn carriages, and over the cobblestone courtyard to the far-right entrance to the back apartments. There were no markings or identification of any kind, and cameras dotted the area. I stopped at the security vestibule and signed my name in the registry before being escorted to the third floor.

"Mademoiselle! We've missed you! She's missed you too," Etienne, my mother's private nurse, said in heavily accented English when I stepped out of the elevator and into the hallway that led to several private suites. It was good to see him, even though it had only been a week since my last visit. "She has been *très méchant.*"

"*Je suis désolé*," I said. "I should have let you know I'd be away. I just didn't expect to be gone so long."

I smiled and headed to the end of the hallway, where the large wooden door to my mother's accommodations stood open, as though she had been expecting me. I passed into the foyer, which opened onto a brightly lit room with furniture that likely dated to the original occupants, and was more like a penthouse suite than what one typically sees in an inpatient psychiatric facility. Beyond the living area was a small galley kitchen and a large bedroom. The place was, as ever, pin-neat, and my mother was at her desk, reading Marcel Proust's *In Search of Lost Time.*

Dressed in an elegant white pantsuit with matching shoes, Maman looked a decade younger than her actual age. As usual, everything about her was pristine and perfect. Everything except her mind. At times she didn't look real to me. She appeared to be a computerized composite of the world's most perfect woman, one who easily met the golden ratio measure of physical perfection: Pale blue eyes that were spaced just right. A nose, lips, and chin that Michelangelo could not have sculpted more nobly. How had I not seen the resemblance between her and Kat? Had they looked different when young but then aged in the same direction, the way many siblings do? The pressure in my chest wasn't new, but it somehow felt different.

Maman flicked her eyes my way and half smiled as if she were contemplating whether she was angry or pleased to see me. I held her gaze and thought about how her eyes had always been the most beautiful thing about her. Now they just looked cold.

"Do you know I used to try to think of ways to make you talk?" I asked her, ignoring her gesture toward the chair opposite her desk. "For example, I once thought if I pretended not to notice that I was about to walk off a ledge, maybe you would yell out my name to stop me. And you know what? I don't think you would have."

She scribbled a note on her small white board while I talked, then flipped it around.

You're angry.

I would have denied this at any other point in my life. I would have reassured her everything was fine. But that was in the past. Her note was so absurdly understated I nearly laughed in her face.

"Correct," I whispered instead.

She erased and wrote.

Where have you been?

I slowly sat down in the chair and contemplated which pawn to move next. It was surreal to sit at that desk, as if she were the CEO of the psychiatric facility and I was there applying for a job, or getting fired from one.

"Helen died this week," I said, crossing my arms over my chest to keep the pressure at bay. "But you probably already knew that. When Helen's lawyer called to tell me, I thought they were mistaken, because you know, you said she died fifteen years ago."

My tone was cruel despite the recent knowledge of how much more she had lost than my father. Perhaps after he died there had simply been no room left in her heart for anyone else. Not even me. Even so, my mother had no choice but to sit there and take the terribleness I dished out to her.

Part of me wanted to hand her Helen's letter to see how she would react. I wanted to blurt out all the things I had learned, tell her all of it. As angry as I was, though, I couldn't give her the power of knowing how much I knew without her first answering my questions. I sat patiently while she wrote on her board—possibly the most I had ever seen her write in a conversation.

I did what I thought was right. It was the only way to keep us safe. You would have run back to Savannah if you could have. I had to erase that part of your life.

"You robbed me of everything," I said with no emotion in my voice. "Going to school. Having friends. Boyfriends. Family . . . Helen."

She shrugged her shoulders in that maddening French way that was a physical "So what?" Her words were draining, but worse ones followed.

We. Were. In. Danger.

"But were we, though?" I laughed, and this seemed to interest her, as she leaned forward and delicately erased the board.

I did my best for you!

This triggered my smaller laugh into a cackle, a noise I'd never made before and caused my head to spin. In that instant, I realized I'd spent my entire life believing that if I tried to love her, if I counted her pills, said and did all the right things, forgave her, kept her insanity hidden, and got her the right help, she would get better. Her sad, broken smile would disappear and a genuine one would take its place, all while living out in the big wide world with her wonderful, ordinary life. Hope is a deadly addiction.

"And by the way, Kat's dead too," I said, getting a reaction that I was not expecting: Fear-tinged rage lit Maman's eyes and made her look exactly as crazy as I thought her to be.

Something in her expression changed. A spark of wheels turning, her eyes narrowing at a point beyond my shoulder. I sighed at her dramatics, tired of it all.

"And also, by the way, I'm moving to Savannah," I said quietly. "It's the only place I ever felt like I belonged."

YOU CAN'T! The letters were so large I read them upside down as she scrawled, her mouth twisted into a thin, white, sideways *S*. I'd always hated the saying that you can't argue with a crazy person, but that phrase came to mind nonetheless.

For a second, I thought that maybe she wasn't all that crazy. Maybe there was a well-considered reason for everything she did or didn't do.

I pulled the pictures I'd brought from my bag and slid the first one over. The recognition on her face was unmistakable.

"I have something I need to show you. To ask you. This is a picture Helen took of me on the riverfront about two weeks after I moved to Savannah with her. See this man?" She gave me an uncompromising stare. I slid the next one over. "Here he is again." I pulled the third picture from my bag. "And here he is again." Her eyes went from the picture back to mine, still revealing nothing.

"We left New York two days after you went into the hospital. She took my picture at the airport right before our flight. He went from New York to Savannah right along with me, so maybe he planned on doing something bad, but he didn't."

Nothing. And then something shifted in her expression. Something icy and primal. Like a reptile ready to strike. She turned her face away.

"Is this man your sister Katraine's ex-husband? Is he Alina's father?"

She tilted her head back sharply, her mouth wide open—her version of laughing, I suppose, though I couldn't remember another time she had done this. She shook her head.

"Who is he then?" I asked, my blood starting to heat up my cheeks.

She picked up her pen.

Kat's twin, Albert. My half brother.

I tried to keep my reaction from registering on my face.

"I have a lot of questions about why you never told me you had siblings, but for now, I'll stick with this. Why was he following me?"

She looked at me with disappointment. Impatience, perhaps.

To keep you safe.

"From whom? From what?" My voice was shrill. "What aren't you telling me?"

From her.

"From Helen, of all people?" It made no sense. "Did you really think she would do something to hurt me?"

Another hard headshake and then nothing, as though I were officially too stupid to know the truth.

Helen wasn't the source of her worry. Time stood still. There was no turning back. Her eyes landed on mine, and her face said she suspected what came next.

"Since the day my father died, I tried to be invisible to you. I can't do that anymore. I don't want to upset you, but I'm asking you to tell me who killed him. I have to understand what happened."

In my nearly thirty-one years I had never seen my mother's composure crack. Not once. I'd seen her stare at walls with a blank face for days on end, but never once had I seen her cry. Tears now trickled down her face, and part of me was glad for it. Still, she never took her eyes from mine. I held a pen toward her. She wouldn't take it, and in that moment, I knew for certain her tears were just another lie, another deflection, another way of stalling me from pressing for the answer.

"Tell me who killed my father. I'm tired of playing this game with you. I need to move on with my life."

She picked up the marker, moving so slowly that she had to be thinking, deciding whether to tell me or not, and whether what she told me would be an answer that would satisfy me and send me away.

Katraine.

I don't know how it was possible that my heart soared and plummeted in that one instant. How I could be relieved and overcome with despair at the same time. The feeling of relief didn't last for more than a few seconds when I thought again about Helen's role in things.

The letter Helen had left for me sat on the desk between us. Was everything in it a lie? Had Helen created a false narrative to protect Kat? Had Helen been so blinded by love she couldn't see that she was harboring a monster? I could not reconcile this with the Helen I remembered. She wouldn't have stayed with someone who had killed her brother. She loved him. She loved me. She believed in righteousness and family and helping people.

My mother had to be wrong. She had been delusional since my father's death. Maybe even before. Why would I ever take her word for something so serious?

I held Helen's letter in the air, desperate to make her change her words. For her to own one moment of clarity. I was even more desperate for Helen to stay in my memory as the person I'd idolized. The person who had saved me. If the love of Helen's life had done this and she had known, that would be impossible.

"You claim Kat killed him, but Helen left this for me before she died. She tells a different story. In her version his death was likely either random or committed by Alina's father after the plane crash. Why should I believe your version and not hers?"

Something folded inside my mother. She picked up the marker, this time with steady, angry hands. Her words came in fast, violent strokes.

She flipped it around. I was in no way prepared for what it said.

Because Davis was Alina's father.

Chapter Thirty-Two

ELLE A DISPARU

I spent the afternoon wandering around Paris, past the Arc de Triomphe, up the long boulevards, past the Louvre, through the Marais, up the steep steps of Sacré-Cœur, across the Seine to Notre-Dame, along the Rive Gauche, to the Eiffel Tower and back around dusk to my apartment, which felt like an assortment of rooms ready to rent to any short-term visitor, its view of the river and its Bateaux Mouches a picture-perfect place to have your honeymoon. Nothing about the place was personal: no photos, awards, posters, or art. The cream-colored bare walls were tall and depressing, boxing in a life that was clearly not worth living.

My mind replayed every word my mother had written, each one I had spoken. As unstable as my mother was, her explanation made the kind of sense that would complete her narrative: If my father had a daughter with my mother's sister, and that daughter died on the day I—his new daughter—was born, then perhaps Kat's grief would drive her crazy enough to murder him. This also would mean that the rivalry between the sisters would be something even Alina's death could not fully erase. I had so many questions. How long did my father maintain a relationship with Kat? Did my father know that Alina was his? Was my mother once again making things up in order to spin me more deeply into her psychotic existence?

Whatever the way it wound, the truth of my life was that I needed to leave Paris, needed to be as far away from my mother as I could be. I felt no remorse as I went into my bedroom and began to pack my clothing into giveaway bags.

There wasn't a single thing from my old life that I would take into my new one in Savannah—the life that I had been kept from living for far too long. It occurred to me that I had not only been ghostwriting other people's narratives, but I had fallen into the trap of penning my own.

And yet I couldn't stop thinking about Helen's role. Had she known about Kat and my father, or that my mother suspected she was responsible for his murder? I thought back to Helen's description of Kat. A completely different version. A divergence that wide didn't seem possible. I grabbed my bag to read her letter again, in the light that Maman's information had shed. Maybe I would see something I had missed.

I dug into my bag only to realize I'd left the letter in my mother's room. It was the one thing I could never leave behind.

"Bonsoir, Etienne," I said as he picked up my call. "I'm so sorry to call at this hour, but could you check Maman's room? I think I might have left a manila envelope on her desk."

"Bien sûr, Août," he said. "*Un moment.*" I could hear him breathe as he walked down the long hallway, knocked on the door, and called my mother's name before turning a key and entering, the heavy wood creaking on its hinges, the footsteps to the desk all part of my imagination. Then a softly spoken "*Merde.*"

"What's wrong?" I asked, fully expecting to be disappointed, as my mother wasn't one to leave anything lying around for too long.

"The letter is here," he said, sounding alarmed. "But your mother is not."

I called for a cab and hurried back to the hospital. A security guard escorted me to a cramped office, where I signed forms and watched a video of my mother walking right past the empty nurses' station. She had disappeared around the corner like a ghost. The next clip showed her getting into an elevator—an elevator that required a key to open.

Her eyes fixed on the camera right before the doors closed, and she mouthed the words "*Je suis d*ésol*é*." *I'm sorry.* There was no footage of her getting off the elevator. None of her leaving the building. A camera facing the sidewalk caught the back of her head minutes later. From there, she seemed to have disappeared into thin air, just as I'm sure she had from the hospital in New York the day I turned twelve.

"We don't know how this could have happened," the head of security said, clearly nervous about my potential reaction.

I stood to go. "Can I see her room?" I asked, unsure what I expected to find.

The guard cleared his throat and dropped his eyes. "Just so you know," he said, "we've never had anything like this happen before."

I did a slow walk around my mother's room. She'd left her cell phone on the bed. The only other thing out of place was the book she'd been reading earlier. She'd left it open, face down. As strange as everything was at that moment, her leaving that book was the strangest of all. She would never leave anything on her desk. She'd never leave a book open that way. I picked it up. Underneath it, I found a note she'd written. It had most likely been left for me, but I wasn't certain.

If we'd been given a different life, at a different time, I would have been so much better than I am. What I became. That's one of the things about the death of someone so dear to you. Grief not only robs you of your future, but it also changes everything about your past. You view all the moments differently than you did before. It carves a chasm between how you once saw yourself and how you see yourself from that point on. A person can only bear to see the grief they caused for so long. There can be no more waiting for me to be fixed. I can never be fixed.

I don't know how much time passed before I stood to go. I gathered up a few of her things and asked the nurse to put her jewelry and personal items into storage in case she came back. I gave her room one last look—and left.

The ride back to my apartment passed in a blur. My mind shifted from irrational things to wondering if the note my mother had left on her desk was intended to be her last. She'd purposefully overdosed several times over the years, and not once had she left anything like that before. I didn't know what to make of this.

Because of road repair, I had to get out of my cab two blocks from my apartment. I walked fast, even though there was no reason to rush home. There was nothing to be done except wait.

I grabbed more mail that had arrived from the lobby and headed upstairs. My mother's perfume lingered in the elevator. I stood at my door for a good while, imagining the things that might be said between us. When I stepped inside, I felt the emptiness around me, so I didn't bother to call out to her. She'd already come and gone.

I gave my apartment a quick glance and noticed the top drawer of my dresser had been left open. It hadn't been that way when I'd left a few hours earlier. I held my breath as I approached it, both hopeful and afraid at what I would find, or not.

When I looked in the drawer and saw that my mother's passport was gone, I blew out a breath of relief and started sobbing because I took this to mean she planned on leaving instead of dying. The evidence for this was thin for certain, but we all take comfort where we can get it. Relieved or not, my anger did not subside; it only escalated, and so did my determination to erase all connections to this dreadful life. I scrubbed my face and sprayed the room with a can of disinfectant I'd bought during the shutdown, enveloping her cloying perfume with cheap floral chemicals. I then booked a flight out of Paris for the following day, and set about rewriting my crappy narrative by pursuing the final glimmers of plot I could lay my hands on.

Chapter Thirty-Three

THE UNTETHERING

Early the next morning, my phone buzzed.

"How are things there?" Thomas asked, sounding, even for him, overly chipper. I nearly laughed from the absurdity of everything.

"That is a very long, very interesting, unbelievable story."

"I've got nothing but time," he said, his tone softer.

I told him what had happened. What I'd learned.

"Wow. You have more news than what I called you with," he said. "I only called to let you know that the package you were expecting from Detective Sanchez came today. Want me to ship it to you?"

The hollow feeling I'd had after seeing my mother changed with the resolve of the life-changing decision I'd already made. I thought back to a time when I believed a different life was possible for me. As a child I had thought there was a different version of life out there, that all I had to do was grow up and go find it. I thought this different version of life was possible right up until my mother told me Helen was dead. From then until the moment I saw Thomas a few days ago, that belief for a better life had never crossed my mind again. Even when I had been engaged to Cort, I couldn't envision a life where I was happy and things were normal.

I pulled myself up from the sofa and considered my apartment. It was the first thing that had truly been mine, and I had once loved it. I didn't love it anymore.

I didn't know where my mother had gone or if I would see her again, but my heart would never be anywhere other than in Savannah. With Thomas. As impulsive as that appeared on the surface, deep down it was anything but that. Everything I didn't know about him was minor details. Details starting on the last day I saw him when I was twelve and ending the second I figured out it was him stretched out in front of me on the lawn eighteen years later.

You don't have to know the details to know someone's heart. Their character. You don't need details to know that a person will love you and do everything in his power to make sure you know it. While I listened to his voice, I closed my eyes and imagined touching his face.

Some people have smiles and eyes that lie. Thomas did not. I was sure about this. My angst was gone. I had already decided what I was going to do before I left Savannah, but I hadn't planned on doing it so soon. So completely.

"Want me to ship it to you?" he repeated.

I sat back down. "Thomas, I need a favor. Actually, I need three favors."

"Sure," he said, that one word managing to sound uncertain. Cautious.

"I don't want to be a bother, and you've already done so much for me, that I hate to ask."

"Don't hate to ask me anything," he said before he blew out a loud, nervous breath. "What can I do for you?"

"This is a long shot, but would you look through the boxes I brought in from the carriage house of my father's things? Look for anything that might help me figure out where my mother might have gone. An old address. Another property she and my father might have owned. Anything at all. I've racked my brain. I can't think of what else to do."

"Sure."

"Favor two: Can I list you as my emergency contact?"

"Is something wrong, August?"

I felt myself smile. I felt tears on my face. "No. Nothing is wrong. I've just never had anyone to list as my emergency contact. I want it to be you."

I heard him sigh. "You can list me as anything you want."

"Next," I said while consulting my watch and figuring time zone differences and how much time I would need. "Can you pick me up at the Savannah airport late tomorrow night? I can get a taxi if you can't."

A long pause. "So, you're coming back? For real?"

"I told you when I left that I'd be back. Didn't you believe me?"

Another long pause. "I believed you, but you didn't say when, and after you left, I got worried you might change your mind. I didn't want to get my hopes up because I can't compete with the things you have there and—"

"Thomas," I interrupted with an overwhelming need to make him understand the magnitude of my newly found hope. "I have nothing here. Nothing. And if you want to be with me, as broken as I am and with all the baggage I bring, I'm there. But even if you don't, I was always coming home."

Chapter Thirty-Four

LUCY

It was time to leave for the airport. I locked the door, left a note with Beatrice, and climbed into a taxi, thinking of my mother the whole time. When she was young and strikingly beautiful, my mother always got what she wanted. Everything around her had to be beautiful. Even the way she moved across a room was captivating. As she got older and her beauty faded a bit, she mastered the art of pity: give someone a half smile, and they would trip all over themselves to help her. To please her. To breathe the same air as her. I tried to convince myself that wherever she had gone this time—likely Vietnam, as she'd always had it on the list if France ever failed her—she'd be just fine. She found the people and food exotic—her word—and the culture French enough to have a baguette on demand.

Once settled into my seat and aloft, my mind drifted through all the times we moved, all the lies she must have told me, the countless midnight wakings to grab a bag and go. It was so frequent that I couldn't even begin to count, nor did I particularly want to. As I dozed, images of deeper losses and betrayals began to resurface, until I zeroed in on something so core that it shocked me.

We'd left Avignon and were living in Lyon. Not long after we moved in, out of nowhere a dog appeared at our door. It was a small, skin-and-bones, scruffy-haired mutt with a worn, tag-less collar. I rushed inside with her, gave her a bath, combed her matted hair for an hour, made her a special dinner of boiled chicken with rice, and put a quilt next to my bed for her. I called her Lucy. We became inseparable.

Two weeks later, in her predictably unpredictable manner, my mother informed me it was time for us to return to Avignon. I had dreaded those words from the second Lucy came into my life.

I asked if Lucy could come with us. I already knew the answer, but I still had to try. My mother stared at me for what seemed like a long time even for her, and then surprised me by nodding. I couldn't believe it. I laughed for the first time in years. I cried and then laughed some more. My mother gave me a strange, disappointed look and then walked away.

I packed my things and went to bed early that night. When I got up the next morning, the back door was wide open. Lucy was gone.

All these years later, I can still remember the sound and feel of my bare feet on that cold stone floor as I ran to my mother's room, desperate to find that dog. I screamed at her to tell me what she'd done, but she stood there staring at me with her mouth open, pretending to be surprised but not trying all that hard to be convincing.

Lucy, like everything else I cared about, was gone from my life.

My mother had broken me bit by bit.

As planned, we left for Avignon that afternoon. As soon as we got there, I went for a walk and checked myself into a hospital. It had taken all those years for me to finally understand that I needed to be locked up to be free from her. And yet even that failed. I had to have been delusional to think that she wasn't still in control. A woman with her wealth and charm was clearly capable of pretty much anything, including overseeing my psychiatric care in a way that only gave me the impression of being free.

Chapter Thirty-Five

MON ONCLE

I startled awake as the plane began its descent into Newark, gathering my notes and quickly texting Tommy my arrival time. My layover to Savannah would give me a little over six hours to do what I'd come to do. Knowing that traffic would shave precious time from this window, I took the train to the subway, and an hour later stood outside of the brownstone where I once lived. To say that nothing had changed would be an overstatement. The exterior was meticulously kept, the windows sparkling clean. The only obvious difference was the garbage cans under the stoop had been replaced by a recycling area.

I walked past them to the kitchen door—we had never used the parlor door at the top of the stoop, and I wasn't about to break habit now—and reached for the lion's head brass door knocker, my hand hovering as my memory whispered terrible things in my ear: *One shot, two lights, three people, four minutes, five police cars, six . . .*

The door swung open and there stood my uncle. A man I hadn't known existed until a few days earlier.

"I suppose you're here to kick me out," he said in French-accented English. The gray hair in the pictures was now a shocking white, stiff and combed in a thick wave away from his still-dark eyebrows. He looked nothing like his twin, Kat, or his half-sister, Claire, but he did have the same crystal blue eyes that were on my level and cut right through me.

"I'm not here to do that," I managed to say.

"Well, don't just stand there letting flies in."

He turned and shuffled into the kitchen, across the checkerboard floor, his gait heavy for a man so thin and frail. I suspected he suffered from advanced Parkinson's.

I followed slowly, my hands out to the side as though I needed the very air to keep me steady. The kitchen was the same as the day I had left it, except that the breakfast table was covered with stacks of coupon flyers. Albert settled himself in the gap between two of these, at an open space where a pair of scissors and a magnifying glass lay.

"How's your mother?" He picked up the giant black-handled shears and began cutting the papers in front of him.

I told myself I had no reason to be afraid of this man, but I also didn't have a reason not to be. Either way, I knew to be on my guard in case he was anything like his sisters. I chose the chair closet to the door.

"You tell me," I said, my mouth dry as sand.

He raised one unruly eyebrow and picked up a fresh sheet of coupons. A clock ticked and then ticked some more. "I don't know how she is, which is why I asked you."

"Has she been here?" I asked, dispensing with pleasantries.

Something that almost looked like a smile rippled across his face. He moved his chair slightly, disrupting a pile of freshly cut coupons and exposing something shiny: six keys . . . and one little pony. My eyes teared up, but I blinked away the melancholy my old key ring brought up. *This is surreal. Breathe. Just breathe.*

"I'm asking because she couldn't have managed all these years without someone helping her. Someone other than me," I said. "I'm pretty sure it was you, because as far as I know, you're the only person left in her life."

"You're nothing like her." He clucked his tongue and waved his hand in dismissal. "You're like him." Whenever someone in the past had said this to me, it sounded like a compliment; with Albert, it hinted at disappointment.

"Do you have an idea where she is?" I almost yelled, then checked my temper.

"I only hear from Claire once in a blue moon," he snapped before looking away. "Only when she needs something. Demands something. Needs me to drop everything and be at her beck and call." Not really an answer. He glanced at me again without moving his head an inch.

I'd have to take a different approach. A more circuitous route. *Make small talk. Breathe. Don't lose your tempter.*

"You're not answering anything I ask you, so I'll move on to something else."

"Such as?"

"How about telling me why you changed your name and how you came to be living in our old house?"

"Humph. That's easy. Would you want people to know your identity if you were me? It's not the case here, but everyone in France knew what happened to my family. A lot of people already hated us back then because of our work. After the accident, they just pitied us. Because of my father, we were a freak show to them. An aberration. Then there was the gossip and the rumors that my father had them killed. It was all nonsense, but there you have it. As to why I'm living here, why shouldn't I be?"

A siren wailed from outside. Then another. It triggered a memory that made me want to hide in a closet.

"Tit for tat," he said. "Why did you change *your* name?" he asked. "Giselle Roamer, *non*?"

I shrugged. "It was her choice, not mine."

My uncle winked at me. "*Giselle* means 'hostage.' *Roamer* is just like it sounds. 'One who roams.' I don't think you or she picked that name out of thin air."

"I assume you know Kat died several months ago?" I asked, unwilling to let him get me off track.

He lifted his chin. "I do. People think twins have a special bond, but that wasn't the case with us. Our connection was flimsy at best."

"Why was that?"

My uncle slow-shook his head like he wasn't sure. "We just were never close." He pushed his glasses up on his nose and didn't seem to mind that they slid back down. "Katraine was a negative, dour child. She was always mad or ruining things for others. Tattling. Being in her presence was not pleasant."

Another long pause. I heard the ticking of a clock in my head. I contemplated changing my flight, but I missed Tommy so much I couldn't make myself do it.

"We were ten years old when I first observed this about her. As a prank, one of our favorite cousins had gotten thrown into a pool, and he drowned. His friends didn't know he couldn't swim, you see. Our grandfather came to our house later that day to tell us, and we were all devastated, except Katraine. She blamed the boy for not learning to swim."

My uncle reached for a new sheet of coupons. "She always talked about the things people couldn't do. So-and-so couldn't ride a bike. This one can't parallel park. Little things, but bigger ones too. She never mentioned anyone's accomplishments, not even her own. She was only interested in a person's failures. Their weaknesses."

"Why did she kill my father?" No time for memory lane.

He put the scissors down and took his glasses off and glared at me. I'd struck a nerve. Maybe he was more protective of his sister than he wanted to pretend.

"Why did Katraine kill my father?" I repeated.

Instead of an answer, I was met with a question. "Why did you go back to Paris this week?"

My joints went cold, and I took a long, deep inhale through my nose to stay calm. We were getting to it now, and I wasn't going to let up until he blinked.

"Was it Kat or Alina's father who killed him?" I baited. He narrowed his eyes, as if measuring me in some way, and nodded slightly.

He put the scissors down and peered over his glasses at me. "It can take your mother a long time to see things as they are, but she's sharp," he said. Another nonanswer. "She was smarter than Katraine and me put together. If she hadn't wasted her life, who knows what she might have become."

"My mother is certain it was Kat who killed my father," I repeated, wanting him to say the words. To confirm what my mother had told me. "Is she wrong? My aunt Helen believed it was the man Katraine was married to before she moved from France. They both can't be right."

My uncle gave me a curious look. "Unless the dead can rise, it couldn't have been Katraine's ex-husband. He died from thyroid cancer two years after the crash. A lot of the people who worked on my father's project got cancer. We didn't understand the risks of ionizing radiation back in those days."

Something inside me wilted. For so many reasons, I'd wanted Helen to be right. I'd wanted her to be right because it was easier to accept that a stranger had done this instead of my mother's own sister. I wanted her to be right because Helen had spent her life in love with the person who had taken my father from me.

"If Kat did do it, why?"

"Why?" My uncle scowled. "I stopped trying to figure out why people do things a long time ago." *Snip. Snip.*

Don't lose your temper. Ask the question a different way.

"If you were to speculate that Kat was the person responsible for my father's death, why would she have done it? Did she blame him for the crash?"

My uncle slumped and blew out a loud breath, as if realizing there was no avoiding the random, manic-like questions I was peppering him with.

"It's an old story. One that in the grand scheme of things isn't all that unusual or interesting," he said a few seconds later, the weird grin back, his eyes softening. "It's the story of a woman who was beautiful and brilliant but who in the end wasn't quite beautiful or brilliant enough. She gave up everything for this man who talked her into doing something she never wanted to do in the first place. She ruined her marriage for him. She abandoned her child thousands of miles away to be close to him, and he repaid her by marrying her younger sister."

"Is that what happened? Is it true?"

My uncle leaned closer. "Truth is an interpretation, is it not?"

"Yes and no," I said, sort of proving his point. "It's either true that my mother stole her sister's boyfriend or it's not. It's either true that my father was also Alina's father or it's false."

An alarm beeped on my uncle's cell phone.

"Ah," he said. "Time to take my ticker pill."

He stood, shook a large pill from a bottle, and swallowed it dry. I'd spent too much time in the marshes not to be reminded of a pelican downing a fish.

He shuffled back to his chair and lifted the giant scissors again. He didn't look to be in any big hurry to do anything with them.

A few seconds passed. It felt like an hour. "As I said, those things are either true or false. No shades of gray."

"What does your mother say about the situation?"

"Lots of things. Some of which I've learned in the last few days are complete fabrications. Before she disappeared into thin air yesterday, she told me my father was also Alina's father. She also told me Kat killed him."

"Your mother is a very smart woman," my uncle repeated, his voice fading as if exhausted. "And, just so you know, I'm not like Katraine. I never blamed your father for what happened. I made a choice. I live with the consequences."

I leaned back in my chair, studied my uncle, and thought about what to say next.

"I was eight when my father was murdered. Why would Kat have waited so long to kill him? He wouldn't have been hard to find."

"Ah," he said. "Another chapter in the same old story. In this chapter the woman cannot get over the man who broke her heart and destroyed her life. It's about someone so foolish she believed that if she called or followed or begged this man, he would eventually change his mind and take her back."

"For eight years?" I said with more disbelief in my voice than I had intended. "She was in a relationship with my Aunt Helen all that time. She stayed with her long after he was gone."

My uncle shook his head. "Your Aunt Helen never knew what hit her," he said. "Katraine would have shoved her into a volcano if your father would have taken her back."

"Think of those eight years as a scale," he said with his shaking hands ready to weigh something. "One side of the scale is calm. Acceptance. The other side is rage. How much do you think this side can hold before it falls? I'm not making excuses for Katraine, but year after year things got thrown on this side of the scale."

He dropped his right hand. "She lost everything, while Claire got the perfect husband. A healthy daughter. Claire inherited her mother's fortune, while our mother died with nothing. Our father doted on Claire and made no attempt to pretend he didn't favor her. It just became too much."

My uncle scooped up the pile of coupons and dumped them in the trash. "I think the final straw for Katraine," he said, "was discovering you were born on the same day as the crash that killed our entire family. Believe it or not, she wasn't aware of that cruel bit of irony until years later. I don't know how she found out, but she did."

Helen had said the same thing in her letter, but she'd softened it by mentioning it as a coincidence. My uncle, on the other hand, had said it so matter-of-factly it was devastating to hear. He'd provided context that directly linked my life with my father's death. He had confirmed my awful suspicion that I was in some way responsible. *Don't think about it now.*

"My mother made us move all the time," I told my uncle. "She would tell me we had to relocate because the person who killed my father was looking for us. Did Kat do something to make her think this, or was it in her mind?"

He shuffled to the table and eased back into his chair.

"Hating and tormenting your mother was a hobby for Katraine long before the plane crash," he said. "Katraine had a cruel streak, and she resented Claire because, as I said, she was our father's shining star. We were well into our teens when your mother came along, but Katraine still craved his attention. His approval."

My uncle closed his eyes as if our conversation had drained him. "There's a lot of truth to Claire's claim that Kat made those threats, but I also think Claire took precautions for the same reason I did. She didn't want people to know who she was. Even early on she was embarrassed by our parents' unusual arrangement, and then later our family's tragedy became a national headline. If Claire wanted to be left alone all these years, her actions were prudent."

"Do you have an idea where she might have gone?"

My uncle almost smiled again. "You keep looking at your watch," he said. "Do you have someplace to be?"

I left New York for Savannah an hour later, grateful for my uncle. Grateful that he came to the door when I knocked and that he'd been willing to tell me the things he had.

He'd told me a lot, but there were still things I didn't understand, so I spent most of the flight to Savannah researching my family further, starting with my grandfather. According to a small online article I found in a Rouen newspaper, Almon Bernard became a virtual recluse after the plane crash that claimed three of his children, their mother, his three grandchildren, and a daughter-in-law. Three years later, while bird-watching alone at a lake in the Champagne-Ardenne region, he suffered a stroke and died a few days later.

My grandmother died not long afterward from a brain aneurysm.

I would have been four years old when my grandfather died, and at around that same time, I'd flown with my parents to France. I didn't have a specific recollection of anything we'd done on that trip, but I vividly remember my father telling me we were in Paris. Maybe that trip had something to do with my grandfather's funeral.

I also thought back to earlier in the week, when I had lain in bed and looked at my father's painted stars. I'd thought about Helen's daily ritual of reading horoscopes and how strange it was that she believed a person's astrological sign determined their entire life. It seemed ridiculous how anyone could believe something as random as the day they were born directed the course of their journey. And yet, as illogical as it was, I now felt in my heart it was true in my case.

I'd asked why someone would have waited eight years to kill my father if it was retribution. My uncle's explanation worked. Kat had lost everything. My father might very well have been murdered because of the tragic coincidence of my being born on the same day Alina died. It could have been what tipped Katraine's scale.

Since the day my father died, for reasons I did and did not understand, I had felt responsible for his death. Now, knowing what I had learned, I couldn't see this changing.

Chapter Thirty-Six

LUMINESCENCE IN SAVANNAH

The next morning, I woke to bright sunshine and Thomas asking, "Do you remember asking me to look through your father's things in those boxes?"

"We had that conversation less than twenty-four hours ago, so sure," I mumbled, still half asleep.

"Let me get us some coffee. I'll show you what I found."

I groaned and pulled a pillow over my head. "I'll meet you downstairs."

When, sometime later, my eyes flew open, I heard Thomas banging around in the kitchen, fixing breakfast. Or lunch. Maybe dinner. I was disoriented.

I took a quick shower and joined him downstairs. He handed over a cup of coffee. I said, "Merci beaucoup."

He shook his head and grinned. "You do know that you've turned me into that guy on that old TV show who goes crazy when his wife speaks French, right?"

I mulled this over, weighing out all the many advantages and possibilities.

"That must be why you wanted to name Helen's old hearse Morticia. Methinks you have a French fetish of some sort."

We smiled at each other for a long moment.

"Did I dream it, or did you say you had something you wanted to show me?"

He held up a finger. "Uh-huh," he said. "I have two things to show you." He picked up a large envelope from the kitchen counter and slid it over. "You asked me to bring in those boxes from the carriage house to see if there was anything in them that might help you find your mother. I didn't find anything like that, but I checked your dad's old cameras. One of them had a roll of undeveloped film. I hope you don't mind, but I had our lab process it this morning. There are several pictures of you with your mom."

I had thought everything of my father was gone, only to discover earlier in the week that his things had been in Helen's carriage house the whole time. Boxes full of his work. Still, the packet Thomas held out for me represented something different. Something unfinished.

It was something my father had started with his own hands but didn't live to see through. It felt like he had reached into the future and passed it on to Thomas to finish for him. I was struck again by how a person can have a big life planned only to have it taken in the blink of an eye.

Thomas asked, "Do you still have doubts about the things your mother or uncle told you?"

The question threw me off-balance. I thought it over. "My mother is nuts. My uncle is an odd bird that goes from being too blunt to talking in riddles and then back again. Helen was, as Grams would say, googly-eyed about Kat, so who knows how good her judgment would have been." I threw my hands up. "I'm ninety-nine percent sure my mother and my uncle are right about Kat. That nagging one percent exists because I don't want Helen to have been so wrong about someone who stayed in her life for thirty years. I don't want to think of Helen as some naive victim. Or worse, as someone who knew what Kat had done and still chose to stay with her."

"Sometimes people see what they need to see, August," he said softly. "I didn't know Helen the way you did, but you're right. It is impossible to believe she would stay with someone she knew killed her brother and who threatened you. But you know what? Maybe it was better that Helen was that gullible. She left this world not knowing what Kat had done. Maybe she turned away from it, but in the end, it got her through the day."

I threaded my fingers into his.

"I feel like a brat saying this, but if I'm honest, part of what bothers me about my mother snatching me up like she did is knowing that it had to be a relief for Helen. It causes me to question how hard Helen searched for me. What would she have done if she had found me? I'm sure Kat wasn't going to let herself be put on the back burner again. Occam's razor. Go with the simplest explanation, and the simplest explanation is Helen didn't search all that hard because it would have meant losing Kat a second time."

Thomas squeezed my hand.

"I hope this will be the most self-centered thing you ever hear me say, but I don't know what makes me feel worse, that Helen chose Kat over my father, or that she chose Kat over me. If everything my mother and my uncle said is true, it comes down to that. It just does."

Light as a whisper, Thomas brushed my cheek. "Helen did

choose you. She came for you that day in New York without Kat being on board with it. Helen had to know it might mean an end to their relationship."

His words suddenly made me feel despair for Helen. Coming for me that day when I was eleven had to be one of the most difficult choices in her life, yet she never complained about it once. All Helen ever did was show me love and kindness, and I needed to hold on to that rather than wallow in the self-pity that came with being disappointed that she didn't show up sooner, rescue me a second time, or reach out in recent years because she didn't want to lose Kat again.

If I had any hope of happiness, of getting on with my life, I had to quit turning things over and looking at them from every possible angle, starting with the last time I saw Helen. The day I turned twelve.

I needed to stop analyzing Helen's unusual silence when she drove me to the library that morning or how her eyes were fixed on my face as if she were trying to commit it to memory. As though she knew she would never see me again.

I had to stop questioning how my mother found me that day or how someone so damaged could orchestrate all the moving pieces that would allow us to disappear so completely.

I needed to quit wondering if Helen had known about the things Kat had done to scare me as a child. Forget that she wasn't exactly truthful in her letter about the timeline of when she found me in Paris. Stop asking myself if she had purposefully avoided the glaring symbolism of my father being murdered on the exact day Kat's family had died in a plane crash eight years earlier, or if the reason she came for me on my eleventh birthday was based on a fear for my safety.

I didn't share my thoughts about Helen with Thomas. I couldn't. At least, not yet.

"You said you had two things to show me. What's the other thing?"

"Detective Sanchez and I have been talking some since you had me send him that photo of Garner. He sent copies of a few things from your father's murder file for me to look at. These are old phone bills he gathered early in the case. They span the entire time your parents lived in New York. Someone called your dad's studio from a pay phone in Savannah six times. It's long gone, but that phone was on the corner of Abercorn and Park. It's not likely Helen would have called your dad from a pay phone instead of her house phone," he said. "It stands to reason it was Kat who called him."

I examined the list. The length of the calls ranged from one to nine minutes.

I found myself wondering why my father would have talked to Kat for nine whole minutes. This thought drifted to wondering why that number looked so familiar. I have a great memory for numbers, especially since I habitually count things. I hadn't done it much as an adult, but as a child I would sometimes lie in bed at night and silently repeat sets of numbers over and over. Phone numbers. Lock combinations. Items on a receipt. Anything with a set of numbers was fair game. I didn't understand my reason for doing it back then, and I still don't.

My mind flashed back to the night I'd answered Helen's phone and the person on the other end wouldn't say anything. I'd only recently learned about the *69 feature, and I used it that night. I'd written the number down on a scrap of paper and put it in a metal box I hid in the bottom drawer of my father's childhood desk.

I hurried upstairs. The box was right where I'd left it eighteen years earlier. Only two things were inside: the charm bracelet Thomas had given me for Christmas when I was eleven and a scrap of paper with the same number as the one on my father's phone bill.

I handed the scrap of paper to Thomas. While I looked over the phone bill again, I explained what it meant. The last call to my father's studio had come from that pay phone two days before he died. If Kat had meant to cover her tracks by calling from a pay phone rather than Helen's house phone, she had succeeded. Apparently, those calls had never been investigated.

My thoughts turned to something Helen had written in her letter. She claimed that she had left for Kuwait a few days before my father was killed. She'd also said Kat was with her when my mother called to tell her about my father. I now realized Helen hadn't said they had arrived in Kuwait together, though.

I needed to see their passports again.

"I'll be right back."

I pulled Helen's passport from the file cabinet first. She'd flown to Kuwait when she said she had, confirming it couldn't have been her who called my father from Savannah. I scanned Kat's, looking for a matching date. It didn't match. She'd arrived in Kuwait five days after Helen had, and she'd flown there from New York. Not Savannah.

I showed the passports to Thomas. He nodded.

My mother had seen things as they were. She had many flaws, but putting on blinders wasn't one of them. Helen, on the other hand, either did not want to believe that the woman she longed for in the moonlight had murdered her brother or was oblivious to the menace in front of her face.

There was no way to know if Helen had known what Kat had done. I was just going to have to accept this. I was going to have to choose what to believe.

Chapter Thirty-Seven

THE LENS

Helen wrote that sometimes things change, and you don't know how or why the shift was made. You just know things are better. As they should be.

I made a lot of changes in a short amount of time. I listed my apartment in Paris and accepted an offer two days later. I gave the buyer a great deal in exchange for two favors: The first was that if my mother ever came there looking for me, they would give her a letter I planned on mailing there. The second favor was that they would contact me right away if this happened.

Because of its proximity to Savannah, Tommy transferred to the bureau's Augusta division, and by all appearances he turned away from his old life without a backward glance. I aspired to do just that, because as many times as I had done that very thing, I never did it without a lot of regret and silent anger.

After going through boxes of my father's things, I learned that right before his death the Metropolitan Museum had scheduled an exhibit of his work. That exhibit never happened, and I was determined to change that. It took a lot of work, but I eventually nailed down a date.

Online, I'd read articles about his career, but until I spent countless hours sorting through the real stuff, I didn't truly understand what an incredible photographer he had been. He seemed partial to black-and-white, up-close shots of people unaware they were in his lens. I detected a pattern. Before my father lost his first daughter, he seemed to have focused on people who looked worn and defeated.

After Alina's death, he sought out faces reflecting happiness, and at first this seemed to be the opposite of how it should have been, but then I understood. He had been seeking what was foreign to him. As a young man with no real exposure to grief, he'd studied it and had tried to capture it. When life turned on him and pain became too familiar, he did the same thing in the other direction. Maybe he'd forgotten what happiness looked like, so he sought it out in those around him.

After my first birthday, his focus shifted to me, different types of birds, and city skyscrapers. I'm not sure what it meant, but I chose to take the lack of smiling faces of other people as a sign he stopped seeking happiness vicariously and found it in his own life again.

There was something else I discovered about my father from his collection of pictures. He had been obsessed with taking pictures of my mother. They were married for only nine years, but he had over three thousand photos of her in those boxes. In at least half of them, my father appeared to have captured her unaware, yet she looked so poised and beautiful in every single one of them it made me wonder if she saw him there. I could not find a single unflattering shot of her. Then again, maybe he kept only the good ones.

When I chose the prints for the exhibit, I struggled whether to include some of her. There wasn't anything obscene about them, although he certainly liked shots offering a lot of skin and cleavage. My reluctance came from a vague but ever-present feeling this was an invasion of their privacy, especially in the ones that showed her staring directly at the camera. Directly at him.

The looks she gave him were subtle but unmistakable. Looking at them made me feel like a person who peeps into the windows of strangers. Would my father have wanted other people to see these, or were they intended for his eyes only? Would my mother want me to share them with the world? I would have asked her, but I had no idea where she was.

Something about that collection bothered me beyond the usual discomfort anyone would have when witnessing something so sensual between their parents. I couldn't put my finger on it. I finally talked to Tommy about it, and he took a pile from my hands and sorted through them for less than a minute before pushing his chair back and finding my eyes.

"I know what bothers you about these," he said. "It's the timing."

"What do you mean?"

He plucked one from the pile and laid it out in front of me. "Look at the date written on the back. You would have been one month old."

"Correct."

He tapped my mother's face with his index finger. "If she were a stranger, and I asked you to guess something about her, what would you say?"

I studied it again. "The first thing I'd say is that she really, really wants to get it on with the photographer," I said, and we both laughed when I did the shudder thing people do when talking about their parents in such a way.

"Your mom is smoking hot, and you're right about the sex thing, but what else?"

"I would say she's sure of herself and confident. Self-absorbed. She's the stereotypical person who knows how beautiful she is and doesn't care that you know she knows." I glanced at the image of her face again. "I'd also say she's happy. Happy and relaxed."

Tommy nodded. "There you go. The timing of all that is what bothers you."

I raised my eyebrow at him and waited.

"Her family members had just died in a plane crash. She'd left her parents and the only home she'd ever known to come to New York with your father right before that, but she looks exactly the way you described. Like she doesn't have a care in the world."

I grabbed the stack and looked through them again. He was right. There wasn't an ounce of sadness on my mother's face. I sat back and thought this over before scooping up the entire stack.

"Decision made. These are going back into storage."

Chapter Thirty-Eight

LETTING GO

A few days later, I got a call from the hospital, reminding me that Helen's cell phone and a few of her personal belongings were still there. I drove over and got her things the next morning. When I got back home, I decided, with some trepidation, to check the videos on her phone. Helen was gone, but her right to privacy wasn't. Still, I watched a thirty-nine-second clip someone had taken with Helen's phone of her standing with Kat in front of the US Route 1 Mile Marker 0 in Key West. Helen shouted something about this being the end of the road, but most of her words were drowned out by traffic.

Hearing Helen's voice and seeing her move in real time took my breath away. Her gestures and expressions were familiar from all my memories of her and from all the times I'd consulted a mirror. I found myself missing her so much my throat ached.

Freezing the video and locking eyes with Kat had the opposite effect. It brought a searing heat to my chest that left me weak and drenched in sweat.

Still, I watched it over and over, comparing her to my mother. Their frontal facial features were different, but their profiles were nearly identical. Roughly the same height and build. Same blonde hair.

The similarities were unmistakable, yet something about them was fundamentally different. Most of the time, my mother had a blank expression. It managed to make her appear serene. Soft and sweet. Like Sleeping Beauty.

Kat, on the other hand, had an odd combination of a blank look mixed with that of a trapped, feral animal.

I also watched other videos from her phone, looking for something that would help me understand Helen and Kat's relationship. I don't know what I thought could be gained from watching them interact, but I became obsessed with even the most subtle nuances of their body language. The intimate glances and quick touches between them. The way they leaned into each other and laughed at the same time. Finished each other's sentences.

My need to know more about them didn't stop there, though. In a frenzy, I snooped through drawers and plowed through closets. I dragged out every folder from the file cabinets. I read legal documents. I studied old check registers, receipts, and any scrap of paper I came across, right down to a grocery list hanging from a magnet on the side of the refrigerator.

I also spent the better part of an afternoon poring over Helen's and Kat's passports. They had traveled a lot together over the course of thirty years, but Kat had also gone several places without my aunt. She'd flown to places my mother and I had lived, during the time we had lived there. Kat had also been with

Helen on those postcard visits to Avignon and Italy. I didn't know what this meant, but I knew it meant something.

I concluded something else about my family. No matter how hard I searched or what I found, it would still be impossible to untangle all their secrets. There were just too many.

Speaking of secrets, I came to a decision that it was time to set mine free. I called Thomas, and before mentioning I needed to tell him something, I asked when he would be home.

"You should see headlights right about now," he said. "I'm pulling into the driveway."

I moved to the window and watched him all the way to the door.

"You haven't asked me something important," I told him after he'd settled next to me on the sofa. I couldn't look him in the eye, so I stared at my hands instead.

"What's that?"

"You haven't asked me why."

"I haven't asked you why," he repeated, as if trying to decipher my words.

"You haven't asked why, without a fight, I let my mother take me from Helen. Why I let her drag me all over France long after I could have walked away. Why I didn't reach out to Helen at some point or ever lift a finger to help find my father's killer."

Thomas put his hand on my shoulder, and something inside me crumbled. Tears poured down my face faster than I could swipe them away.

"I would never ask you something like that, August. Plus, I don't need to ask you because I already understand it. She's your mom. You thought you could help her get better."

"I *did* think I could help her, and that she would get better," I said, "but you give me too much credit. That wasn't the main reason." My eyes felt like they weighed a thousand pounds, but

I forced myself to lift them to his. "From the day my father died until a few days ago, the decisions I've made, the things I've done, and not done, happened because I've spent a lot of time over the last twenty-three years thinking my mother was the one who killed him."

Thomas scooted closer. "I . . . don't understand, August," he said, fumbling for words that would help him make sense of things. "What did she do to make you think that? Did she have a reason?"

I shook my head. "I couldn't think of a single reason she would have done it, but I heard her arguing with him on the phone a few minutes before it happened. I'd never heard her speak to him that way. I didn't know what the issue was, but she was furious. I heard her tell him she'd see him in five minutes right before she slammed the phone down.

"Let me come back to that day," I continued after standing to pace, "and tell you about the ones that followed. Once we got to France, we moved all the time. Sometimes we hadn't even gotten unpacked before she'd say we had to leave again. She'd hand me this rambling, paranoid note about how we weren't safe. And as strange as this sounds, I wanted to believe her. I wanted to believe we were in danger, because that meant someone else had killed him. That I'd somehow gotten things all wrong. Most of the time, though, I assumed her need to move wasn't based on a fear of harm like she said. It was a fear of being arrested."

Thomas held out his hand. I sat back down. "Did you tell anyone?"

"Not a soul, and I've felt complicit in his murder for twenty-three years because of it. I didn't even tell her I thought she'd killed him. What was I going to do if she admitted it?"

Thomas pried my hands apart and folded his into mine. "You were just protecting her. You were doing what any kid in that situation would do."

"I was protecting myself, Thomas. When I was eight, I didn't understand anything about the foster care system, but I did the math. I knew if my mother got arrested, I would be sent somewhere, and that it wouldn't be good. By the time I found out I had an aunt who would take me in, I told myself it was too late to tell anyone. It wouldn't change anything. Nothing would bring him back. Year after year I told myself this, and after a while I just became part of the lie."

Thomas leaned closer. "I hear what you're saying," he said, "but I still don't understand why you thought she killed him. Couples have loud disagreements all the time."

I blew out the breath I felt like I'd been holding for twenty-three years.

"Right before my mother slammed the phone down, she told my father she had to run to the corner store and that she'd see him in five minutes. After she left, I went to the window to watch for him. I saw him coming up the sidewalk. He spotted me in the window and held up a package for me to see. A few seconds later, a woman walked up to him, but he didn't notice her because he was looking at me. I only saw a flash of her profile, but I thought it was my mother, Thomas. I saw her shoot him."

Chapter Thirty-Nine

GIFTS

I'd told myself thousands of times over the years that my mother did not choose mental illness, but in a small, dark corner of my mind I didn't always believe it. There were times, especially when her issues impacted me directly, I became too easily convinced there was an element of intentionality on her part. That things were exaggerated and manipulated. Staged.

I had also silently blamed her for taking my father from me. An unspoken accusation is still an accusation, and I'd been wrong. Much of the time I'd been convinced she was responsible for his death, but thankfully there were times I questioned my memories of that day and I was able to assure myself it simply wasn't possible. There were even rare moments when I convinced myself both truths were possible. That in some parallel universe she had pulled the trigger yet somehow hadn't.

Sometimes I think about a TV show I saw once where adults were tasked with writing a letter to the child version of themselves. The purpose of the letter was to encourage the child and help them understand the journey ahead. To show how each link would lead to another.

I was eight years old when I saw my father's murder. I know I need to forgive the child that I was. When I saw it happen, I did nothing but run to my room, cover my head with a pillow, and pretend it wasn't real. I pretended even after I heard the screams of the woman who found his body, and later when those were replaced by the anguished cries of my mother. After that, I kept right on pretending.

If I ever write that letter to the child version of myself, I'll explain to her that denial is one of the best defense mechanisms the human mind was ever gifted with and that she should be thankful she'd been able to use it. Life would have been too overwhelming otherwise.

I'll also tell her to stop being so hard on herself. Her brain did exactly what a child's brain does. It took the events of that night and blended them in a way that made things seem one way when they were another. *You heard your mother arguing on the phone with your father. You heard your mother leave the brownstone. You saw your father's murder. You heard your mother come back inside seconds later. You concluded she killed him. You convinced yourself you were wrong . . .*

I didn't know if my mother knew or suspected I had these thoughts, but even if she was unaware, I still wanted to explain things. The letter I mailed for her in care of the new owners of my apartment in Paris was one of apology.

My conflict about that night and my mother's role in it had left me battered and bruised, but worse yet, it had kept me from trying harder to get her the help she needed. The words I left for her weren't adequate, but they were all I had, and I must believe she'll read them someday. I also need to believe she'll forgive me when she does.

I called Detective Sanchez to thank him for mailing my father's things and to explain everything that had happened since the last time we had spoken all those years earlier.

I had another reason for calling the detective. A few days earlier, I'd gone to the Tybee house to check on things and to throw everything of Kat's into the trash. When I'd emptied her top dresser drawer, a heavy, old-fashioned key clanked to the floor. The sight of it triggered a memory that nearly buckled my knees. It was the key to the gate at our New York apartment. The key I used to play with as a child. The key Kat had ripped from my father's hand after she murdered him.

I overnighted it to Detective Sanchez for confirmation, but I already knew what that key opened. And what it closed.

There were things I didn't share with the detective. I didn't tell him that I'd seen my father's murder, or that I'd spent all those years believing my mother was responsible because she looked enough like her sister that I'd gotten them confused.

I also didn't tell him that my mother had either known all along who killed him or figured it out somewhere along the way. She'd been declared incompetent, more than once on two different continents, which made it doubtful she'd get into any sort of legal trouble for withholding that information. I saw no reason to speak of it, though, just in case.

One of the things Detective Sanchez had sent me was the gift my father was holding when Kat murdered him. The detective had even gone to the trouble of rewrapping it. When he asked how I liked it, I offered an excuse about waiting for my next birthday before opening it, rather than telling him the truth.

I didn't open it because that box was a moment frozen in time. It was the last thing my father ever touched, and it represented something he was going to do. *Things undone.* I may never open it. That piece of my father's story can remain alive as long as that gift remains a promise. A possibility. Much like the light that is just now leaving a star but won't be seen for hundreds or thousands of years—that light belongs both to the past and to the present.

That box now sits on the shelf in his old bedroom, next to an old origami swan who had spent a lot of years alone and is finally glad for some company.

Chapter Forty

BIRTHDAY GUESTS

A year flew by and June 4 rolled around again. Thomas and I were at Grayson Stadium, in Savannah. At the top of the ninth inning, the scoreboard flashed HAPPY BIRTHDAY, AUGUST CAINE!

"That is twenty years late, and it was a much bigger deal when we were twelve," he said, and we both laughed.

I squealed and clapped like I was still twelve years old. "I love it!"

Thomas lightly squeezed my shoulder, and it made me smile. One of the many endearing things about him was his constant need to be touching. Sometimes he snuck a quick stroke of my hair or nestled his hand into the small of my back when no one was looking. He always reached for me in his sleep, and I sometimes wondered what was behind it. Perhaps he did it for the same reason I lightly touched his scars at night after he had fallen asleep. Those scars were what kept me grounded. They assured me he was real and that he was there by luck or fate or the grace of God or some other collision of random and determined events not meant to be understood.

However it happened, he was right where he was supposed to be. We both were.

"Why do you keep tugging at your sleeve?" he asked a second later. "Have you developed a nervous tic?"

The Savannah Sand Gnats had long ago moved to Columbia, but I still wore a decades-old shirt Thomas had given me that said NOBODY CAN DO IT LIKE A SAND GNAT CAN!

I glanced down at my shirt and dusted away the crumbs. "No tic. I'm tugging because the sleeves are too tight," I said, then took another huge bite of my hot dog. Thomas smiled and shook his head. This was dangerous ground when talking to a woman. He couldn't resist, though. We liked teasing each other.

"You've packed on weight lately. The whole shirt looks a little tight, but more so right in this area here, if you know what I mean," he said, still grinning and waving his hand in front of his chest. Sometimes I can't help but make him squirm, his shyness at times surprising, which makes him all that much more endearing to me.

So I pointed to my ear and said, "No. I have no idea what you're talking about. So tell me. Whisper it right here and tell me what you mean."

His wobbly grin lasted a fraction of a second longer before he whispered the answer I already knew. It felt strange to be flirting at my age, but in my defense, I hadn't gotten to do it at the time in life I was supposed to.

"You gained weight because I'm such a good cook," he said a beat later. "But you're still too thin."

"I gained weight because you're good, all right. But truth be told, your cooking is average," I said, instead of telling him the truth. I was pregnant with twins.

"What do you mean my cooking is average?" he asked, his

eyebrow arched. "I'll show you average when we get home."

"Promises, promises, Thomas."

"Meh . . . that didn't come out like I planned, now that I hear it out loud," he said, and we both laughed.

Before heading home, we drove over to watch a Tybee Island sunset. When we pulled into the driveway, I pretended not to notice the setup for a surprise party. Grams and her live-in caregiver, Janice, were bustling around arranging flowers on two large tables. Five men in tuxedos stood under a tree with string instruments and were getting instructions (bossed around) by Liz. Carly and her new boyfriend were hanging streamers and balloons and beautiful paper lanterns from the trees, while Lucy, the dog we adopted, chased a jarfly and barked like crazy.

Thomas gave a loud sigh. "I guess either we're early or they're running a little late."

We smiled at each other before stepping out of the Tahoe and waving to everyone. The band hurriedly started playing "Happy Birthday." I covered my mouth and acted surprised for a bit before letting my eyes drift to the carriage house. Somewhere along the way, for reasons I'll never understand, I had come to believe the departed can cross back and forth across time and that my father led me to the carriage house that day. That his truth clamored to be free and he wanted me to find his things.

My eyes drifted from the carriage house to the front porch. My father was standing there, fifteen years old and still wearing his Georgia State Champions baseball uniform. Confident and happy.

This was the version of him I liked most. The version with more future than past.

I blinked, and my aunt Helen had joined him. She waved to me like she used to wave at ships coming into the harbor. She then shooed me to go on, her expression telling me to get out from under her feet. Guests were waiting.

Chapter Forty-One

APPARITION

It must be a myth that women in labor scream terrible things to their husbands or curse the day they ever met. Before I went into labor, I'd been confined to bed rest for three weeks. I was big as a house and not all that friendly. My hair was plastered to my head from sweat, but from his small, uncomfortable chair, Thomas still looked at me like I was the prom queen.

Dr. Hinton reappeared at hour nineteen. "You want to deliver these babies on your own, but we've had some major changes in the last few minutes," he said in a stern tone. "We need to do a C-section, and our window is closing."

My eyes found Thomas. He mouthed a desperate "please." I nodded and started to cry.

I had told Thomas weeks earlier that I didn't want a C-section unless I could remain fully awake, but I never shared with him that I had this paralyzing, unrelenting fear something would go wrong if I had to be put under. I was afraid of dying without ever seeing their faces. *Please let me see them at least once.*

I'd been that way a lot lately. Worrying had replaced counting thing.

Dr. Hinton patted my arm. "Give us two minutes," he said. "This is the right decision."

My nurse had reminded me three times her name was Tia. Maybe I had called her something else. Tia rushed back into the room and pushed a syringeful of something into my IV. Within seconds the world became a fuzzy, wondrous place.

She left, and it was just the two of us again. I wanted to tell Thomas not to cry. Even though I was loopy, I couldn't bear to see him upset. He had been a trooper right until the point Dr. Hinton said we were in trouble.

My mind shifted to the practical, and I had this sudden urge to tell him where things were. Where I kept the extra keys. Passwords to accounts and computers. Dry cleaning that needed to be picked up. That practical urge passed, and I felt myself smile at him instead.

My smile disappeared, though, when I noticed my mother standing right behind him. It had been two years since I had seen her last, but she looked the same. I found myself wondering if she'd been a ghost all this time.

Maybe she and my father died the same day and drew straws to see which one of them had to stay with me. As I thought this, I realized it was crazy, but I allowed myself to believe it. Maybe it wasn't crazy. It made perfect sense. She didn't talk because she was a ghost and ghosts can't talk. She never aged, and everyone knows ghosts don't ever grow older. Why hadn't I seen it before?

Thomas leaned down to kiss me, and when he stood, my mother was gone. I started crying again, and he reached for my hand.

"I thought she was here," I heard myself say between gasps. "I thought her ghost was here."

"Who?"

"My mother. She was right behind you."

Thomas peeked over his shoulder. "Just the drugs," he whispered, and I suspected he was right, but I kept crying all the same. A second later, Tia rushed back into the room and gave Thomas a silent glance that meant she wanted to speak with him alone. Loopy or not, I understood what that look meant. Something was wrong. When Thomas came back, his face confirmed it.

"What?"

He gave me another stunned look. "She said your mother just handed her a note asking permission to come in here."

My eyes wouldn't focus, and I couldn't make sense out of what he was saying.

Nurses appeared out of nowhere, added and removed things. Unlocked wheels and rushed to take me somewhere because something had gone wrong. I saw Thomas nod to someone. My mother, or the apparition of my mother, whichever it was, floated to the other side of the bed. Her skin felt soft as velvet when she took my hand and leaned down close to my face.

I thought I heard a woman's voice, but the words were drowned out by a loud monitor next to the bed. Another voice from a different direction yelled, "We've got to go. Right now!" And then I heard nothing except the softest of whispers telling me that everything was going to be all right.

EPILOGUE

Ava-Helena and Thomas Caine Reese had to stay in the hospital twelve days. They were fine, but I couldn't leave, and Thomas wouldn't go.

Dr. Hinton's voice waxed and waned over the days, telling me over and over that amniotic fluid embolisms are very rare and very deadly. I was very lucky to be alive. Him saying the word *very* stuck with me, but the rest of his words passed in a blur until he said them again.

When I could be rousted awake, Thomas was always there. He usually held both babies, but sometimes my mother held one or the other. Or maybe it was someone else I thought was my mother, because I still wasn't sure if she was real.

The days twisted and faded from one to the next. Light turned to shadow. Shadow to light.

I woke once to find Thomas snuggled up next to me, his presence warm and impossibly light. His words were jumbled, but his voice was as soothing as the gentle rain I could see sliding down the window.

Sometimes I heard the woman I believed to be my mother humming, and at times the rhythm of the chair as she rocked the babies. I had the strangest dreams, some vivid, others vague as a vapor. I sometimes couldn't tell if I was dreaming or floating or standing on solid ground. Helen came to visit in a few of those dreams, and it wasn't lost on me that she died from one type of embolism and I, almost, from another. She and I had been alike in so many ways. Even this.

We went home that twelfth day, and Thomas moved the babies into our room. Just for a little while. Until things became normal.

We had turned my father's old room into a nursery. His old furniture was in the carriage house for storage, but we left his painted stars just as they were. I can't wait to show the twins the constellations and to tell them about their grandfather.

I once read somewhere that the footprints left by the Apollo astronauts will still be on the moon a hundred million years from now. I like to think about this when I see my father's stars. Sometimes I can almost let myself believe that his sky is as permanent as the real one. That his handprints and those tiny painted stars will still be there long after I and everyone I love are gone.

My mother made a significant life decision. For the time being, she moved into the house on Tybee. If it bothered her to be in the same space her sister had occupied on and off for three decades, she didn't show it.

Thomas goes to pick her up every morning and then takes her back each evening. It would be more practical for her to stay with us, but she always half smiles and shakes her head whenever we ask.

After she leaves each day, I count the minutes so I can take the journey with her in my mind. Twelve minutes after she and Thomas pull out of our driveway, I visualize them crossing the

Thunderbolt Bridge toward Tybee, and I imagine my mother's face as she gets that first glimpse of orange light rippling across the marshes. The singular beauty of it takes her breath every time, and after reflecting on it, she realizes she's always been drawn to water.

Three minutes later, I imagine her smiling at the sight of herons high-stepping through the twisting tidal creeks and tall cordgrass.

After that I suspect she watches a few stray seagulls, perplexed at how some of them cut and curl their way across the sky while others in their flock stay suspended—aloft in motionless flight.

Honestly, I don't know what my mother sees or thinks on the drive over to Tybee. She may close her eyes and sleep. Still, I spent most of my life traveling with her, so I take this journey with her too. Only this time, I take it in the way I want it to be.

Each time I drift off and wake, I remain still and listen to the sounds of our wonderful old house, glad these beautiful notes form the melody of our life. The babies coo, and Thomas tinkers in the kitchen. He talks to the twins in a silly, high-pitched voice that makes me laugh. Crows caw and marsh birds screech. The floorboards squeak and oak branches creak against each other from the wind. Lucy's nails tip-tap across the floor, and Helen's cat Sergeant F. E. Lines mews as he tries to adjust to living back in his old house. He mews *a lot.*

My mother hums when she rocks Ava and Caine, the tune foreign yet strangely familiar. Some days she plays the piano for them. Always softly. She hasn't said anything since that day in the delivery room, and even though I'm not sure she did say those things, for some reason I have it in my mind that when the twins start talking, she will too. They will learn to speak together.

At the rate I'm going, the twins and I will learn to walk together.

That's just some negativity. If I take things slow, I can already manage the twenty-seven steps from our bedroom door to the nursery.

It has been interesting watching my mother change, but in my heart, I know she will never be normal. She is far too broken, and there isn't enough medicine or time or magic to heal her. There just isn't. And although she did not choose this terrible illness, I've always suspected there is a part of her that doesn't want to get better. She would see this as a betrayal of my father. She lived. He died. She split the difference.

I also know there are many things I will never understand about her, such as why she refuses to disclose anything of her past or why she won't speak a single word. I may forever have to wonder what she was arguing about with my father that day on the phone, or when and how she figured out that her sister killed him, or more important, why she never told anyone.

I may also never know how after not seeing each other for two years she knew to come to the hospital that day, or how she managed to get to Savannah on her own. Her presence that day, though, was an unexpected gift beyond measure that in the end doesn't really need an explanation.

It's fine that I don't know these things. People aren't entitled to every detail about another person. We all have parts of ourselves we want to keep in the shadows.

Still, when I look at my children, knowing my own mother is a stranger to me, it brings an incredible ache. I can't imagine being that way with them. Not ever.

I knew from the second I became aware of their existence that I would want to know everything about their lives. That I would forever annoy them with questions and bore them with more information than they would ever want to hear.

But they'll listen. That's the price of love.

Right after my father died, I tried to make myself remember things about both my parents, and with the clarity the years bring, I realize these are not memories so much as wishes.

Truthfully, my mother was never openly affectionate, nor was she actively involved in my life. She was around and attentive in perfunctory ways, but all the laughter and normality and spontaneity of my childhood came from the wonderful father I'd been blessed with. I know, though, that she loved me. That she still loves me. But something about her makeup was cold and broken before my father's murder. Maybe before the tragedy of her family. The only time she ever glowed and shined and sparkled was when he was near, and those shards of light shattered the second he died.

Still, sometimes when she holds the babies, I notice the tiniest spark of something in her eyes that wasn't there before. And while this gives me hope, it also brings an awful reminder that she did everything she could to keep me safe all those years, but the cruelty of her love was always the most dangerous thing in my life.

I sometimes wonder if she realizes this. I hope not.

Most of the time I'm happy. There are times I can't believe a person can be so lucky. At other times I become overwhelmed with fear and doubt. I feel the anchor of history pulling me back down to a bottomless, lightless place I once knew too well. When that darkness comes over me, I try to think of Thomas, our children, and the life we're building together. Sometimes it helps.

My thoughts also drift back to the day when, like a ghost, my mother appeared by my side. I wasn't a hundred percent sure she spoke when she leaned down next to my ear, but my suspicion had invaded my thoughts. The words shifted into phantoms just out of reach. They haunted and consoled me. The very possibility of their existence was the first thing I thought of when I woke in the morning and the last thing I thought of at night.

Helen was right: Things do come to us in dreams. Twenty-six days after I came home from the hospital, I dreamed of being a toddler. My mother held me on her lap and whispered "*mon amour*" in my ear as she scratched the translation into the sand. *My love.* Then, just as mysteriously, the waves washed the words away and she was gone, leaving nothing but the faintest scent of lavender and the ghost of her touch.

I woke to the early morning sun streaming through the windows and smiled.

When she was still a talking person, the only pet name my mother ever called me was "my love." If I close my eyes in the quiet, the memory of her saying those words is a once-lost treasure that took me so many years to find.

I want to think, to believe, she will say those words again someday, and that nothing—not even the weight of history—will wash them away. She'll squeeze my hand just when I need her most and tell me that everything is going to be all right.

And she's right. It will be.

Hope is a wonderful addiction.

ACKNOWLEDGMENTS

It took several years and many attempts to write this book, and it wouldn't have seen the light of day without the help of some incredible editors, including James Powell. His work on the early draft was invaluable, as were the kind, much-needed words of encouragement he so generously gave. A million thanks to the brilliant Amy Scheibe for her willingness to shape the book into something it wanted to be, and to Katherine Caruana and Sterling Hooker for the final copyedit. I am also forever grateful for Brooke Warner, Lauren Wise, Shannon Green, and the entire force-of-nature team at Stable Book Group for their willingness to take this journey with me and for holding my hand every step of the way.

Finally, I want to thank my parents, Doug and Ann Kiser, for their unfailing love and support.

ABOUT THE AUTHOR

Photo credit: Ric Griffith

Sandra K. Griffith is a doctorate-level psychologist with extensive clinical and forensic experience, the owner of a behavioral health agency, and an adjunct instructor at Marshall University. When she's not writing, she enjoys traveling, antiquing, cooking, and spending time with her family, friends, and much-too-large collection of pets. She splits her time between Kenova, West Virginia, and Tybee Island, Georgia, just outside of Savannah.

Looking for your next great read?

We can help!

Visit www.shewritespress.com/next-read or scan the QR code below for a list of our recommended titles.

She Writes Press is an award-winning independent publishing company founded to serve women writers everywhere.